To Tame the Wolf
A Shadow Walkers Novel

Angie Hulme

PublishAmerica
Baltimore

ISBN: 1-4241-2605-3
PUBLISHED BY PUBLISHAMERICA, LLLP
www.publishamerica.com
Baltimore

Printed in the United States of America

For Jude – not much I can say that I don't say as much as possible already; thank you for you, and for the friendship we share, both are very precious to me.

For Ali – you're one of a kind, hon. Life is definitely richer for knowing you.

For everybody else – you know perfectly well who you are! The extra added support and love you give me has helped me keep going through some dark times.

For my favourite bar staff – it's only a safe place because you all make it so, thanks.

And for Grandad. The world is lesser for your passing, but the love you gave will last forever as we, whom you touched, share it further.

Prologue

She heard the familiar cry, the signal for her to move. In a flash she was gone, running lightly through the undergrowth. No twig broke, no eye could give shape to the copper-grey blur.

Drawing near, his scent filling her nostrils, she slowed to a trot and allowed him to detect her.

His snout rose, sniffed, and he sauntered over to her, touching her nose with his.

"Ahead, 200 metres," he said softly, more growl than speech.

"Attack It from both sides," she replied and set off, stealthily, to the right.

Her partner, sleek black and touched by silver, slid to the left and moved forward.

Together they crept close, as one, years of assuramce requiring needing no assurance that the other was doing the same.

It came into view in a small clearing. She circled around, gaining his side, knowing he would gain the other.

For a moment she stood, hackles up, crouched and ready to pounce at some unknown, instinctive signal.

The signal came, and she leapt. Flying through the air, she was darkness come to life.

She had time to see the crouching, hideous figure turn to her partner. Its eyes blazed yellow under an overhanging brow, teeth pointed and glinting in the faint moonlight.

It launched toward him, arms outstretched, and caught his muzzle in both hands.

She landed on It's back and dug in with sharp claws. It's head turned and she snapped her jaws, heard a tear, spat out the grisly, cold flesh.

It let go of her partner for a second, rose, flung her violently to the floor. She hit hard and lay dazed as It turned back to her partner.

With a shake and a howl, she leapt once more, barrelling into Its side.

It tumbled onto Its back, leaving her partner to fall to the floor. In a flash, she was on It, biting, scratching, until Its struggles grew weaker with exhaustion.

Then, in the blink of an eye, she shifted.

Now on it's chest was no large, 200lb wolf.

Now on It's chest was a 6ft tall, naked woman. Blood dripped from her mouth and hands as she pulled up Its head and gripped it, front and back.

With a swift, easy flick, Its neck swung round and cracked deafeningly. So injured, It lay still, accepting defeat and hoping for freedom.

Then It saw.

Attached to her back was a scabbard of battered leather. She reached behind one shoulder and pulled out a 15-inch silver sword.

Knowing, It tried to struggle but was too weak. She stood, one bare foot pinning It to the forest floor.

In a fluid movement, she lifted the sword above her head and brought it down onto Its neck. Unable to move Its head, the blow struck and It burst into searing blue flame and was gone, leaving no mark save a scorch upon the forest floor. Then she turned away, an unconscious sneer of disgust turning her lip upwards, and went to her partner.

He was now a naked man, lying helplessly on the ground. Bleeding, one eye gouged loose, the other half-closed, rips and tears scoured his body, a chunk of flesh was missing from the base of his throat.

She dropped to her knees beside him. "Danieel," she whispered.

He touched her, tried to speak and found only blood. He spat it out and tried again. "I can feel...the poison...Sansé."

"No..." she told him, eyes glistening wet.

He matched her tears and swallowed. "Yes...he was a bad...bad one...you must do it...before...before it is too...late..."

"I cannot," she pleaded. "Perhaps—"

"You know," he interrupted, "there is no perhaps...better this...death...than that...life..."

Sobbing, she kissed him gently on the forehead, then lifted herself up and took hold of the sword once more. She bent and wiped it clean on the grass, then stood over him.

Her tears touched his ravaged face and he tried to smile. "Go on...my love...never forget...I'll be waiting..."

Sansé lifted her arms, the silver weapon shimmering cruelly, gaining weight every second she held it, but finally it rose above her head, triumphant in the forest sheen.

"What good is good if life is just to make no difference and then die a nobody, after giving everything?" she asked.

He had no reply, simply caressed her ankle and traced the shape of a heart.

She pursed her lips and kissed the air. Then, as of their own accord, her arms fell and his head rolled away like a final punctuation.

"What use, if the evil always wins and grows ever larger?" she asked, dropping the sword and loosing the scabbard from her back.

She let the leather fall behind her as Danieel's body melted silently away into the dirt.

"What use to always love—and always lose?" she asked, then shifted again, back into the copper-grey wolf form.

"No use at all!" she growled, then slunk away to find a place to sleep until the dawn.

Chapter 1

"I think she's waking," an old man said, holding the hand of a young girl.

She lay on a bed, surrounded by three men. Her right calf was heavily bandaged, but still faint patches of drying blood could be spied through the layers.

The oldster, a gaunt figure with flat, white hair and a kindly face, watched anxiously.

Across from him, a 30-something, stocky, pale faced man with intense blue eyes and copper-red hair removed the cool cloth from the girl's forehead and waited.

The third, watching from the foot of the bed, had skin the colour of milky coffee with dark hair lolling aimlessly down to almost cover large, dark eyes, seemed to be closest in age to the unconscious girl.

The girl stirred, her brown-blonde hair settling chaotically upon the pillow. She opened soft, gentle, intelligent brown eyes and stared, uncomprehending for a moment, at the three men. Then the eyes turned afraid and she started to yank herself away, trying to speak, staring accusingly around.

The middle-aged man held her down as gently as he could. "Don't move," he recommended.

It was his voice, perhaps—warm and caring—but the girl settled down and stopped struggling. In a moment she found her voice, spoke shakily. "W-who are you? Where am I? What...what are you going to do with me?"

"Nothing, my dear," the old man said. His voice was gravely and tired. "Do you remember? You were in the woods..." he prompted.

The girl's expressive eyes flew wide as the memories flooded back.

Sunnyhurst Woods...she walked idly, humming to herself...a branch cracked and she started, then shook her head with a smile and continued...a rustle in the bushes...she stopped dead, faced the undergrowth...her mother's nagging words reverberated in her head "You'll be out of luck one of these days, lady, walking alone in those woods all the time."...a growl

9

froze her thoughts and her blood for a second, before she turned back the way she had come—the fastest route out of the woods—and pounded the ground as she ran hell-for-leather...but though it seemed like the eternity of a bad dream, soon the growling close behind convinced her it was all too real...the beast was upon her, teeth clamping around her right calf...tall as a man, but stooping, it shoved her down as she tried to turn and fight before dropping to all fours...a line of slobber touched her unbelieving face...this thing was covered in hair, with a long snout that snarled and showed razor-sharp teeth...but it's eyes! Oh god, it's eyes were human!...little else registered as she began to swoon, only a faint thrumming sound and a cry—from where or who, she did not know...then darkness enveloped her and she heard no more.

Until now! She gasped. "You! You saved me?" She still sounded half-accusing, but her eyes were calmer and the urgent panic had left her voice.

The old man nodded. "The beast that attacked you is no more. We brought you here, to a place we know, and cared for you while you slept through the night and into the day."

The girl looked for the first time at her surroundings.

The room was spacious and unlived in, lit coldly by a lamp in each corner. It contained only a desk and the bed she lay on, plus three backpacks stuffed to bursting, each with a sleeping bag attached.

"Who are you?" she asked now, looking back at the old man—the only one who seemed ready to explain.

He smiled, a melancholy sight until she saw his eyes glitter—though with what, she could not quite say, as their colour seemed to change constantly. "We are they who walk in the shadows to fight for the light," he said simply, his mouth twitching in something she took for amusement.

"Er…" The girl frowned. "Ok, I'm sure that makes sense to someone…What are your names?"

The middle-aged man chided the old one with a tutting sound and a smile that lit up his ghostly face. "I am Camhlaidh," he said, "the old one is Menw, and the youngster is Julio. What is your name?"

She smiled. "Unusual names…mine is Jodhi. I live in Blackburn, but your speech—and your name…tells me you don't?"

Camhlaidh shook his head. "A long time ago I came from the Highlands of Scotland. More recently, I come from nowhere and travel everywhere."

"Scotland! That's the place!" Jodhi smiled. "I have a hobby, dialects and names and things. Yours sounds strange, older, even for the Highlands." She mused a moment. "Your accent is faded, older like I said, with only a bit of a lilt to it. It's been long since you went home?"

Camhlaidh shrugged. "It has been long and long."

Jodhi was sad for him, she could see how he used to walk the mountains and sit to watch the view, and she could see how he missed it. "You miss it," she voiced her thoughts.

He nodded. "I do. But it is always in my heart." He placed a hand over his chest and smiled that radiant smile.

Menw nodded. "You may notice how Camhlaidh speaks very little, yet you know more than he has said."

Jodhi started in surprise. "I…but I…I saw so clearly! His mountains, the way he climbed and camped out just to watch the sky at night…wha-how-?"

Camhlaidh shrugged. "Telepathy."

"Huh?" Jodhi was unsure whether to laugh at the joke—unsure, in fact, if it was a joke.

Menw tilted his head. "He is a powerful telepath. I hope you will find this out, Jodhi, and more. One of the things Cam does without trying is to say little, but yet convey more than speech ever could."

"Telepath…" Jodhi couldn't hide her bemused eyes. "Well, I always kinda believed in spooks and ESP and stuff but I dunno much about it. And how am I expected to find out more?" she added, a little suspiciously.

Menw gave his tired smile and this time his eyes settled to amber long enough for Jodhi to see his sadness. "You were bitten, Jodhi. If you believe in telepathy, which you must because you have experienced it and are intelligent enough to accept the evidence of your own senses, then you must learn to believe…in werewolves."

Jodhi let out a sharp, terrified laugh, but said nothing.

"You were bitten by one, Jodhi, if you believe it or not. Tonight was the third and last night of the moon-wolf's changing time—so you will find out next month just what this means, unless you are of the other kind." Menw hurried on before she could say anything. "You can learn to control it and use it to your advantage; we will help you do this if you join us in our fight against the darkness. We will tell you all we know of werewolves and every other type of being. We will show you how to control the wolf inside and bend it to your will. We will—"

Jodhi cut him off by rising and hopping off the bed. She collapsed in agony when she hit the floor, holding her bandaged leg. "I want to go home," she told them coldly. "If I've been out all night then my mum'll be afraid. I don't believe in werewolves, I'm not a werewolf, and next month I'm gonna go to bed and sleep, just like I always do, and just like I want to do now."

"We'll let you go, Jodhi," Menw told her as Julio rushed to her aid, and then dropped back as she shoved him away, "but first you need to know something about the monster you will become if you cannot control it. Once you know, then you will be prepared and we will let you go, and remain here a while so you can return to us if you wish."

Jodhi laughed hysterically. "Sure, right! Let me go!" she cried; Camhlaidh was lifting her bodily back onto the bed.

"Let me talk to her," Julio said. "Wait outside."

Jodhi giggled. "And what're you, another telepath?"

He shook his head. "I'm an empath."

With an effort Jodhi calmed herself and changed the subject to his accent. "You don't look American."

Julio nodded, his dark brown eyes staring intently at her. "I am American, but my family is Mexican." He grinned suddenly, showing sparkly-white teeth. "My grandparents were wetbacks." Chuckling at the confusion on Jodhi's face, he explained. "It's a word for illegal Mexicans—means they swam from Mexico to America." His face turned serious. "But never use that word to anyone, to a Mexican it is an insult equivalent to…some used against African-Americans. Besides, my abuelita, my grandma, she'd skin my hide and hang me from a flag post if she knew I'd called her one!" He grinned again and turned to Menw. "Leave us be a while."

Menw rose reluctantly, but sprightly for one who looked so aged, and Camhlaidh followed. "Call if you need us," the telepath told Julio, who nodded—seeing the full meaning in his head: "Call us if she turns violent…"

Jodhi stared coldly at Julio who smiled warmly. "Like I said, I'm an empath. I know how you feel; I know everything you feel at this moment."

Once the door closed, Jodhi turned on Julio with a snarl. "What?! What, you gonna amaze me by telling me I feel like shit?! Like you guys are crazy bastards? Like I'm crazy for actually believing you?! Like-like…" she faltered, lost in her anger, disturbed by her unusual viciousness.

Julio waited patiently for her to look at him again.

When she did, it was with tears in her eyes. "I'm just…normal. This can't be happening," she sobbed.

Julio sat and held her as she wailed angrily into his shoulder. Once, she tried to pull away, lashing out when he refused to let her, but then she calmed slowly and sat up and Julio saw the sad acceptance in her eyes.

"You're too clever to convince yourself this isn't real," he spoke, finally. "You saw the beast yourself. You know Cam's telepathy is real because he showed it to you. Now we can help you, and we want to help you, all you have to do is let us."

"Help? Help me?" She laughed hysterically. "I'm gonna turn into a-a monster every full moon and you want to help me?!"

Julio shook his head. "The thing you were attacked by is what happens to those without control. If you become that type of wolf, then for three nights a month—the moon itself, and the two days either side—you will become that thing. You will be that beast, and you will turn other people. Unless, that is, you have control."

"And…with control?" she asked fearfully.

"You can choose to control the wolf, to give it no power over you. With control, you won't be a slathering, mindless beast but a sleek, beautiful wolf with your own mind, and the wolf's senses. And on the nights of change, you'll be no more vicious than if you had PMT." He gave a cheeky grin.

"What would I have to do?" She ignored his attempt at lightening the mood. "What about my life? The one I have now?" Tears welled forth again.

"Your life will never be as it was before last night," Julio admitted. "Your choice is the hardest you will ever make. To remain here and become the beast every month—but not give up all you know and love. Or…to leave, join us, let us help you—let us be your family."

"How did you join up?" Jodhi asked, unable to consider anything until her mind was calmed further.

Julio shrugged mildly. "I'm an empath. I feel people's emotions, and their…auras? Something like that…I was only 18—two years ago—when I was taking out the trash and felt an evil presence. I don't mean just a bad person, I mean an evil something…something inhuman. Less than, more than, other than human. Like an idiot, I stayed still instead of running and it came for me. I fought it off, somehow, but I could not stay where I was, in the life I was living not with the knowledge I suddenly had. I could not remain oblivious. So I chose to leave home. Once knowing what really lurks in the shadows, how could I have stayed and pretended different? Though the Lord knows I still wish I had sometimes." He smiled wryly. "So I wandered and was eventually found by Menw and Cam. I joined them, and lost everything I had—family, friends, job, girlfriend, most of my possessions. But I found everything, too…" Now his smile was warm. "My family, my friends are those I travel with, those in our group. My job is to fight the creeping darkness so others can live in freedom. My girlfriend…" here he bowed his head sadly, "I don't know what happened to her, but I have none now—nor would I wish to, for I could die in the next fight. My possessions, we have things we need, some luxuries, the life is hard for the fighting, but we do a good thing, and mostly I am content." He nodded. Jodhi saw it was one of satisfaction.

"What was it? The presence?" Jodhi held her breath.

"A vampire," was the calm reply.

She gasped and a hand flew to her mouth.

"Vampires are much as described in legend, though there are some differences. But, like you, if the person can control the vampire, then instead of becoming a monster, they can be as a normal human being. Under control, a vampire who does good deeds looks mostly as you or me, with differences best seen rather than described. When feeding, the eye-teeth lengthen, but such a vampire only feeds on the flesh and blood of the animal. Any butcher will sell blood…" He smiled at her horrified expression. "You look like I did when I first met a friendly vampire."

She covered her face with her hands and shook her head. "I feel like I'm in an episode of Buffy!" came the muffled whine.

Julio grinned. "I feel like that every day!" he confessed.

Jodhi peeked at him. "How do you watch TV?"

"We have ways." He shrugged. "Until I'm sure you'll believe me, I can't say any more."

"If you steal TVs you can tell me," she gave back with bitter sarcasm.

"We never steal." Julio frowned deeply and looked away. "We accept only that which is given freely in gratitude or payment for labour. The cholos I grew up watching, hating, showed me only that their way was not the right one. I'm no gang member, Jodhi, never hint that I am. All of us, our whole group, live the same way. We have friends who give when they can, when we have to work for food we do. And Menw—" he stopped short, "Menw has some ways, too. Legal ones." He finished the last two words in a half-growl.

Jodhi glanced around, afraid to meet those darkly flashing eyes. "Sorry," she whispered.

Julio jumped up, shook his head, hit his forehead. "No, truly I'm sorry!" he said again with a depreciating grin. "I still feel the pain of many of my own things, as well as that of others. Forgive me, I'm sorry."

Jodhi gave him a tentative nod for which she got a winning smile.

"So, when do we leave?" she asked quietly, sadly.

Julio gently placed an arm around her shoulders. "You've decided to join us?" he asked.

"What other choice have I got?" She shrugged him off. "But don't expect me to be happy. Once I have control of this thing I'm coming straight home!"

Julio nodded. "I understand." But his eyes twinkled that he knew differently. Looking elsewhere, Jodhi did not see.

Julio opened the door and called Menw and Cam back inside.

"The lady joins us?" Menw asked hopefully.

Julio nodded. "The Slayer has arrived."

"Huh?" from both men.

Julio chuckled and saw, from the corner of his eye, Jodhi crack a small smile. "Nothing, fathers, nothing." He patted them both patronisingly on a shoulder and grinned widely at their bemusement.

"I have to see my mum," Jodhi said in a sullen voice. "I dunno what I'll tell her, and you might have to wrestle me away when she tries to stop me…but I have to say goodbye. Even though she'll hate me for it."

"She would only hate because she loves you," Julio said. "Because she'll be worried, afraid, hurt. But she'll always love you."

"Don't preach to me, Julio." Jodhi stood tall. "I also want to say goodbye to a-a close friend."

Cam raised an eyebrow. "Does she have a name?"

Jodhi grimaced and snarled. "Not your goddamn business! Let me keep my thoughts, at least! My memories! My privacy! If you must take my life, leave me my brain."

Cam bowed his head in shame. "I did not look. The picture came to me."

"Next time try ignoring it," she retorted.

Cam nodded and said nothing, but guilt fell over Jodhi like a blanket and she cried out. "And don't give me these feelings either!"

Julio stepped in. "He didn't give you any feelings, Jodhi, though you might be picking up some of his. He also didn't look inside your head. It was his talent not him. Cam would never see something without permission or accident. He feels as bad as you do, believe me."

"I doubt it," she said stubbornly, knowing who she was talking to.

Julio shrugged. "Hey, what would I know? I'm just the empath," he said pleasantly.

Jodhi's anger crushed itself as she collapsed into sobs once again.

Julio led the others outside, shut the door and walked them a few feet away, facing out into the woods. "She needs her peace," he told them.

Menw was confused. "Why was she so angry about you getting to see her friend's picture?" he asked them. "What's wrong with you seeing what her friend looks like?"

Cam hesitated. "I…think they are more than just friends, only it's a secret." He looked for confirmation.

Julio nodded. "That's what I get. They haven't told yet, because the world is too cruel."

Menw knitted his grey-white brow. "So it was a man? Her boyfriend? Would her mother disapprove?"

Julio smiled *"Menw always seems so awkward when using words more current than the 1500s."* he thought.

"No, it was a girl," Cam told him, patiently waiting for the penny to drop.

"Oh," the old man said, and then, "Oh!" He threw his hands in the air. "My brain, my mind, they cease to work!" He grinned. "But I still have no understanding of the problem with this."

"Not everyone around here likes dykes," came Jodhi's voice from behind them.

All three whirled around.

"Sorry," she shrugged negligently, "didn't mean to interrupt. Still want me along?"

"Of course we do," Julio said. "I swear—"

"Course you do!" Jodhi mocked surprise. "You're guys! You love the idea, right?"

"Now that is simply unfair, young lady," rebuked Menw.

She sighed and nodded. "I know. Sorry. Not much used to your kind of reaction is all, got on the defensive."

Julio nodded. "We know," he said. "But...none here judge by anything but deeds. Where your heart goes is its own business and no choice or fault of anyone. Therefore," he grinned impishly, "perhaps we could go out sometime and see what pretty girls are around. You could give me a few tips."

Jodhi laughed.

"Inside." Menw commanded, shivering though the sun peeked through the trees. "We eat, and then we let Jodhi visit her mother and girlfriend."

"Alone?" She suddenly looked small and frightened.

"One or all of us can go with you if you want. If not, we'll be right outside," Julio reassured her.

Jodhi nodded. "I think I have to do it on my own, if you can come with me but wait around the corner or something. But thank you." She looked around at the three faces before her. "I guess I could try a bit harder to be nice...I know it wasn't your fault I got bit."

"We understand," said Cam softly.

But then Jodhi shook her head. "I wish...but no, I have to do this alone. I have to tell Rachel whatever I can—and my mum. And..." her shoulders tensed, "I have to tell Mum the truth about Rachel—and about me."

Julio put a comforting hand on her shoulder. "We'll be right outside. Cam won't listen, but if you call he'll hear. Right Cam?"

Cam nodded.

Menw stood. "We shall eat first," he told them and went to open one of the overloaded backpacks, "then we go. You have been missing the full night; I believe another hour will cause little extra trouble."

Jodhi gasped. "Oh no, she'll have the police out!"

Cam smiled. "Pardon me a moment." He bowed his head for a moment...the room was silent. Then he raised it and nodded once, his eyes shining with the effort expended.

Julio clapped and chuckled. "No more police!" he guessed.

Cam simply shrugged and gave a ghostly smile.

Jodhi stared. "This...I'm not gonna get used to all that fast."

"He has his uses." Julio grinned. "Why else would we keep him around?"

"Why, for his stunning good looks, of course," Menw joined in as he returned with paper bags of food. "It is no feast, my dear," he warned, "but it does the job of fuelling us as well as anything."

Jodhi took a cautious peek inside the bag. A bottle of water took up one corner. Airproof ziplock bags took up the rest of the space. Delving in, she discovered ham sandwiches, an apple and banana and a single-serving sized packet of custard creams.

"We rarely eat like Kings," Julio agreed.

"This looks yummy to me," Jodhi replied, tucking in with a suddenly hearty appetite.

Chapter 2

As Jodhi opened the front door and tentatively walked in, casting a last glance behind to her new companions, a small, plump woman came running from the front room and barrelled into her with a screech. The woman threw her arms tightly around Jodhi's torso and sobbed into her neck.

Jodhi hugged back, much gentler but matching tear-for-tear.

When the woman calmed and let go, Jodhi steered them both into the front room and sat down on the sofa, patting the cushion next to her.

The older woman sat down; touching Jodhi's face as if afraid she would disappear.

"Are you all right, Jo?" the woman asked shakily.

Jodhi nodded and smiled. "I'm fine, Mum. I was bitten in the forest by a big dog; someone was passing and saved me. He bandaged my leg and fed me until I was awake and able to come home."

"W-where is he?" The woman looked around.

"He didn't want to come in...he's shy. He said to say hello, though."

Sharon Maye frowned then shrugged, too happy to have her daughter back to worry about the man who helped her—she was obviously unharmed aside from the bite on her calf.

Jodhi took her mother's hands and held them close to her. "Mum...I have to go away for a while."

Sharon shook her head, smiling. "What?"

"The man who helped me—he asked me to join him and his friends on a trip. I'm not sure where—nowhere in particular I don't think, just a trip to learn and grow in myself." She bit her lip. "I know what you're going to say—but I trust these people as much as I trust you, and I have to do this or things will be...very, very bad."

"Are they forcing you?" Sharon stood up, ready to fight.

Jodhi shook her head rapidly, realising how her words sounded. "No, I don't mean bad like that...Mum, I'm 18, and I'm going to go on a trip to learn lots of things and see lots of things. I know you won't understand, because I know how crazy this sounds, but please accept it. For me. I swear to you I'll be fine."

Sharon sat down and said nothing. Tears clouded her eyes once more, only these were not of happiness. "Go then," she muttered. "Go, see if I care. Out all night, got me worried sick…now you come back and tell me some stranger has invited you on holiday and you want to up and leave…" She shook her head. "Jodhi, I know not having a dad has been hard sometimes but…"

Jodhi stopped her. "No, Mum, this isn't your doing!" she protested. "I know how it looks, but you used to trust me…can you again, just one more time?"

Sharon shrugged her daughter away. "I suppose I have to. you'll leave anyway…Jo just promise you'll write?"

Jodhi nodded. "Whenever I can find pen, paper, envelopes and stamps I'll write you a huge letter. And I'll call whenever I can too."

Sharon nodded. "I wish you wouldn't, Jo…but I know you. I know you'll do this no matter what and I won't have us parting in anger." Sharon sighed. "Me and my dad parted in anger, and I never saw him to say I was sorry. Just, just swear to me—this is what you truly want to do?"

Jodhi nodded. "It is, Mum. I-I have to do this."

Sharon nodded and reached for her purse, sitting behind the sofa.

"I have money, Mum," Jodhi protested, knowing what her mum was doing.

"Well, now you'll have more." Sharon half-smiled as she rooted and found her chequebook.

"Mum, there's something else…"

Sharon looked up. "What?" she asked, a little sharply.

"You know Rachel?"

"Rachel?" Sharon thought for a second. "Oh, oh Rachel from Livesey, of course, lovely girl. Is she going too?"

"No, I'm going to see her before I go though." Jodhi sighed. "I need to tell you something about Rachel."

"Yes?" Sharon smiled pleasantly.

"We…I…me and Rachel…we're…we were—have been…you know…more than friends…?"

Sharon nodded. "Yes dear, lovely girl she is. Was that all?"

Jodhi stared, open-mouthed, and then burst into laughter.

Sharon joined her with a twinkling grin. "What, you think a mother doesn't know?" She chuckled. "But is this part of why you need to leave? I know this isn't the most welcoming place for a young lesbian. You need to 'find yourself,' or whatever it's called this week?"

Jodhi shrugged. "Something like that, I suppose." She nodded.

Sharon nodded and signed the cheque with a flourish. She folded it and tucked it into Jodhi's pocket. "Well now, you best get yourself a shower before you do—there's a backpack up in the loft or a suitcase, whichever you prefer? Then you can go visit Rachel—and you be sure to tell her she can come visit me anytime, now."

Jodhi nodded. "The backpack would be best. I'll take a shower and pack. I'm sure Rachel will come and visit if you invite her." Jodhi stood. "Thanks, Mum."

Sharon shrugged. "I know my daughter wouldn't do anything without thinking it through first. I trust you, Jo, you know that. Just you keep in touch, or I'll be changing the locks." She grinned.

Jodhi nodded with a smile and began her usual staircase ascent of two steps at a time, then groaned in pain at her calf, and limped the rest of the way.

In the bathroom, she removed her bandage gingerly. The bloodshed was worse than the wound, which was already scabbed over. Jodhi "hmmd" in surprise.

Washed, packed and ready to go, Jodhi hugged her mother tightly. "I swear I'll be back and I swear I'll write and I swear I'll be alright," she said, bravely.

Sharon nodded and forced a smile. "My little girl grew up." She sighed. "Have fun, baby Jo, and call if you need anything at all."

Jodhi nodded. "I will, Mum. Thank you for-for being my mum. And for letting me go."

Sharon burst into tears again and Jodhi held her until the sobbing subsided. "Bye for now, Jo." Sharon waved her off, watching as she disappeared around the corner to where, presumably, her friends waited.

"My little baby Jo…" Sharon shook her head sadly and went inside. "I hope I raised her well…there's nothing else I can do now." She rooted on the messy coffee table and came up with a bag of hard-boiled sweets. She sucked them peacefully, memories of "baby Jo" keeping her company in the now-empty house.

Jodhi nodded wearily at her companions as she spotted them sitting on a wall, waiting for her.

Cam nodded and smiled softly, and Jodhi eyed him warily. "What?" she challenged.

"I caught those pictures again…" he apologised.

Jodhi shrugged. "She was OK, I think she hates it but she loves me I guess, and she knows I wouldn't do anything stupid…" she snorted. "Which is more than I know right now!"

"To your girlfriend now?" Menw asked.

Jodhi nodded and set off at a slow walk, not wanting to go but knowing she must. "I have to do this one thing then we can leave," she promised.

"Is it close?" Menw asked, strolling alongside her.

"Just a couple of streets," she told him. "You guys stay here, I'll be back. Oh, and look after my bag." She dropped her backpack on the floor and left Menw to heft it and return to his fellow travellers with a grunted. "Such a polite young lady."

Julio grinned. "Well, you know those darn kids these days…not an ounce of respect for the people who tell them they're a werewolf and then drag them away from everything they know and love."

Menw rolled his eyes and ignored the stifled laughter coming from Julio, amused at his own sense of humour.

"Leave her to it," Julio advised once he finished patting himself on the back. "She'll come around, it's hard to up and leave for something like this— I remember." He gave a wan smile. "I remember leaving behind everything I knew. Both of my cultures, family, friends, all the places I'd seen all my life…and I did it of my own volition, not like this." He tilted his head. "She'll come to love us, just don't press her."

Menw listened to all this with a raised eyebrow. "I thank you for the lesson, Julio, for I am but a humble nobody, young and foolish."

Julio shrugged off the annoyed sarcasm but shut his mouth and watched his legs dangle from the wall.

"Now, now, children," Cam muttered, used to their age-difference squabbles.

In silence, friends again as usual, the three waited patiently for Jodhi's return.

Rachel answered the door, wearily, but snapped upright upon seeing Jodhi. "Jodhi! Oh god, where've you been!"

Jodhi let herself to be pulled inside then, as soon as the door had closed, allowed herself to be enveloped in loving hugs and kisses.

Steeling herself, Jodhi pulled away and faced the confused face of her girlfriend. She set her face firm, almost cold. "I'm leaving, Rachel. it's not to do with you, I promise, but I have to do some travelling, some experiencing, and some learning. So I'm leaving as soon as I'm done here."

Rachel stood, her arms dangling aimlessly by her sides, face frozen in shock.

"Mum would like it if you visited her. She knows about us, and she likes you, so it'd be nice if you kept her company once in a while."

"You told her!" Rachel accused, pointlessly.

"I did," Jodhi shrugged, "but she'd already guessed anyway."

"Where're you going?"

Jodhi recognised the pain behind the cool words. "I don't know. Please don't ask me to explain, Rach. I have to go away a while, maybe I'll be able to tell you someday, but right now that's all I can say."

"Who is she?" came the expected reply.

"There's no-one else."

"You're going alone?"

"With friends."

"Since when?"

"This morning." Jodhi realised she had begun imitating the short, thrusting sentences that were being directed at her and sighed. "I'm sorry, Rach. I'll be back sometime. Please let me go."

Rachel laughed. "And if I don't?"

Jodhi hung her head. "Please don't do this, Rach."

"Don't do what?" Rachel moved closer. "Don't thank you for tearing out my heart? For not giving a flying crap? Don't love you? What, you want me to wish you all the best and wave bye-bye with a jolly smile?!"

"I seem to recall a time when you were begging me not to let you love me." Jodhi's voice scraped through the lump in her throat, holding back the tears. "I remember all those times you begged me not to tell, not to be who I really was because you were so afraid. It tore my heart every day not to be allowed to tell the world that I love you, that you were mine."

Rachel let tears run down her cheeks and drop onto her jumper, staining the light blue a dark, spreading navy. "So, now I'm repaid." She sobbed. "God, Jo, tell the world! Shout it from the roof! I don't care, if that's what you need to stay!"

"Rach, that's not—"

Rachel threw open the door and strode out into the middle of the road. Cars honked and neighbours peeked out of the windows as she spread her arms wide and lifted her head to shout. "I, Rachel Amory, love with all my heart Jodhi Maye! And I don't care anymore who knows it, because She's threatening to leave me! Jodhi, please, please stay with me! I'm sorry! I love you!"

22

Jodhi stared at Rachel, mouth open, heart wrenching. She edged out of the door and beckoned Rachel over.

From the corner of her eye she saw Cam, Menw and Julio tiptoeing closer and shook her head slightly. They moved back, disappeared around the corner, unseen.

Rachel stopped and waited at the end of the driveway.

"Rach, please!" Jodhi begged. "It's not about that! I'm glad you finally got the courage to do it, but I still have to go."

Rachel turned and marched back into the road.

By now the pavement was filling with observers, and drivers gawped through their windscreens.

"Then run me down!" she ordered the cars. "Do it now and may the image never leave that heartless bitch's brain! May she never forget is was her who caused it!"

"I'm sorry, Rachel." Jodhi turned and walked quickly to her friends, who let her go past a pace or two, then followed.

Once away from the traffic, Cam touched Jodhi's arm. "She'll be all right. I can help a bit later."

Jodhi looked at him, uselessly swiping at her damp face, succeeding only in spreading the wetness around a little. She saw he would help her send thoughts to Rachel, would help Rachel herself find a calm place in her head. She smiled and nodded.

Menw handed her an enormous handkerchief and Jodhi took it with a small grin, drying her face and eyes, taking her pack from the struggling Julio and plodding on bravely back to the cottage in the woods.

It was a long walk, and well after dark by the time they arrived. The men were barely tired—used to plenty more exercise, Julio explained, but Jodhi threw herself down in the nearest corner and rested her head tiredly against the wall.

Julio gestured to the bed. "Take that, Jodhi, we can get you a new sleeping bag tomorrow. You should sleep now."

Jodhi shook her head. "Do you guys have a radio?" she asked, consulting her watch.

"Sure, I have one somewhere." Julio scratched his head and poked his head into his bag, rummaging. "Something you want to hear?" came his muffled voice.

Jodhi nodded, then realised he couldn't see. "Not really, just felt like a bit of music."

"Cool," Julio escaped, holding a battered old radio in one hand. He looked at it mournfully. "Sorry, it came second-hand and it got…bashed up a bit following us around. It works great though. Where do you want it?"

Jodhi shrugged and held out her hands. "I'll keep it low."

Julio handed it to her and settled himself a short distance away. "Cam stays up late, Menw sleeps like a dead thing, and I'd like to listen to the music too—if that's OK by you? I'd like to hear something new."

Jodhi nodded absently, turning the tuner and flicking the on switch. A crackled song came through and she hummed it to herself as she adjusted the reception and drew out the aerial. She left the volume to a murmur and set it beside her.

"I'm sorry about your girlfriend," Julio ventured, cautiously.

Jodhi looked at him sharply, then relaxed and nodded. "Yeah…she was always something of an overreactor…"

"Cam will help you make her feel better—about you leaving, and about herself. If you let him."

"I guess I should." Jodhi sighed. "Least my mum was all right. Hey, she gave me…" Jodhi rummaged through her pocket, finally pulling a folded cheque from her jeans. She opened it and her eyes grew wide. Made out to CASH, Jodhi held a cheque for £5000. She showed it Julio who whistled appreciatively.

"Wow…" he smiled and handed it back, "that ought to keep you well."

Jodhi frowned. "Maybe it should keep us?" She gestured in a general way. "You guys are letting me come along, I know it's 'cause of the…the bite thing, but still. I might as well donate it to the cause. I know you mean well." She handed it back to him.

"Keep it for now," he told her. "You can cash it tomorrow and then decide what to do."

Jodhi nodded and they listened until Julio, making a surprised sound at the 1am news jingle, suggested they get some sleep.

"I enjoyed listening," he said quietly.

"Me too. But don't think this means we're friends," she warned.

Julio saw her smile and matched it with one of his own. "Wouldn't dream of it.

Jodhi lay awake in the dark, feeling the lumpy mattress under her back, buckled and bowed into the shapes of how many other people's bodies, that had once slept here in the darkness.

I'm leaving, she thought, hardly believing it to be truth until now. But it's

24

always easier to think such things in the small morning hours. She drifted into an uncomfortable sleep just before dawn could disturb her.

When she woke, it was to a mock cheer from Julio. "Evening, sleepy." He grinned and brought her some cold breakfast. "Sorry, you missed the hot stuff...but it tastes fine cold."

Jodhi looked at it—bacon sandwiches. She screwed her mouth into a smile. "Healthy." She took a bite and savoured it. "Never had cold bacon before...nice."

"Cam's our resident chef."

"Thanks, Cam," Jodhi called, then realised he wasn't around. "Where'd he go?"

"He takes a run most mornings," Julio explained. "While me and Menw sit around and be repulsive in all our body fat."

Jodhi laughed through another mouthful of food. "Sorry!" she exclaimed, realising she had sprayed a few crumbs on Julio's jacket.

He wiped them off with a chuckle. "No problemo."

"So when do we go?" she asked now, carefully swallowing before she spoke again, and then taking another huge bite as Julio spoke.

"When Cam comes back, he'll be carrying a big bucket of water. Menw will heat it, we'll wash, and then we'll go. First to the bank, for you, and to pick up anything you want to buy. Then...actually I'm not sure." He looked for Menw, found him seated outside, drawing patterns in the soil. "Menw, where are we going next?"

Menw hummed for a moment. "Not sure..."

"Helpful," Julio commented and shrugged. "He'll lead us wherever his instincts say to go, or Cam will take us someplace his talent tells him to—he is either blessed or cursed, depending on his mood, with precognitive visions. Sometimes we follow me, but not much, mine's not that kind of a talent."

"I still don't know what Menw's talent is," Jodhi told him, licking the last of the bacon grease from her fingers. "Come on, I really should know."

Julio gestured for her to follow him outside. "Menw, time to show Jodhi what you do. She's right, she really ought to know."

Menw nodded, stood and dusted soil from his hands. "See that tree?" He pointed. Jodhi nodded. "Ok, go check it—make sure it's just a normal tree."

Jodhi looked at him strangely but went, walked around the tree, knocked on its surface, pulled away a small strip of bark and walked back nodding. "OK, it's a tree...want me to check you got nothing up your sleeves too?" She grinned.

25

Menw shrugged and held out his arms. "By all means."

"He takes his talent seriously, Jodhi," Julio murmured. "You'll see why when you see it in action."

Jodhi kept her face straight as she peered up each sleeve and saw it was clear. She nodded solemnly and stepped back.

Menw nodded and faced the tree Jodhi had checked. He raised one hand, snapped his fingers and pointed to the tree—almost idly.

Jodhi gasped and stared. The tree had turned blue! She ran over to it, touched it, peeled bark from it…it was blue underneath. She rubbed the colour with her fingers, and nothing came off save splinters of blue bark. As she stared in amazement, Menw snapped his fingers again. The tree turned back to its normal dark brown in front of her popping eyeballs.

"I am a mage," Menw called. "We presumed you would believe it more readily if accompanied by a demonstration. We know well enough about cynical natures and those charlatans who style themselves 'Magicians.'" He scoffed at the very thought and sat back down.

"Wha—" Jodhi managed to say, but just then Cam came jogging back into view.

He carried a bucket almost half his size, with a lid secured on the top to prevent the water splashing out. He was topless, dirtied, sweaty and exhausted, but as he collapsed to the ground beside Menw he grinned up at Jodhi by her tree.

"Nothing like a long run to wake you up in the morning," he proclaimed. "I presume Menw did his tree thing?" He nodded, without waiting for a reply. "He likes that trick."

Menw nodded. "I like that trick." He mimicked Cam's faint archaic accent fairly well and grinned to himself as he took the bucket inside. There was a faint crackling sound, making Jodhi whirl towards the cottage, then Menw poked his head out. "I shall be finished in a few minutes, and then you all may follow in an orderly fashion."

"Huh," was Jodhi's reply.

"He heated the water, now he's going to wash first," Julio explained.

"Heated? Oh, with the…the…" Jodhi snapped her fingers and pointed in the style she had just seen.

"Basically, yes," Julio agreed.

"Right…" Jodhi went to the rock Menw had been sitting on and let herself sit down with a thump. "Who the hell are you people?" she muttered loudly.

Neither man said anything; allowing the question to be rhetorical as Jodhi accepted what she had just seen.

"So…how powerful is he?" she asked finally.

"Very," Cam said.

"He's the most powerful mage anyone has record of," Julio agreed. "Course he's also the oldest."

"How old?" Jodhi cringed in anticipation.

"I believe he's forgotten!" Julio laughed. "But ask him to tell you about just about anything important human history knows of, plus a few things it doesn't, and he'll have all the answers—and most of them first-hand at that. He seems to be quite good at being in the right places."

"I think he was attracted to them," Cam said.

"With his instinct thing?" Jodhi asked, already knowing the answer.

"Yep," Julio answered her anyway.

Then Menw emerged from the cottage, some steam following him out. "That's better," he said, grandly. "Who's next?"

Julio and Cam both looked at Jodhi who shrugged and made her way to the cottage. "You promise not to peek, right?" she said with a faltering smile.

"There's curtains on the windows, and a bolt on the inside," Julio reassured her.

"Yeah, but, Cam…"

Cam's eyes widened. "Never!" he said, hurt by the insinuation that he would purposely peek.

"He can also tone down his talent, for just-in-cases." Julio directed the comment towards Cam.

"I already had!" he protested. "I can't turn it off," he explained to Jodhi now. "I have to keep it on, but it's down for now, if that makes you feel better."

Jodhi caught his full message—he usually kept it on full or high to catch calls for help, or calls to travel somewhere. He couldn't block it off entirely, but turned down as far as he was able it wouldn't pick up accidental pictures of any sort. She nodded and smiled at him apologetically. He nodded at her and smiled back; he understood, no hard feelings.

When they were all washed and ready, the four of them hefted their backpacks and set off to walk towards the small Darwen town centre.

Chapter 3

Jodhi insisted on sharing what remained of the cheque. After buying a sleeping bag, warm clothes, walking boots and some other things recommended by the three experienced travellers, there was still plenty left.

Cam—generally in charge of the group's money—insisted she keep hold of it, to spend if she wished.

Smiling, Jodhi had ordered them into a nearby restaurant where she proceeded to feed all four of them until her companions begged for reprieve. Jodhi finished her last bite with relish and grinned happily.

Drinking their complimentary coffee, talk finally turned to the near future.

"I am unsure..." Menw admitted. "There is some place tugging me towards it, but I can give it no name."

"But you'll know it when we get there, right? You know which way to go?" Julio phrased it as a question, but knew the answer from experience.

"I do," Menw confirmed. "I can take us in the direction of the tug and I will know as soon as we arrive. I have done this before, as you both know. Jodhi, I hope you can simply trust me."

"He never fails," Cam said confidently. He knew Menw's instinctual "tug" would lead him to wherever they were meant to be, and would do so in good time for whatever they must face.

Seeing this, Julio nodded and Jodhi shrugged her acceptance.

"However, I do not need to take us yet. The tug is there, but gentle, we will be there during the next full moon, I think. So tonight we will begin your meditations, and in good time before the change days we will find a place for you. If you work hard, we should be able to control you easily from a lock-up place away from people."

Jodhi stared at him in horror. "What!" she spluttered. "You're gonna lock me up! I thought the whole point what that I wouldn't need to be locked up!"

"Eventually, yes," Menw replied calmly. "However, you were bitten by a lunar-wolf and so for now we must assume that you are one also. Therefore until we can trust the wolf, or trust your control over it…there is no other way to prevent you from killing every full moon. Unless, of course, you wish to wake to the day…in a strange place…your stomach strangely full, wondering whose blood is drying on your skin. Would you like Cam to show you the picture?"

Jodhi looked at Cam who could not hold her gaze. She turned her stare back on Menw. "I get it! I got it without the description, thanks! Sorry for being a bit edgy…this whole werewolf killer thing is pretty, you know, FUCKING SCARY!" she cried and pushed away from the table, leaving behind the money for the meal and racing past the curious eyes of the other diners.

Julio nodded for the other men to stay and took off in pursuit.

Jodhi had made it only to the bus stop, where she was now perched on a seating bar and weeping quietly.

Julio approached slowly, knowing she wanted to be alone as much as she needed someone around. "No matter what," he realised, "she will always associate us, to some extent, with being turned." His shoulder drooped in sadness for Jodhi, and for all the people she would push away, and he moved away a bit. Not intruding, but there, just in case.

When Menw and Cam ventured out, he told them to find a place and they would turn up sooner or later, and they left for the library.

Jodhi had sensed Julio's presence, felt him move close then back away to wait patiently.

Grateful resentment flooded her as she stared at the floor, blurred through her tears, and wished for death. "Anything is better than this."

***

"So where shall we go next? If we are not needed," Cam asked over a book.

Menw grunted and shrugged. "Pick someone you haven't seen in a while and pay a visit. I'll let you know when we need to rush off."

Cam nodded and thought. "Ask Julio," he suggested.

"Hmm. Think a little longer before we resort to that. Although he does tend to come up with good suggestions for aimlessness," Menw agreed. "And speaking of the devil, here he is with Cerberus," Menw said quietly, and then burst into laughter.

Cam gave him a dirty look.

"Oh now, Cam, I don't mean it like that," the old wizard said, injured. "But I apologise anyway."

Cam shook his head. "Never do that again. If either of those two heard…"

Menw nodded in a hurry. "I prefer to keep my bones intact. I shall find another way of being humorous."

"You've been trying that for centuries," Cam said with a sly smile and stood to greet Julio and Jodhi, leaving Menw chuckling and pretending to frown.

Julio nodded to Cam and Menw and pulled out a chair for Jodhi. She sat and he joined her and patted her arm.

"How do you feel, Jodhi?" Menw asked gently.

She nodded. "Sorry about…before. I know why you have to…lock me away. I'm just scared, is all."

"I know love," Cam told her. "But you'll remember nothing. Not until it's controlled. You'll wake up yourself, and you might be a bit tired and achy but that's all."

Jodhi nodded. "That's what Julio said. He said I'll maybe feel like my skin is being tugged when I'm changing and it'll only hurt a second…then when I change back it's just like shrinking."

Menw nodded. "Many studies have been done. They all come out saying much the same."

Jodhi nodded. "God, I feel like Oz."

"Oz?" Cam queried. "As in L. Frank Baum or Judy Garland?"

Julio shook his head. "Not a place, Cam. A character."

Cam nodded. "Then it could only be Buffy. You found a fellow obsessive I see."

Julio nodded and Cam turned back to his book with a "Kids these days" shake of the head.

"Wanna see if they have the books?" Jodhi asked. Julio nodded and they took off into the stacks.

***

"I know where we can visit," Cam told them all as Julio and Jodhi returned. "We haven't seen our friends in Department E for a while…maybe they need a helping hand. Maybe they have some tips for you, Jodhi."

Julio grinned. "Cool! I've not seen those guys in ages! You heard about their new recruits, right?"

Cam nodded, Menw nodded, Jodhi looked blank.

"Department E," explained Julio, "deal with all sorts of supernatural, extraordinary, extrasensory, weird-ass things that go on in the world. They do research and experiments on willing subjects, they discover those with powers—latent or not—and bring them in to study them and enlist them in the fight against the occasional bad guys that hit their turf. They don't fight much though, and they at least claim to never keep people in who don't want to be there—though we know they have in the past...it's a complicated place."

"Okay," Jodhi sighed, "I'm getting way too used to all this strange crap."

"So how are the new heroes holding up?" Cam asked.

"They're alright from what I heard. They're doing tests, helping out; I think Cydir is one of their agents. Sara and Amy are, like, scientists I guess. Janna and James are planning to get married, last I heard, and they both work together with their powers, you know."

Jodhi listened to all this in bemused ignorance. "I'm sure you're about to tell me who you're talking about, right?"

"A few years ago, three friends had a special talent that they didn't know about. They made a computer game together, and brought the characters in it to life. Their talent—to create things with their imagination. They based the characters on themselves, so when one got hurt their model did to a lesser extent. They lost one of their good guys, but defeated the bad guy, and the remaining creation is now a field agent. Sara and Amy are a couple, Sara worked for the Department before they arrived and by all accounts they just hit it off from the second they saw each other, now Sara does the research while Amy stuffs it all into a computer and tries to force it to make sense. Janna and James are the other two talented, they're getting married but don't really do all that much in the Department."

"Right..." Jodhi murmured. "This is weird stuff."

"Even from our point of view, yes," Julio agreed. "But these guys at Depot E are experts in research; they taught us most of what we know about our talents too. And also curses like yours. Which then, naturally, led onto cures and control. So you might want to thank them in a while, when you see what their methods let you do."

"Right...I'll be sure to do that," Jodhi agreed bemusedly. "So...how do we get to them?"

"Well, they're in London, so we take a long stroll," Julio explained.

"We walk to London!"

"Sure, how'd you think people got around before trains and cars and the like?"

"Shanks' Pony…" Jodhi reluctantly acknowledged.

"Shanks' who?" It was Julio's turn to be bemused.

"Uh? Oh, feet, walking." Jodhi gave him a smug grin. "Ha, I finally knew something you didn't!"

Julio stuck out his tongue.

"Now, now, ladies," murmured Cam with a smile.

Menw sat up and stretched. "Well, no time like the present. We usually go at our own speed and take detours on the way to stay each night at a friends," he told Jodhi. "It does take a little longer this way, but we're in no hurry right now and it costs us less than to stay in hotels. Plus, it's worth it to catch any news we missed, and occasionally help with a minor problem."

"Or a major one." Cam grimaced, sitting erect suddenly and grabbing his head in both hands.

Jodhi leapt to her feet, but Menw and Julio simply muttered calming words at him and waited.

"It happens," Julio explained quietly, telling Jodhi to sit. "Remember I said he gets precognitive visions sometimes, they hurt but only for a minute, then it's fine. He'll need to rest for longer tonight, and have a cracking headache for a while, but that's all. Give him a minute, but if you touch him it can screw up the vision and leave him totally dazed for days afterwards. I tried it once…never again."

Jodhi sat and waited impatiently until Cam relaxed and rested himself bodily on the table. "Oh wow," he gasped.

Menw was already handing him pills and he swallowed them eagerly. "Thanks."

They waited for him to breathe easier and speak to them.

He did soon enough in broken sentences as he tried to remember. "Someone…someone old. A woman…werewolf…controlled…she used to be a good guy…tall…strong…name?" He thought hard and shook his head. "That's all I got…something bad, though, to do with your tug Menw. Guess we have a reason to go visiting after all."

"We do?" Jodhi asked, confused.

"We know there's something and someone, and that we're being pulled to it," Julio explained. "We need to find out if anyone else knows of it, or if there's anything they can give us or tell us or advise us."

Cam nodded then winced in pain at his tender temples. "I'll be ready in a minute," he promised.

And he was. Once the pills kicked in he nodded, head still aching but the throb subsiding a little, and they stood and left the library.

"Where to first?" Julio asked as they started out in a seemingly random direction.

"I thought Lana in Burnley," Menw said. "Not very far away, so Cam will be able to rest as much as he needs. And if anyone knows ought of this woman she will, or she will know where to find out."

"Lana is untalented, technically," Julio explained to Jodhi. "But she is the wiz when it comes to tracking down information. She has a photographic memory, so if she's seen this woman she'll remember, or she'll tell us where we can go to find out what we need, and if it's not in her memory then she has this amazing way of knowing exactly where to go or how to find out."

"Wikipedia personified," Jodhi said and nodded, then, "Never mind, computer stuff," at the blank faces of her companions, then concentrated on conserving her energy for the trek ahead. "I'm so spoiled with cars..." She decided some time into the trip when her feet ached and her calf muscles screamed.

"Want to rest?" Cam asked gently, seeing her pain.

She shrugged bravely. "I'm alright."

He nodded and spoke anyway. "Can we stop to eat for a short while? I need to rest."

"Of course." Menw nodded and Julio found a small café where they piled in and ordered food.

"Thanks," Jodhi whispered to Cam who nodded and smiled faintly.

After slowly eating, Cam gave Jodhi a sly questioning look and, upon receiving a small nod in return, he stood. "I feel better," he said, meaning it was time to continue. They left and set off again, by now halfway there.

***

Close to the heart of Burnley, Lana Newley was poring over a stack of books in her library (the library taking up essentially of the whole of the large house she lived in). With titles such as "Oxygenation of a Vampire's blood" and "Gremlins—a history of fact and folklore", it was no wonder she seemed to be nodding off when a booming knock from the front door startled her to her feet.

She yawned widely, staggered a little and pinched her cheeks to bring herself back to reality. Pulling off her glasses, she dropped them onto an open book then closed the book with a thud and a tinkle of broken glass. "Shit..." she muttered. Then "Whozzat?" as the door knock came again.

She waddled a little stiffly to the door and peeped through the spyhole.

"Ah!" She smiled and threw open the door. "Welcome! Come in, come in! You and your new friend. I'm Lana," she babbled as everyone filed in.

"Jodhi," murmured the stranger, taking in the shabbily dressed owner of a near-mansion.

Lana's dark brown hair was a permanent horror, her clothes were old or, as she preferred, comfy. She was small but stocky, with a hawklike smile of deep intelligence, quite unlike the sparrow Jodhi had imagined.

"Poor girl," went on the unusual figure, her dark eyes, framed with the squint lines that came with reading old and faded texts, scolding Menw. "You look exhausted! You too!" She ushered Jodhi and Cam into the library, swept some books off four chairs, and sat them down. She took the third chair for herself, gave the fourth to Julio, and simply glared at Menw. "Now why would you do this to these two poor people?" she demanded. "I bet you walked all day, miles and miles! I can tell Jodhi's not used to it, and I'm betting Cam had a vision! What were you thinking?!" Her voice rose to a crescendo as Menw flinched apologetically.

"It was important," Julio said. "Something big. We rested on the way, but Cam and Jodhi weren't forced to walk so far, they chose to."

Lana nodded at Julio kindly then turned back to Menw. "Still!" She frowned. "Well, as you're here you can fix my reading glasses—they're in the big book on the table. The green coloured one. Then you can rustle up some food from the kitchen. And make it a good one!" she warned.

Menw nodded meekly and opened the book. He spoke a few words under his breath, and then placed the repaired glasses on Lana's lap as he hurried in the direction of the kitchen.

Lana dug a glasses case from her desk and carefully inserted the repaired pair inside, then she sat calmly and waited for the food as Cam dozed softly and Julio and Jodhi chatted about television and music.

Soon, Menw arrived with a tray bearing chicken and salad. "This was all I could think up at short notice." He smiled, setting the tray on the floor and helping himself.

While eating, Lana finally asked what brought them to her door.

"Well," Menw explained, swallowing quickly. He explained Jodhi, then Cam's vision.

Lana mused on the vague descriptions a moment. "It sounds like…there was a werewolf once who fought on our side. But she vanished about 250 years or so ago, her partner was found dead by the remains of a vampire. She's not fought on our side since, but there's been no exact proof of her fighting for the other side either, not recently anyhow."

"Are you able to find out more here?" Menw asked.

Lana shook her head. "I don't think I have the right information here. If she has laid low for so long there'll be nothing in my books that's not already in mine or your heads. But you could try Mark Gossamer. If there's anything to be found on the Internet, he'll have it for you, and as we know he has an amazing network of rumours, so if there's anything on the grapevine he'll know."

Julio nodded. "Mark, where is he now?"

"Nottingham, last address I have," Lana said. "I'll let you have it before you go."

"Thanks, Lana." Julio smiled. "Can we borrow your TV?"

"I thought Buffy was on at night." Cam smiled.

"It is, but there's plenty more TV to watch." Julio grinned.

Jodhi nodded eagerly and Lana pointed them in the direction of the barely-used living room.

Hiding behind more stacks of books was a large TV, complete with VCR and DVD player.

"Wow!" Jodhi grinned at the size of the TV and sat down on a slightly musty-smelling chair.

"Let's see if it works first..." Julio crossed his fingers. "It gets so little use it could've died months ago, and Lana'd never know." He pushed the on switch and the TV worked. Then he pushed the DVD power, and that worked too. He clapped playfully and motioned for Jodhi to stay put.

"What you want to watch, Jodhi?" Julio asked, motioning to the DVDs. "Most of these aren't even Lana's, it's kind of a dumping ground for everybody on the way through, so anyone can use them."

Jodhi started browsing but eventually gave up. "Just recommend me something?" she suggested.

Julio looked thoughtful and then smiled. "Sure thing." He grabbed a disc and pushed it gently into the slot.

***

In the library, Lana and Cam were discussing his vision.

"It was definitely her!" He nodded emphatically, looking at a page in a dusty tome. "Oh how I hoped I was mistaken, but I can't have been."

35

Menw looked over his shoulder at the caption. "Sansé," he said. "I believe the name is familiar, but there has been more than one by that name in the history of the world, I am certain." He hedged his bets hopefully.

Lana nodded, oblivious to the particular tension. "Of course, but this is a special Sansé. The werewolf Cam saw. The book says she was a fighter for the good, she and her husband, Danieel—also a wolf. She vanished one night. The conclusion from what was found is that they both attacked a vampire, who bit Danieel. Sansé saved him by severing his head with her sword, and was never seen again—not on our side, anyhow…"

"Yes, we do indeed know that Sansé well," Menw mused, giving nothing away. "Might she be involved, but have come back to our side?"

Cam shook his head. He sent a vivid picture of her to Menw, the ones from his earlier vision, complete with the feelings of hatred and disgust she radiated.

"Not back on our side, then," Menw agreed.

Lana was wandering her maze of a room, muttering to herself. "I have no way of knowing what she's up to right now. Mark is your best bet that I can think of. Menw, are you being pulled anywhere?"

The wizard nodded. "I don't know where, but somewhere not too far away. It's not for a while yet though, so we have time to visit Mark. We were also planning a trip to Department E."

Lana smiled. "Good plan. Hey, they might be able to help you with Jodhi's werewolf thing."

"That's what we thought." Cam nodded, still studying the picture, trying to remember…trying at the same time to forget. Finally he snapped the book shut with a shrug.

"Take it with you, might come in handy," Lana told him. "Now, let me go sort out beds for you all. It's evening now and, Cam, you look ready to drop."

Cam gave a rueful nod. "A bed would be very welcome," he admitted.

"Won't be long then." Lana scurried out of the door and towards the stairs.

Chapter 4

A large copper-grey beast bearing some small resemblances to a wolf prowled around the cobblestones of a stereotypically quaint village. She sniffed the air and drew back into the shadows as two laughing girls walked past.

The wolf continued walking, approaching the entrance to the Church grounds cautiously. She stuck a paw tentatively over the threshold of the vestibule and bared her teeth in a smile as she felt nothing. Some Churches had been blessed, long ago, to keep out her kind. But some, alas for those who frequented this one, were not.

She darted along the open path as stealthily as her bristling frame would allow and paused outside the big doors.

A moment later a naked woman stood tall before them.

She shook herself a little and held up one hand, which had retained its claws.

With a wail of terror, she slashed down across her skin, ripping and tearing, before collapsing to the floor to writhe and sob, crying in terror about a great demon.

The door opened and a kindly smile dropped to a grimace of horror as an old vicar hurried to the figure lying on the floor.

"By the great God, girl, what happened to you?" He gasped, kneeling over her.

The girl called out incoherently and the vicar removed his overcoat, which he had just put on, ready to go home, and spread it across the girl's nakedness.

"Come on, lass." He grunted and willed her to help him move her. "Get you inside." He panted as the girl finally began to uncurl and move.

He took her through into his vestry, where she collapsed on a comfortable red sofa, sobbing.

"Now, girl, what happened to you?" the man asked gently, touching her shoulder.

She jerked and hit out, making him leap back.

"Now, now, it's all over now, dear. I'm going to help you. Let me call the police out, they'll get whoever did this to you."

The girl shook and sobbed as he dialled the phone and spoke quickly to a local policeman before hanging up and returning to the girl's side.

"I'd give you a wash, dear, but Bobby says I'd best not until they've looked for DNA samples." The vicar sighed sadly. "Whoever did this to you, well, he's a demon for sure, whatever else God might have made him."

The girl looked at him for the first time, eyes glittering with what he thought to be tears.

"There, there, you're all safe now." He smiled gently.

The girl smiled back, a cruel glint of sharp teeth suddenly showing in her strangely fur-lined face. "There, there," she said mockingly, "you'll be in Heaven soon enough." She grinned and leapt onto him, the change completing even as she moved.

Chapter 5

Julio and Jodhi were left to their own devices.

"At least she isn't running away again," was Cam's viewpoint, seconded by Lana, arriving back into the room with a nod.

"It is not Jodhi that concerns me. More Julio. He fails over and over to take these things seriously."

"Menw, not everybody has to have kittens to take something seriously. Now, he's looking after Jodhi, which is something we need until everybody is certain she has accepted us properly, and he's doing a far better job of it than you could and that's a fact you know full well so don't look at me like I just kicked your favourite puppy. I think we are best to leave him to it until we need him for something else."

Menw nodded. "Very well. I still think his attitude needs some readjusting, however I will give this one to you. We can plan and discuss far more easily without his constant pointless interruptions."

"Alright," Lana interrupted now, "we can play at insulting Julio later. Now, you are going to get some sleep. Menw, top of the stairs turn right, second door down. Cam, same but the first door. I threw a couple of sleeping bags into the TV room for the young ones and left them to it. If we're going to visit Mark, we should probably get some good sleep."

Menw and Cam allowed Lana to usher them from the room and up the stairs. They said their goodnights, and the three of them crawled exhausted into their beds.

In the TV room, Julio and Jodhi swapped yawns and reluctantly turned the TV off to get some rest of their own.

Jodhi tossed and turned a little, unused to sleeping in strange places, unable also to turn her mind from the things she had done and learned over the course of this single day. A werewolf. Her—a creature from a bad Hollywood gorefest. The idea was laughable! And yet…and yet it was true. She could feel the wolf growing inside of her, waiting for the chance to stretch its claws and sink its teeth into something soft. She shuddered and curled up into a ball, staring at the wall until she drifted into a restless sleep.

Julio slept peacefully as always.

Lana lay on her side and yawned. So she was to see Mark again, it seemed. They had remained friends, but only from a distance; the past five years, since the break-up, they had not met face-to-face. And now she would see him again. In company of Cam. Sighing, she tucked the duvet under her chin and closed her eyes.

Menw thought of Julio and frowned. *Young upstart*, he thought. Soon, though, he turned his mind to the ocean and meditated himself to sleep.

Cam could hardly settle on a topic of thought. From Lana, the way his heart had leapt and then seemed lighter upon seeing her again. To Julio and Menw and the storm that was directly over the horizon. To Jodhi, their new charge, a human—but occasionally one in the guise of a wolf. To Sansé, at which point he closed his eyes and forced his head clear, a task which had always come easy to him, though the Lord knew he had often done nothing to deserve such peace. Nevertheless, it was a long time before he relaxed enough to allow sleep to overcome him.

***

In the morning they arose one by one, the group in the living room slowly swelling to its full number. When they were all there, Menw stood. "Breakfast, all?"

All nodded.

He smiled and spread his arms. Suddenly each knee balanced a wooden tray, on which was a plate featuring a full fried breakfast.

"Well, if we have a long day ahead, we may as well begin it correctly." Menw smiled and began eating his.

Jodhi hesitated, but only long enough to realise the food was doing nobody any harm. She took a tentative forkful of egg and tasted. Soon, she was tucking in happily with the rest of them.

Once breakfast was finished, Menw banished the plates and trays and grew solemn. "Sansé has returned. Of this, Cam's vision has informed us. Jodhi, you know nothing of Sansé, but Lana will gladly fill you in. Julio, you know of her but have never encountered her in any form. I warn you both, and us all: she is dangerous. Incredibly so. She can seduce the body and the mind, she is a mood-wolf and can shift her shape from human to animal at will, and even in human form can force your eyes and mind to see, your skin to feel, your nose to smell, your ears to hear whatever she wishes—be it real or false.

40

She kills without thought for anything save perhaps how much pain and trauma she can inflict on you, or the unlucky person who finds you. She is cruel, vicious and evil. She—"

Julio groaned. "We get the picture, Menw. Don't mess wit dat bitch."

Menw stared at him. "If you truly got the picture you would not be so flippant about it!"

Julio rolled his eyes. "Look, gringo, I'm not about to walk up and tweak the lady's tail, alright? I see her—I'm out."

Menw stood up. "If you see her, Julio, the chances are you will be dead before you can run."

"What, she got Medusa vision or something?"

"She doesn't need Medusa vision, boy. She can rip you apart like melted butter the second she gets bored of turning your brain into soup with her mind tricks."

Julio raised an eyebrow. "Alright. So, like I said, she's a scary one. Can we move on to something of more immediate importance now?"

Menw opened his mouth to reply angrily but Lana cleared her throat. "Immediately, we plan to travel to Mark in Nottingham. He may be able to help us. He has some other avenues of research plus an uncanny grapevine for rumours, and also may possess one or two volumes I am missing from my own library. From there, we move on down to Department E. Settled?"

Julio nodded. "Sounds like a plan. When do we go?"

"Now, I believe would be the optimum time," Menw answered scornfully. "Unless you wish to sit around a little longer doing nothing to help the people being injured by Sansé? Or perhaps to wait and see if she will come and find you—after all, that way you could prove you were paying attention to my warning."

"Now you're just being silly," Lana scolded, but Julio hushed her.

"No, no, the old man has something he wants to say. Let him say it."

Menw shrugged. "You care little for what we do, you care nothing at all for other people, you do not bother to involve yourself in our discussions unless you have some wise remark to make, you are lazy and selfish and when you do decide to join us in carrying out our plans you are always the one who does not listen carefully enough and winds up making a mockery of the whole thing!"

Julio clenched his jaw, stood up and spoke tightly. "Now I know how you feel. Thank you. Goodbye." He turned on his heel and stalked out of the room. A few moments later, he stalked back past them with his pack over one shoulder. Another long moment later the front door slammed.

"Well done," Cam said with sarcastic pleasantness. "Anyone else you'd like to get rid of, while you're at it?"

Menw scowled. "Shut up, Cam. He will be fine. He knows what to do; he can take care of himself. Now perhaps we can begin our journey?"

Cam sighed, knowing better than to argue and more concerned about the dangers lying in their path if, indeed, Sansé had returned. "As you say, he will be fine. And yes, we should begin."

Jodhi watched this interaction curiously. Neither seemed to take the win, yet at the same time Cam seemed to submit unwillingly to Menw. She wondered about their leaving Julio alone, but presumed they must know better than her and had no wish to become embroiled in the argument. Even Lana watched with resigned disinterest.

"Then pack your bags, and let's go!" the researcher ordered before fighting could begin again.

They relented and headed to their separate rooms. A few minutes later they returned, their packs full. Lana was a while longer, as she was beginning her packing from scratch, but soon enough she was ready also and the four of them rested for a speedy drink before leaving.

As Jodhi tilted back her head to take the last dregs of hers, she felt the wolf growl within her and yelped, dropping the glass.

Before the other three had time to react, there was a sound of smashing glass and a figure hurled itself through the window, landing upright on the floor and glaring around.

It was humanoid; it's shape and size that of a grown adult. But its skin was light green, luminous, and its eyes black orbs. And when it snarled, they saw two rows of small, pointed teeth to match its vicious-looking nails.

"Cantor…" Lana breathed.

"Wha—" Cam half-turned and the Cantor leapt at him. In a flash he was on the floor, dazed.

Lana was next. The demon picked her up and threw her bodily out of the window.

But as it turned to Menw, there came a guttural growl from the other side of the room and it turned, just in time to see a huge wolf leap.

The wolf came down upon it with a crash and immediately reached for its throat.

"Jodhi no!" Menw cried, flashing a quick spell to throw the wolf. Another moment, another hasty spell, and both wolf and demon were magically bound, unable to move.

The Cantor scowled and sat silently. But the wolf howled and snarled, trying to loose the binds, throwing itself around the room until Menw, to prevent it breaking the furniture, or itself, threw out another binding, lashing it to the far wall. "Sorry, Jodhi," the wizard muttered, trying to figure out whom to look to first.

Cam groaned and pointed at the window. "Lana…"

Menw nodded. "You can make noise, you can wait," and he leaned out of the broken window, carefully removing the remaining glass shards. "Lana?" he spoke to the body heaped on the floor. "Lana…" He raised a finger and a small bolt of electricity nudged her.

"Wha-? I-? Huh?" Lana was awake in a second and looked around, confused. Menw waited, and remembrance clouded her eyes. "Oh. Cam…?"

Menw nodded. "He's groaning away like usual."

Lana took his proffered hand and pulled herself back through the window, falling with a thud when she saw the wolf stuck gracelessly to the wall and the Cantor bound sullenly on the floor. "Oh…shit," she said. "Jodhi—She's a mood-wolf."

Menw nodded. "More dangerous now, but better to control later."

He shuffled to Cam who was sat up, rubbing his head and grimacing. "I'm OK," he promised and Menw backed away.

"Who do we deal with first?" Lana asked, sitting by Cam and checking his head for bumps.

Cam nodded towards the demon. "That. Jodhi's contained, she will change back into herself once she calms. There is nothing else we can do for her but wait."

Lana thought. "Wait. We should cover her up."

Menw looked at her strangely and she pointed to the torn clothing on the floor.

"Cover the poor girl up, save her some embarrassment if she changes back while we're all here. There's a screen somewhere…ah, cupboard, over there." Lana pulled a black screen from a cupboard neatly concealed between bookcases. "Blocks the sun. Some of these books would turn to dust if they could and I can't stand the curtains being closed all the time," she explained and concealed the slowly calming wolf with it. "There now. Sorry, Menw, go on."

Menw nodded and flicked a hand towards the Cantor, who was immediately upright, hovering a foot above the ground and looking sullen.

Lana shook her head. "Do you know what that is? He's a Cantor demon, a witch's familiar. He'll die before he talks to you—even through torture."

Cam grinned. "He doesn't have to. Menw, ask away." He closed his eyes and concentrated, to pick out the answers from the images that would flash unbidden through its mind as Menw asked his questions.

"You came to kill us," Menw began.

The Cantor nodded easily enough at this, and Cam nodded also.

"Why?"

The Cantor smiled.

Cam frowned. "Witch…She's a friend of somebody else, somebody this creature is afraid of…Sansé? Yes, yes, he knows the name."

"Sansé sent you to kill us?"

Cam nodded.

The Cantor howled.

Cam raised a hand. "Menw, instead of 20 questions—ow about if you give me a some time. I'll get in his head and pull out whatever might be of use to us later, and when we need it I'll have it. That way, we risk missing nothing."

Menw nodded. As you will.

"Use the TV room." Lana gestured to the door.

Cam nodded and, taking the Cantor firmly by a shoulder, pulled him along in mid-air and out of the room.

By now the sounds behind the screen were fewer and softer. The wolf was beginning to calm, and, as Lana peered around, a flash of humanity made its eyes Jodhi's again.

"She will be back soon," Lana observed. "Perhaps it may be useful if I spoke with her alone—upstairs."

Menw knew what "upstairs" meant—Lana's own most private of rooms, even he did not know what was contained within. He nodded now. "As you wish," and loosening the wolf from the wall, but not from its bindings, he chose a book and sat down to read. "I shall be here, call when the binds are ready to be broken, or if you need me."

Lana nodded and, gathering up Jodhi's torn clothes with one hand, took hold of the beast's shoulder, as Cam had done, guiding it through the air and lifting gently to pull it up the stairs.

***

As Cam delved inside the Cantor's head, Jodhi was slowly returning to her human form. Lana watched her carefully until she was fully herself and looking around, bewildered.

44

She turned quickly to shout. "Menw, the binds."

Jodhi was freed almost instantly and she hit the floor with a thud and groaned. "What—"

Lana handed her a dressing gown and Jodhi put it on painfully. "We were attacked. A demon. You probably saved our lives—at least, your wolf did."

"Wolf...that's why I was tied up? Where is the-the—"

"The demon is bound, as you were; Cam is rooting around in its head."

"What was it?"

"A Cantor. They're witch familiars—powerful witches, a weak one couldn't control one of those things. They're basically humanoid in shape, but green-skinned, claws, teeth, black eyes. They are the best sort of familiar—stronger than any human, impervious to pain, loyal even until death. Only a telepath can get any useful information from it, and only because it comes directly from it's head—they will die before revealing anything of their own accord."

"And he-it attacked us?"

"Yes."

"Why?"

"At the behest of its witch; these things don't attack like that for fun."

"Somebody wants to kill us?"

Lana smiled. "Somebody usually wants to kill us. But I can guess that this, something this major, is something to do with Sansé. We'll know more when Cam is done. Come on, I left your bag downstairs; but we're about the same size, raid my wardrobe a bit, find you something to wear for now. We should probably hit the shops when we can, though, get some extra outfits."

Jodhi smiled, faintly troubled. "Good plan. I can see I'll be going through them like nobody's business."

***

Downstairs, Lana, Menw and Jodhi; dressed in a loose-fitting button-up shirt and tracksuit bottoms; waited for Cam to finish.

Eventually they heard a tread and he entered the room, hot and exhausted. "Okay. I got all I could. We can bury it before we leave."

"You killed it?!" Jodhi gaped.

"What choice did I have? We can't take it with us. To send it back to its owner is a fate worse than death—first it will tell her willingly everything it knows of us, then she will likely torture and kill it for failing to complete whatever task she set it."

45

Jodhi nodded. "Okay, okay. I know you guys know best."

"What did you find out?" Menw asked.

Cam sat. "There is a witch working with Sansé. She is powerful, but rather crazy; and well and truly under Sansé's spell. The Cantor was sent essentially to surprise us, strike and do some damage, and retreat with any information it could glean. They obviously weren't expecting us to have picked up a mood-wolf in our travels." He smiled at Jodhi, seeing her burning to ask a question. "We'll talk about that later though. I think an extra day of rest is needed. The thing is that this witch is powerful enough to control two Cantors. The second is here, somewhere, waiting. It will attack once the other does not return, and this one is a master of its breed."

There was silence for a moment, followed by a knock at the door.

Jodhi felt her hackles rise. "Don't move!" she growled. "It's that—the thing—Cantor."

Nobody moved.

The knock came again, harder this time.

"You're sure?" Lana asked.

Jodhi nodded, the wolf inside her snarled and twisted, trying to find a way out. "Wait here," she growled.

Cam stood and she turned on him, eyes feral. He sat again and she left the room.

The three listened carefully. A door opened. A moment of nothing. Then a squeal and a snarl, something broke and footsteps raced down the driveway.

Cam was first into the hall. The door hung off its hinges, splintered, and there was no sign of either Jodhi or the Cantor.

Cam swore to himself and his fist hit the wall.

Lana took his hand. "That won't help." She led him back into the living room.

Chapter 6

Isabel braked heavily as a figure raced out in front of her. It stopped for a moment, shocked by the sudden glare of headlights, and what she saw froze her blood.

A human figure, but green, with eyes like pools of darkness. It bounded away and she saw another figure race past, only a glimpse; yellow eyes, fur, claws, teeth.

She sat still for a moment, swallowing a scream, and then slammed her foot down and sped away.

Reaching work, she sat in the car park for a while, her head hanging against the steering wheel. "I didn't see it. I didn't. I saw nothing. I saw…oh God I saw it. Them. Oh God."

She shrieked as something tapped on her window and a shadow backed away.

Looking up she saw Darren, one of the helpline co-ordinators, looking concerned.

She forced a weak smile and climbed out of the car. "Sorry. Was miles away."

"You don't look so good, Isabel, you okay?"

"I'm fine, fine, really. Sorry." She dashed inside, down the corridor, up the stairs and into the ladies; leaving a row of confused faces behind her.

"She okay?" they echoed to Darren, who shrugged his own confusion.

Isabel sat quietly in a stall, staring at her hand and willing the tremors to stop. When they were almost gone, she stood and walked out, leaning over the sink and staring at herself in the mirror.

"Who are you?" she asked her reflection, who stared back, dumbly.

The door opened. "Oh, sorry, hi, Isabel. Listen, are you okay?"

Isabel looked, saw a concerned face, nodded her head, and then shook it and shrugged. "I don't know, Janey, I really don't," she mumbled.

Janey rested a hand on Isabel's shoulder. "You know if you need someone to talk to, I know you don't know me very well but sometimes it helps to talk to someone you don't know so well."

Isabel almost shrugged the hand off, but saw the sincerity in Janey's eyes and paused. "Thanks Janey, I'll remember that. I best get ready."

Janey nodded and moved aside, watching her leave the room.

Isabel checked the time and saw she was down to just 4 minutes before her shift started. She walked into the office and sat down at her desk. As usual the phone lines were crowded and she slipped the headset on, shook herself to clear her mind and pushed the button for the next caller. "Hello, Hopeline…"

Over the next few hours Isabel listened to the distressed tell her all about their problems in love, in work, at home, with life, with themselves. Problems with violence, confidence, the world at large. Private issues, public issues, small issues and giant issues.

Eventually, talking to a teary housewife whose husband had just left her for a younger model, Isabel's fraying link to her normal life collapsed under the strain of her earlier vision and she snapped. "Look honey, some things just can't be explained, okay? They happen. It's bad. We deal with it the best we can!"

The woman hung up with a loud click. Isabel sighed and dropped her head on the desk, resisting the urge to bang it until her brains rattled. She started when her boss tapped her on the shoulder. "Isabel, can I see you in my office?"

Isabel stood and followed him, the rusty-red curls of his hair bouncing lightly on his collar as he walked. In his office he turned clear blue, worried eyes upon her and closed the door, motioning for her to take a seat.

Isabel sat.

"You've worked here for 3 years, Is, and you've always done brilliantly. Tonight you're fobbing people off and, worse, scolding them. What's wrong?"

Isabel bowed her head.

"Look, Is, I'm being honest with you, I expect the same. Tell me to shut up if it's none of my business, else tell me how I can help."

She shook her head, still avoiding his eyes.

"Alright," he sighed, "I don't want to lose you but I would like you to take a short leave of absence—sick leave, full pay. Sort out whatever it is, get in touch in a couple of weeks and let me know what you want to do."

Isabel nodded, mumbled a grateful thank you and stood to leave.

"We'll miss you, hon," Mitchell said, just before the door closed. Isabel hesitated, half-turned, changed her mind and continued. "I'll miss you," he murmured as she disappeared from view.

Isabel left the building, climbed into her car and faced it almost absently towards home, paying little attention to the journey. In every roadside shadow, every moving tree or bush, she saw a wolf, a demon, a not-so-unreal terror.

***

She slammed the front door and flicked on the light switch, taking in the familiarity of her home. But suddenly even the familiar became a threat. Her home. Yes. But bought by whom? Not by her. They had bought it for her, when they let her go. It may be her name on the deeds, her chosen furniture, her CDs, her TV; the walls may be her colour and the carpet may have been worn down by her own feet. But it wasn't really hers, was it? Not really. Not ever.

She turned to leave, opened the door and stared out into the darkness, but even that—even the woods around the corner, the small stream, the garden and the flickering stars; even that seemed menacing tonight.

Was anything as she had told herself it was all these years? Her house— but not her house. The darkness; her friend until it had sent its minions out to scare her on a lonely road. Her job? Even that had come about because of Them, not because of her, not really, not originally. Was anything she had really, truly hers? Had she ever earned anything?

She closed the door and shuffled behind the sofa, back into a corner where she huddled, arms holding her knees up against her chin, staring at nothing. She replayed images in her head; the green face, grinning madly at her for a split second. The hairy creature. Only this time it stopped, looked at her and came around to her door. She screamed as it opened the door and took her hand, pulling her out, pulling her along the road, pulling her back into the past.

A corridor, with black walls that gave off their own heat, their own light. A room, brightly decorated, displaying toys and gadgets, more than most people would dream of, yet grim and confining as a prison cell. A soft mat on a table, a white coat, a needle, flashing lights, tests, pain.

Isabel screamed, screamed, cried out for help and opened her eyes to find herself stood in the middle of her living room; only her living room was no longer neat and cosy. The sofa was shoved out of place, the coffee table lay on one side, shelves had been emptied directly onto the floor, things broken, nothing left in it's accustomed place.

She looked around for a moment, bewildered, before her knees gave way and she fell to the floor and curled up, sobbing into her sweater-covered arms.

***

Cam opened his eyes. "I know where she is," he said. "She has been taken, captured. She is in a normal house, on a normal street, locked in a cage in a cellar. She cannot speak to me, but I can locate her."

Menw and Lana breathed a small sigh of relief.

Cam nodded. "I can feel others in the house. One is the Cantor, I recognise his scent. There is another I do not know, but her print is similar to the Cantor so it must be his witch. The third is masked; I cannot tell anything other than he or she exists in that space."

"Only three. We can do that," Lana said with a grim smile.

Cam looked doubtful. "Chances are that third is Sansé…"

"What's the house like?" Lana asked.

Cam closed his eyes once more and reached out his hands. Menw slid pen and paper into them and he drew a layout. When finished, he looked at the three sheets and placed one aside. "This is upstairs, we will not need it. These, however," he laid out the remaining two, "we need. But there is also another who needs our help, I heard her cry while I searched for Jodhi."

"Who?" Menw asked.

Cam shook his head. "I do not know yet, but once we have Jodhi we will find her." He bent his head and began to study to layouts, giving no opportunity for further questions.

***

Jodhi groaned and rolled over and stretched, reaching to tuck a hand under her pillow. She frowned as a pain shot through her fist and realised the only thing she was hugging was stone.

Her eyes flicked cautiously open, guarded against…whatever she might see. She saw a blank, bland, brown wall, pockmarked and dimpled.

"What the—" she whispered, sitting up and slowly turning around.

She saw a room. Dull and dusky, roughly made as if hewn by hand from the ground itself.

Her cage was large, filling the shorter wall. Along the full wall to her right was a long workbench with a cupboard above. To the left, half of the wall was

50

more workbench and cupboards. In the corner was a set of wooden stairs. The slatted type that always existed in film cellars. The ones where a hand would reach out and grab the ankle of the unlucky walker; tripping them so they fell. Either upwards, to fall with their face at the perfect angle to confront the horror beneath, or downwards, landing with a jarring thump that left them cold for a moment, waiting for the evil Something to creep out and attack.

There was definitely a Something under these stairs. Curled up on what looked like a giant dog bed was a human figure; its head was buried and hidden, but one of its hands flopped sideways and Jodhi saw it was green. The second Cantor, then. And this, this must be its Witch's lair.

The stairs creaked and Jodhi tensed as a silhouette appeared. Slowly it descended into the light and she took it in.

The witch was small and blonde, with brown eyes and full lips. Her skin was unblemished and her teeth as she smiled were pearly white. Yet there was something odious about her. Something forced, something unreal, something that hid under her skin and made her as grotesque as any warty caricature could ever be.

Jodhi cringed as she walked to the cage, the witch gave off psychic offal so strong even she, telepathically talentless, could feel it, and her thoughts squirmed unhappily as her skin crawled.

"Well hello." The witch's voice immediately defied all outer appearance; it was made of poisoned gravel. "Nice to see you awake, my dear. Tell me, is your room to your satisfaction?" She cackled and gave a little hop.

Jodhi said nothing, only raised one eyebrow slightly.

"Not feeling talkative, eh? Well, we can change that, I think." The witch walked over to one of the cupboards on the left. "Let me see, now. I can…make you scream? No, too noisy, I have such a delicate little head." She batted her eyelids ghoulishly. "Speak in tongues? Pah, too overdone. Speak in rhyme? Now that is a fun one, but not today. Here we are, then. Speak everything that comes into your head." She removed a bottle of pale blue powder. "Just a pinch, I think. Don't want it to last forever; a half hour or so will get me everything I need to know—ah, if only the police knew about this little bit of magic, eh? Criminals? Hah! They'd stand no chance! Which is precisely, of course, why I'm not going to tell them." She gave a toothy grin and opened the bottle. Smiling, she took a pinch and placed it neatly onto her palm. "Now then, I do hope I got it right this time. The last mix I tried…well…suffice to say it was kinder to kill her, in the end. Oh but I do like when I'm allowed to experiment!" She gave a double hop and raised her palm to her mouth.

51

In a flash, Jodhi was on her feet and at the opposite side of the cage.

The witch frowned. "Now, do stay still, dear." She pursed her lips to blow and Jodhi scurried to the other side.

"Oh, silly girl. You think these little powdery magic tricks are the only power I have? I own—owned—two Cantors! Until you people killed one of them." Her tone turned sulky and she pouted for a moment.

Jodhi prepared to move again but a searing pain shot through her chest, taking her breath away and leaving her limp on the floor, gasping.

"How's that, dear? A hundred little pinpricks. Move again and it shall be a thousand." She hummed a little ditty and waited. "No?"

Jodhi shook her head, still panting.

"Good girl." The witch aimed and blew the powder into the air. Instead of dispersing in a general direction, however, it gathered into a dart and flew directly into her left ear.

Jodhi yelped as a tickling sensation crawled up to her brain and was gone. She waited. Nothing. *Guess she mixed it wrong again*, she thought with relief.

"No, dear, I think I got it just right this time," was the reply.

I said that out loud? Jodhi thought, then clasped a hand to her mouth as she realised she'd done it again.

The witch laughed heartily, hopping from foot to foot and clapping her hands. As Jodhi watched, she stood on her hands, then her head, then did a tap dance before stopping abruptly and staring, straight-faced, at Jodhi.

"She's mad. She's completely nuts!" Jodhi said, shaking her head. "Oh shit, that's out loud too."

The witch cackled.

"I wish she'd quit that, it's like nails on a bloody blackboard!"

The witch stopped and scowled. "So, you think I'm odd, hmm? You think I'm...unusual?"

"Odd is not the word. Timmy Mallet is odd. Dennis Rodman is...unusual. Insane may fit you better, although maniac and psychopathic also spring to mind."

The witch growled.

"Evil, horrid, mean—ugly, definitely," Jodhi continued, amused to watch the witch's plan backfire into insults.

"Enough!" the witch snapped.

Jodhi looked innocent. "You're the one who made me speak my thoughts, don't complain because they weren't as complimentary as you would have liked."

The witch ignored this and strolled peaceably up and down alongside the cage, hands clasped behind her back.

Jodhi watched. "What's she up to? Trying to psyche me out? Not likely. This rate, the others'll have rescued me before she gets anything useful."

The witch stopped and smiled. "Indeed, I expect your friends will attempt a rescue. Putting off their plans to go elsewhere to do so, no doubt."

"They won't leave for Nottingham without me," Jodhi assured her then swore loudly.

"Nottingham, hmm? There is a Walker there who is of use to you?"

"Mark. He's got some books and a grapevine and extra knowledge. We're going to find out all about some woman called Sansé and will you stop doing that you insane bitch!"

The witch laughed. "Careful, you'll change into the big bad wolf if you get too angry."

"It's not a full moon."

"Nor does it have to be, for you, my dear. Oh. They haven't told you, have they?" Her lips curled upwards in a pleased smile.

"Told me nothing. Meant to tell me. Something about emotional werewolf."

"Allow me to assist." The witch continued smiling. "You will not turn into a monster according to the lunar cycle. You will turn into a monster every time you are overwhelmed by a negative emotion—anger, fear, hate, jealousy, greed, and so forth."

"No…"

"Yes, my dear."

"I'm a danger to everyone. The incredible hulk, only a wolfy version."

"And even uglier. Yes. You are going to kill them all, if you are not careful."

"There's a cure. Something. Has to be. Some way to stop it. Control the moods. Something. Please tell me?"

The witch smiled, not answering the question. "You are a liability, my dear."

"Arlene!" a voice cooed from upstairs. "Playtime over, come on up. And bring your beastie."

"Yes, Sansé," Arlene acquiesced.

"You're with Sansé! Oh help me. I'm dead. Done for. Roast wolf for dinner," Jodhi began muttering to herself.

Arlene ignored her and psychically poked her Cantor into movement.

"Come, pig." She giggled and went back up the stairs, the demon following closely on her heels, leaving Jodhi to curl up and talk to herself all she wished.

***

Sansé grabbed Arlene by the scruff of her neck. "They're coming. Get out now, you know where to go. Take the car. I will follow later." She released her.

Arlene nodded and picked up her bag, sat already by the door. "Come," she ordered the Cantor, accepted the car keys from Sansé and bowed deeply. "Thank you, for the car, most kind, we will be waiting. Thank you." She bowed her way out of the door and, with a screech and a grating cackle, was gone.

Sansé shook her head. "The most powerful witch I could find, also the most insane. Why me?" She stood at the top of the stairs, wondering what the person below was like. "A wolf…" she mused. "A girl wolf. You'd think they'd be a little more cautious nowadays. Some of these female werewolves can go bad…" Chuckling to herself, she waited for her captive's gallant rescuers to arrive, planning no real harm to them just now, yet unable to resist presenting herself and proving her worth by escaping.

***

Lana parked the car well out of sight and waited.

Cam nodded. "It was definitely that house. But…the witch and her demon have left."

"Just the one you can't see, then. Plus Jodhi." Lana frowned. "That's not…usual, is it? Forgive me, I rarely find myself out in the field like this, but—"

"It is highly unusual," Menw acknowledged. "I think we would do best to be very cautious. Also, to expect the worst."

Cam clenched his jaw. "I've been ready for the worst for a long time." He beamed his plan into their heads and nodded. There was no point trying to sneak up on the house, if the remaining person could cover themselves as they had, and if the witch and the Cantor had exited already, the chances were high enough that the one left was simply waiting for them. To walk in the front door, bold as brass, was how they would gain their upper hand and rescue Jodhi. And now, with only the one shadowy presence remaining, there was at least no danger of being caught from behind.

Lana started the car and rolled forwards until they were parked outside the house. For a moment they waited. Upstairs was dark and still. Downstairs there was a light and as they watched a shadow moved across the window.

"There," Cam said. "Shall we?"

They climbed from the car and walked down the path to the front door; Cam first, followed by Lana, looking sympathetically at the dead flowerbeds on either side, Menw bringing up their rear with a half-cautious eye.

Cam knocked on the door and tried the handle. It was unlocked. "Take that as an invitation," he muttered and walked inside.

"Jodhi?" he called as he entered the living room. He was answered by a snarl as a wolf leapt, its jaws aiming for his neck. He ducked, shoving Lana to the ground, and Menw, almost leisurely, stopped the beast mid-flight. Before he could bind it, a woman took its place and rose gracefully to her feet.

"Sansé." Cam stood, his fists by his side, clenched.

The woman smiled. "Darling, you remembered." She drifted towards him, naked, unembarrassed, and caressed his cheek. Her grey eyes burned into his until his knees grew weak and he leaned in to kiss her.

"Cam!" Menw snapped, and he jumped back, shooting him a grateful look. Lana took his arm and pulled him back a step farther.

"What's wrong lover?" Sansé flicked her hair and nodded to Lana with an amused smile. "Going for brunettes, nowadays?"

Cam reddened and Lana dropped his arm. "Going for people less evil than you," he replied.

Sansé giggled. "And Menw, my dear, you don't say hello to an old friend? How rude." She pouted and walked to him and he backed away.

"The old friends I have don't usually try to kill me; therefore, you are not an old friend," he said coldly.

"Aw." She pouted again and took another step towards him.

He grimaced a little and took an involuntary step backwards. Before his back foot connected with the floor and his balance returned, Sansé shoved him to the ground and took off through the open door, wolfing even as she streamed out of sight and away.

Cam and Lana were by Menw's side but he shook them off and pulled himself upright, grumpy-faced.

"I fell for it," he scolded himself. "And so did you," he scolded them. "Should have gone after her," he told Cam.

"I could never have caught her if I had, and I could not have gone far with you lying here," Cam argued softly.

"And anyone would've stepped backwards a bit," Lana added. "Someone gets that far in your face it takes a bigger will than most people have to stay put."

Cam looked around. "Jodhi is in the cellar, by the way."

***

The powder worn off by now, Jodhi was listening intently to the noises from upstairs. Now, as three figures descended the stairs, she stood and waited; sure this would mean her rescue.

Cam was first out of shadow and smiled broadly. Menw was next, and Lana stood by.

"Stand back, Menw advised and sent a spark shooting through the iron lock on the cage door. He beckoned to Jodhi, who reached for the door of the cage and pushed gently. It moved and she smiled and shoved hard enough for it to swing open.

Cam cheered softly and gave her a hug. "Come on, celebration on the way—bad idea to stay here."

Jodhi paused. "I-I'm sorry," she whispered.

"Apologise on the way too," Lana ordered and put an arm around her waist, escorting her gently. "Anyhow we already forgave you for everything we know and everything we don't."

Jodhi smiled softly and allowed herself to be taken to the car where Lana carefully pulled away.

"Now we are moving once more, tell us what they know," Menw said.

Jodhi hung her head. "The witch, the mad one, Arlene, she had—she put some powder in me. Made me say everything I thought."

"Which was?" Menw pushed.

Lana gave him a look. "Gently, Menw, gently."

He shrugged. "I apologise, Jodhi. But we must know."

"She's not an unwilling interrogant though," Lana reminded him. "Jodhi, it wasn't your fault hon, but if you can tell us what they made you tell them it could help."

Jodhi related all she remembered, and what she had told.

When she was finished, she realised their speed had increased and her companion's faces were grim; but none more so than Lana's.

"Lana? I-I'm sorry, I—" Jodhi began but heard a gentle "shhh" in her head and looked at Cam.

"Mark was Lana's fiancé," he explained into her mind. "Five years ago they split. They still loved each other, but they needed different things. They have been friends, as Menw and I have been friends with them both, but their bond was deeper."

"And I just told…" Jodhi half-thought back.

"They made you tell," Cam reminded her. "You chose nothing. We shall get to him, and then we may worry about the rest."

Jodhi nodded and Cam sent soothing thoughts her way. Soon she slept.

Chapter 7

Jodhi awoke as they pulled into a nondescript driveway. It belonged to a plain, neat, detached house with a concrete garden and newly-painted eaves.

The four of them left the car and Lana knocked politely on the front door, which swung open gently at her touch.

Tentatively, they walked in one-by-one.

Upstairs, something opened yellow eyes and growled softly.

Cam opened the living room door and stepped through. Lana tried to follow, but he stopped in his tracks and trod on her foot as he retreated.

"Hey!" Lana yelped, hopping backwards.

"Um…" Cam rubbed his forehead, "Mark, he…um…I didn't see this one coming…"

Lana shoved past him and into the room, eyes searching. She stopped dead and uttered a short scream.

It was echoed by a muffled cry from Jodhi. All turned to see her held from behind by a tall, blonde, feral-eyed, pearly-toothed vampire.

"Tell me something good or I rip her throat out." She snarled, and then registered surprise as Jodhi unwittingly snarled back.

The vampire dropped her. "A werewolf?!" She looked around, studying, her mild vampire telepathy picking up bits and pieces. "A mage. A telepath. A…librarian?" She moved into the living room. "And Mark…" She stopped and stared.

Mark lay in the dining room, his throat and torso slashed in claw-shaped patterns. The vampire turned on them, blazing. "I'm guessing you know more about this than I."

Cam stepped back, his usual role as mediator reduced to desperately trying to control the vampire's anger.

Unexpectedly, Jodhi spoke up. "We were going to come and see him. Only I got caught, and they made me say where we were going and—"

Menw stepped in. "We are Shadow Walkers, as you no doubt realised, I presume you are yourself. As you no doubt know Mark was also."

"He was my fiancé once," Lana whispered.

The vampire whirled. "You are Lana," she said, softening. "I see how he described you. Then I have no choice but to listen. Tell your telepath to get out of my head, and I will listen."

Cam removed himself. "I wished only to prevent your anger from doing us harm before we could explain, somehow. Most would never have felt me, but a vampire…is hard to get into."

She nodded. "Fine. I forgive. Lana, speak to me."

Lana told her about Sansé, the Cantors and Jodhi's imprisonment. The vampire listened quietly and then faced the cringing Jodhi. "You fear it was you that killed him?" she asked.

Jodhi nodded.

"Fear not. If they wanted to do this thing to hurt and delay you, they would have done so somehow without forcing information from you. Mage, telepath, wolf, sit," she ordered and watched them enter the living room and perch nervously. All averted their eyes from the body.

"Lana? Help me?"

Lana nodded, her eyes still fixed on Mark. "He wanted to be cremated, in his garden. Left among the flowers."

The vampire nodded. "Then we shall do this."

***

Outside, the vampire struck a match and held it to the trail of gasoline that covered his body.

"My name is Alnthea," she said. "It was a name that he loved, in his way…but one that could never replace yours." She smiled sadly. "He never told me what he wanted for his death."

The death requests of the Shadow Walkers were rarely told to others. Living in the dark, they preferred to acknowledge death only by rescuing others from it. Often, a Walker might die and his requests only be found in his will, or a letter sent, or a note placed where it might be found.

"I love him." Alnthea sighed. "Some say a vampire is incapable of love, and most are I think. But some of us, good and bad…some of us are."

"How did you know him?" Lana asked.

"I escaped from Department E, years ago, an evil creature. And I remained evil, truly evil, until the day I returned to feast my eyes upon the scene of one of my crimes. It was a farmhouse where I had taken pleasure in devouring the farmer and his wife and slaughtered the animals in the fields for pleasure. I did not know that they had a daughter, one with telepathic tendency, one who heard my evil mind coming a long time before it arrived. She hid, in the smallest, darkest place she could, and I did not find her.

"I returned, amused by the fact that they had been dead a week and nobody had noticed the absence of this reclusive family. The daughter was still there, this time unhidden; having no evil intent meant my mind had not warned her fledgling talent of my impending arrival.

"I entered the kitchen to find her dirty and eating from a can of cold beans. The second she saw me she just froze, said nothing, but her stare was more accusation than any words could have expressed.

"I don't know what happened. I guess it just broke my heart. A heart that hadn't beat for a long time. A heart I didn't even know was capable of feeling anymore."

"But you began to try and do good things?"

"Not exactly." She said nothing more until Lana shuffled uncomfortably.

"You look almost human, you must do good things."

"I do, I try, but that isn't how it began."

Lana looked at her. "How did you meet Mark?"

Alnthea shrugged at the fire, beginning to die down now. "A story for another day, I think. Today's tale is for you and friends to tell me."

Lana frowned. "But we already told you why we're here."

Alnthea nodded. "I want to know where you go next. And if I may join you. I have nothing left to keep me here but the tears I will shed for him."

Lana rested a hand gently on her shoulder. "Then join us, we'll be glad of you."

They stepped inside, not seeing the yellow eyes watching from the bottom of the garden.

***

Menw was speaking as they returned. "…the call for help you heard? We forgot all about that. Shouldn't we…"

Cam nodded. "We'll go back up and find her, then down again to Depot E."

Alnthea cleared her throat. "Or perhaps take it in groups. Cam's group to find the girl he heard, Menw's to Depot E for whatever you need to do there. Cam and company can join Menw and company later."

Cam and Menw exchanged a look. As usual, Cam was the first to speak. "Slight problem Alnthea. Menw and myself, we are attached. By magic."

"What?" Alnthea's face screwed up in confusion.

"I am attached to Menw. By magic."

Now Jodhi's face mirrored Alnthea's. "What?"

Cam sighed. "The short version, then. About 200 years ago, I did some very stupid things. Menw prevented me from being punished by taking responsibility for me. I am attached to him by my life-force. So long as I remain close by, I live for as long as him. If I move away the link weakens and I with it, far enough and it breaks or can be snapped by somebody else. If that happens, my age will simply catch up with me. It is possible to do it by magic, and let me live as anybody else but…"

Menw spoke up. "But he refuses."

Alnthea grunted. "I will never understand magic. But very well, we travel together. Lana says I might join you?"

There came a pleased agreement from all but Jodhi, whose neck was still smarting from her earlier assault, and simply nodded grudgingly.

Alnthea smiled. "Thank you."

Menw took up the earlier conversation. "We must find the person you heard cry for help. Can you locate her?"

Cam nodded. "Yes. And more specifically the closer we get. If we return to Burnley to begin with, I will find her."

Alnthea cleared her throat. "I am seeing a small problem…"

Cam smiled. "You can travel only by night. This is easily overcome. Once you are able to travel, simply call for me, I will be listening, and I will direct you. Do you drive?"

Alnthea shook her head. "Yes, if I have a car, but I have other ways of travelling."

Cam nodded, accepting the vague answer.

"Well, no time like the present." Lana stood.

"Wait. What are we gonna do when we find her?" Jodhi asked.

Cam shrugged. "Try to help her," he said, "if she will let us."

Chapter 8

Isabel entered her living room cautiously. "Who's there?" Her voice shook and she cleared her throat to repeat herself with more force and jumped as the front door swung closed.

A man stepped from the shadows. Dressed in a charcoal suit, built like the side of a house, his eyes burned into hers. "Department E, ma'am. We gather you experienced something…untoward…unusual…"

Isabel stared.

"We would like you to return to Department E."

"Never," she whispered. "Never!"

"Ma'am—" He stepped forward, reaching for her upper arm.

Then Isabel did something she thought she had forgotten how to do, had worked so hard at forgetting she had ever been able to do.

She went *dim*.

The man in charcoal stopped dead. "Hey!" he exclaimed.

But she was gone, in more ways than one. Taking no time to reflect on her actions, she had opened the door and flew into the nearby woods almost before the man in charcoal could figure out what had happened.

He looked around, bewildered, and then left to climb in his car and report back. He was not dealing with any funny business, that was their job—not his.

Isabel watched him drive away and remained where she was for a time.

Shortly, another car pulled up to her house. Out got two men and two women.

"The door's open…" the older woman said.

"She's here," said the younger man who turned, suddenly, to stare directly into the shadows where Isabel was hiding, "but she doesn't want to be found." He continued, "Well, if we just hang around in that big ol' house of yours, Lana, maybe she'll see fit to find us there, when she's less afraid." As he spoke, he sent warm feelings and a picture of the house to the scared bundle in the trees.

Isabel almost walked directly out, but stopped herself. She would follow. The "big ol' house" must mean the place she had seen the…things. They were involved, somehow, but surely not in a bad way. Yes, she would go there and watch, and see.

Cam smiled to himself. "Let's go." Once inside the car he answered the questioning looks. "She's seen us, she knows where we'll be, she'll follow us and be outside, watching."

"What was the cry for help?" Lana asked.

Cam shrugged. "Not really my business unless she chooses to make it such. She'll let us help her, though, if we do this carefully."

"Help her how?" Jodhi chipped in.

"However we need to," Menw said in a conversation-ending voice.

As usual it worked and they drove in silence to Lana's house.

The front gates were shut as they drove up. It wasn't until they came within sight of the front door that they saw something was wrong.

The window broken by the Cantor was no longer boarded up. The front door was wide open. As they looked, they realised every window, at least at the front, was broken.

Lana pulled the car to a halt and raced inside, forgetting to even kill the engine.

"Wait here," Cam ordered the rest and followed hot on her heels.

Inside was a mess. Wood splintered the floor where doors and furniture had been broken. Glass glinted everywhere the eye could see. Anything that could be torn was now in long, thin, claw-like tatters.

Lana, with Cam quietly behind her, walked from room to room. Nothing, it seemed, remained intact. Finally she stood outside of her own room. Her library had been stripped of every book, scraps of which littered the entire house. But her own room, her sanctuary, what had been done to that?

She pushed the door. It clicked open easily. She stepped inside. The room was tidy. Everything intact. Only, she saw, the bed was in a ruckus, the covers lumpy, as if something lay underneath.

Instinctively, Cam walked to it and pulled back the duvet. In the bed lay a peaceful looking body, the image of Lana. But this body was cold, lifeless. A spot of blood had seeped through her top and Lana stepped up to pull it open.

Inscribed on the chest was a heart, pierced by an arrow.

Sat patiently in the car, Jodhi and Menw heard the scream and arrived at a run.

On seeing the body, the message, Menw walked back out of the room. "Sansé's doing," he said.

Cam nodded his agreement. "It has to be."

Jodhi remained in the room. Staring from the body to the living Lana and back again. She snarled viciously and Lana looked up.

"Shit!" she gasped, seeing Jodhi's eyes melt to yellow. "Jodhi, no!" She grabbed her arms and motioned for Menw and Cam to stay back.

"Jodhi, listen to me. That's not me. I'm right here, you see? Sansé is playing with us. But remember who you are. Remember Jodhi. You are not the wolf, the wolf is not you. Fight it, Jodhi. Come back to me. I need you here. Come back!"

Jodhi ceased to change and stood, shaking, halfway between beast and woman.

"Jodhi. Jodhi you know me honey. Come on. I need you. Here. Now. Remember. Remember you. Come back."

Jodhi cocked her misshapen head to one side and whined questioningly.

"That's it sweetheart, that's you. Come on. Kick the big bad wolf back where he belongs. You can do it. Come on. To me. Come on."

The bristling fur that had begun to grow now started to subside.

"Good girl. That's it. We'd like Jodhi back, please." Lana smiled.

Jodhi nodded and gave a smile, almost a grimace on her shifting jaw. But her eyes lit upon the body once more and in a flash she was the wolf.

Lana threw herself backwards and yelled to Menw. "Bind her, bind her!"

Menw flicked his wrist and the wolf was bound to the wall, howling and struggling in vain.

From farther down the road, only a few steps away from where she had left her car, Isabel heard the curdling howls and stopped in her tracks. "That thing, the creature, the wolf thing…they've caught it?" she wondered aloud. Walking a little faster, wanting yet almost not wanting to see them, she continued along the road.

As Jodhi began to calm, Cam grinned. "Our lady is here. And she's curious."

"Where here?" Menw asked.

"In the bushes outside the gates," Cam replied. "I'm going to go and talk to her."

"With a werewolf and a dead girl in the bedroom?" Lana asked.

Cam stopped. "Good point. But we can't just leave her out there."

Lana nodded. "We can until Menw shifts this poor girl somewhere she will be found and treated properly and Jodhi turns back into, well, Jodhi again."

Menw rubbed his hands together and concentrated. Slowly, the body dimmed, flickered and was gone. "She'll be found; poor girl," he said sadly. "You two go downstairs; I'll watch Jodhi and set her free as soon as I am able."

Lana nodded. She needed to see her library once more. Cam simply followed, comforting her with his mind as well as he could, comforting her more with just his presence.

She stood in the middle of the room, just looking. Everything she had spent so long building, studying, storing, learning. All gone. Or rather, all ripped into tiny, irreparable pieces and scattered around the house.

She knelt amongst the ruin, sending a cloud of paper into the air, and cried.

Cam, hovering at a distance, ran to her, almost falling as the confetti tried to steal his feet from under him.

He knelt and put his arms around her, desperately hunting through and rejecting countless worthless platitudes; eventually settling on silence, filled only by the occasional hitching sob from the broken heart inside the shaking figure he held close.

After a time—who knew how long?—she quieted and simply leaned against him, letting shimmering tear tracks dry upon her cheeks and his sodden shirt.

She gestured weakly. "This was everything I had, all I had...gone. The only thing I had to love."

He couldn't help himself. "I'm still here. I can help you rebuild it all. And more than that, Lana. I-I can love you back."

She stared at him, flushed and puffy from crying, but her eyes glinted with something more.

He looked back at her. *Too late now,* he thought, and plunged. *In fact I...I already do.*

She touched his cheek with the tips of her fingers, drawing him to her. In a moment, she had covered his mouth with hers.

Menw and Jodhi entered and then slowly backed out of the room and returned upstairs, both grinning.

"I knew it!" Jodhi said triumphantly.

"I think everybody did but them." Menw smiled. "I think they will come to find us when they are ready."

"Maybe we can help move things along then," Jodhi mused. "Let me go and talk to the woman Cam's called over. Bet She's still waiting and if she is

I might be able to talk to her." She saw Menw's doubtful look and shrugged. "OK, so I can't do his funny telepathic tricks. But I'm a woman like her, younger, so not any sort of threat."

"I understand your thoughts, Jodhi, but if we lose her…"

"Which we might anyway if Cam's so preoccupied. I know it's risky but we can't afford to waste time, can we?"

"Alnthea will be calling him at any moment." Menw gestured towards the rapidly fading light. "He will hear, he cannot help but. Then he will talk to the woman."

"And if she goes home again because it's cold and dark? Cam'll get her back, or go find her, sure, but think of the time wasted."

Menw gave her an appraising look. "It is not that I doubt your true motives, Jodhi. Yet I cannot help but wonder why you are quite so forcible about this."

Jodhi looked at her feet. "Have you any idea how it felt to wake up, after seeing something so…unreal—to wake up to you, Cam and Julio?"

Menw nodded his understanding. "Ah, I see. You wish to be sure she sees a female presence, to perceive she is safe amongst us at least in that way."

"I guess so." Jodhi nodded.

"I will trust your thoughts on this. When Cam goes to her, perhaps if you go with him. Allow him to talk and explain in the way he does, add what you must. Would this be acceptable to you?"

Jodhi nodded. "Definitely. Thanks Menw."

***

Isabel jumped as she heard one of the gates opening. She was sat in a clump of bramble bushes, knees to her chest, chin resting on her knees. The prickles in her back had long ago stopped causing pain and begun to conform to her shape until she found herself in reasonable comfort.

Now, she crawled to the side and parted enough of the bramble to peek out. She saw the younger man who had spoken before, and the younger girl who had not. With a jolt, she realised they were heading straight for her.

By instinct she almost stood, and then realised that would give her away. Instead she kept as still as she could, breathing only as much as she dared.

They stopped yards from where she knelt, with tremors beginning to travel through her arms and legs.

"Isabel?" the man said, "Isabel. I know you are knelt in the bushes there. I know you saw us before and came to watch us. Come out, talk to us. We know you are in trouble. I believe we can help; at least we would like to try. We would like for you to let us try."

She stayed where she was, sweat breaking out on her body as the tremors began to change into painful shudders.

"Okay, how about this. I know you have no reason to trust us. So, we will go and stand on the other side of that gate and I will lock the padlock. So you can come out and talk to us in safety." He displayed the insides of his pocket, waistband, shoes and motioned for Jodhi to follow suit. "We have no weapons, as you can see. Some part of you, I know, wants to talk to us. That same part knows you can trust us and knows we are here to help. Please, listen to it, just come and have a chat."

The man and girl walked back through the gate and closed it. He fiddled for a moment and Isabel heard the rattle of a chain and the clank of a locking padlock.

She collapsed onto her stomach, panting in pain, and lay there for a moment. When the pain subsided and her muscles stopped quivering she sat and thought. Almost every part of her brain, it seemed, told her she could trust these people. Only the part that still remembered, still feared Them; Depot E, white coats and tests and needles and "This won't hurt a bit" followed inevitably by some form of blinding pain. The part that still remained afraid of everything said "No!" But that was what it always said, wasn't it? Surely she couldn't listen to it forever, especially not now They wanted her back again. Isabel braced herself, told it to shut up and found the hole she had climbed in by.

Cam studied her subtly, matching her with the girl he had half-seen in his mind. She was perhaps 5 feet 5 inches, though the once-cream, now grey with dirt, flared trousers made it difficult to judge. Her shoes were comfortable, white, though not much use for things like hiding in bramble bushes—they were punctured and dusty, as was her once-pink t-shirt. Her hair was dotted with loose brambles, but he guessed the tousled look was less to do with her time in the bushes than it was personal choice—dark blonde, with darker roots, obviously styled by a professional. What concerned him right now, however, were the numerous lines of blood that told where she had been scratched.

For a moment she looked herself over, touching the bramble scratches on her face, arms, back, and stomach. Then she shrugged, there was nothing she could do about that right now. She climbed completely out of her hidey-hole and walked to the gate, standing well out of reach, but close enough to allow them to speak in conversational voices rather than shouting.

"Why do you want to help me?" was her first question.

"It's what we do," Cam replied.

"Why?"

"Because we want to. Because we can. Because when nobody else believes, when nobody else understands, we do."

"How do I know you're telling the truth?"

"You don't. Catch 22 says we can only prove ourselves by helping you, and we can only help you if you trust us enough to let us."

"Then why would I let you?"

Cam tilted his head to Jodhi. "Same reason she did. There was nobody else who could."

"And I just knew," Jodhi added. "Like I bet you do, if you look inside."

Isabel nodded. "So what are you? How did you know where I was? How did you know to find me? How did you know my name?"

Cam smiled. "Keep an open mind, Isabel. I am a telepath. You screamed for help and I heard and came to answer that as soon as I was able. The old man you saw, he's a mage. A highly skilled, if slightly grumpy, wizard. The other woman you saw, she's a researcher, a special sort—kind of an info-locator."

"And you?" Isabel asked Jodhi.

"I'm a werewolf. These guys're helping me too."

Isabel said nothing for a second. Then; "I saw you."

Jodhi's eyes widened. "What?!"

"You were chasing something, like a person, but not."

Jodhi shrugged. "I don't know. I don't remember things from when I'm a wolf. I guess you saw me chasing the Cantor though."

Isabel nodded. "Is that what it was? I was in a car, nearly ran it over. Probably should have done, hmm?"

Jodhi laughed without much humour. "Might've saved a whole lot of trouble."

"I heard you earlier. You were howling." Isabel looked suspiciously at Cam.

Jodhi nodded again. "It's complicated, something happened to make me change. Our mage, he bound me up with magic to keep me safe, and let me go as soon as I changed back. Only, wolfy doesn't like being bound up—obviously."

"What're your names?" Isabel asked now, deciding to accept the explanation for the moment.

68

"Camlaidh." Cam replied. "But everyone calls me Cam."

Isabel gave a small smile. "I can understand why."

He chuckled. "Our little wolf-girl here is Jodhi. The mage is Menw, and our researcher is Lana."

Isabel paced for a while. The two behind the gate waited patiently.

"So…" Isabel said, finally. "You're people with various special talents—or afflictions," she deferred to Jodhi, "who like to use them to help out complete strangers for no apparent reason other than you just can. You telepathically heard me call for help and came running as fast as you were able, what with all your other complicated commitments and all. And you'd like me to believe all this and let you help me simply because you have an honest face. That about it?"

Cam nodded. "Put like that it sounds less than impressive, but essentially…yes."

"What are you, Joinees?" Isabel grinned, her pleasant face more suited to a smile than the previous grim seriousness.

"What?" Cam and Jodhi echoed.

Isabel shook her head. "Never mind. Anyhow, on the basis of all this you expect me to believe you and let you help me however you can, with whatever my particular problem is."

"Would you like a drink?" Cam asked suddenly. "I'm parched for a cup of tea. Jodhi?"

Jodhi nodded slowly, wondering what he was up to. "Sure, coke?"

Cam nodded. "Isabel?"

She shook her head, also wondering. "No, thank you."

Cam shrugged and closed his eyes for a second. Then he held out his hands and stared at them.

Suddenly, he was holding a mug of coffee and a can of coke, which he handed to Jodhi who grinned as she popped the top and drank. He looked at Isabel, taking a sip of tea, and grinned at her shocked expression.

"What—how—hey!" She put her hands on her hips. "You won't get my trust by playing party tricks, you know."

Cam shrugged. "And if I were a two-bit party magician that would be a problem."

Isabel frowned, thinking, and then laughed. "Right…so you, the telepath, told the wizard to send you drinks." She applauded heartily. "Fantastic. Well done."

"Wow, you are hard to please aren't you? Don't move."

They all stood and stared around for a few seconds. In a flash, Menw stood beside Jodhi with a beaming smile. "You called?" he asked Cam who beamed back.

"I did indeed. Meet Isabel. Isabel, this is Menw."

Isabel laughed. "All right, all right, fine, okay. May I please test you now, Cam?"

Cam laughed. "You're having more fun here than you're probably meant to. Go ahead."

"Look in my head. Find the most horribly embarrassing thing I've ever done."

Cam closed his eyes a moment and then opened them. His eyes glinted laughter, a second later he was guffawing his amusement.

Menw presented him with a pen and slip of paper, and he bent and scribbled something upon it.

"Hold out your hand," he told Isabel, who obeyed.

In a moment, Menw had transferred the paper into her hand and she blinked in surprise, then opened it and gave an embarrassed laugh. "OK, so I'm reasonably sure that wasn't just a lucky guess. And, like Jodhi says, there's just that feeling...but still..."

"You don't have to tell us anything you don't want to," Cam promised. "But whatever it is, we will help. Only, can we at least let Lana join in? I'll ask her out here."

Isabel rubbed her bare, scratched arms. "Actually, if the offer of a drink is still going, and I could persuade you to add a chair to it as well..."

Cam smiled and produced the padlock key from his pocket. "Come on in."

Soon, the five of them were settled inside with warm drinks. Isabel had raised an eyebrow at the mess, but said nothing and allowed Lana to tend to her scratches with water and a dab of Savlon.

Once she was cleaned up, and wearing Lana's new clothes—of a drab colour that scarcely suited her—Isabel looked a little more animated.

"We're just waiting for a friend of ours." Cam said. "Alnthea is a vampire. A good one though, we promise. With your permission, I'll simply relay our conversation to her telepathically once she arrives, to save some time."

Isabel nodded her permission.

"And you only need tell us what you're comfortable with," Lana reiterated. "Nothing more."

Isabel nodded again and sipped her coffee, thinking.

"I was born in Burnley," she began. "The youngest of two—I have an older brother. I was always the unusual kid out of us both—and out of

70

everybody else as well. It seemed like I could just disappear at will. I always won hide and seek—well, the hiding part at least. didn't realise what I could really do till I was 8. Mum and me were out for a walk in the woods. Some guy came up and grabbed her bag. She did the sensible thing and let him take it. But I'd never even imagined being so scared! When Mum turned to look for me, I was standing right there still, but she couldn't see me. She started calling for me, panicking, thinking I'd just run off in fright. All the time I just stood there, wondering why she didn't see me, even when she was looking right at me.

"I pulled on her sleeve and she screamed and jumped about a mile in the air, but still didn't see me.

"I said 'Mummy?' and she heard me and started looking for me frantically, but she still didn't see me!

"I was invisible. It explained a lot, but just then I really wasn't thinking about that. I closed my eyes real tight and just wished and wished I could be seen again.

"I knew it worked when Mum grabbed me and shrieked, 'Oh, my daughter, there you are, there you are!' It turned out she'd seen me reappear, right in front of her eyes.

"At first she made no mention of it, and I practised secretly until I could dim and return with barely a thought or a moment's hesitation, not even a flicker.

"Somehow, I always suspected my parents, Depot E heard what I could do and they took me away for a long time.

"I got out in the end, they set me up with that house and I found myself a job, and tried to forget. I didn't see or talk to my family and I just tried to live and be normal and forget everything. I was doing okay, not great but okay, in waking hours at least, until I saw Jodhi and the—the Cantor? Until I saw them running in front of my car.

"I was on my way to work. I'm a phone counsellor for a place called Hopeline. I was in such a state; I wound up not being very pleasant to some of the people calling me for help and my boss suggested I take some sick leave. I got home in a total mess and went a bit…nuts. I guess that was when I cried for help. Anyhow just before you guys came—you're right, Cam, I did see you—some goon from Depot E had been there waiting for me. He was meant to take me back, quietly. I didn't go, obviously. I relearned the art of turning invisible and legged it at high speed." She looked around fearfully. "But that means they're gonna keep trying until they get me again." Her lip quivered and her voice shook for the first time in her story. "Please don't let them take me back there."

"We won't let them get you," Lana promised. "We know Depot E, and we do work alongside them sometimes. But we don't like so much of what they do, their methods, all that side of things. I can only imagine what they did to you, honey, the sort of life you had there, and I promise you, Depot E will not get you back."

"And that," Cam said, standing, "would be my job. They have a bank of telepaths. Let me talk to them." He gave a small nod and left the room.

"Wow," Isabel said. "You really can help. Do I have to join you or anything?"

"Not at all," Lana replied. "As far as we're concerned, you can go home, get on with life and forget we exist—just know that we will help you again anytime. All you ever have to do is call Cam."

"You really think he can get Depot E to leave me alone?"

Lana nodded confidently. "I'm sure he can."

They sat mostly in silence until Cam returned, looking troubled.

"What?" Isabel asked. "What did they say?"

Cam sighed. "They said you were theirs first, but they'll let you alone only for so long as you remain with us—at least for a while."

Jodhi looked up. "Yeah, and we're going to see them anyway, so we can show them you're safe with us—"

Isabel leapt to her feet. "What?! Oh, so they want you to escort me to them? Not likely." She turned and left the room.

Cam followed. "No, Isabel, that's not—we wouldn't—shit," he cried as the door slammed. "Now what?!"

"Let them get her," Menw suggested. "We can pick her up again while we're there and can talk properly to Zeke and Morgan."

"Seems like our only choice really, doesn't it?" Lana said, a tad grumpily.

"Sorry," Jodhi whispered, looking guilty now. "That was a really stupid thing to say, wasn't it?"

"Yes," Menw agreed. "But that cannot be altered now. We might simply return to our original plan—go to Department E and find out what they have on Sansé, and any extra tips they may have to assist Jodhi in controlling her wolf."

Chapter 9

Isabel walked out of the gate at the end of the driveway and began stomping her way back home. She failed to notice the yellow eyes that watched her, following close behind, studying, waiting.

She picked up her car and drove home, walked slowly through her front door, still open after the earlier hasty retreat, and after checking nobody stood in the shadows, and all her belongings remained in place, thanked herself for choosing a rather remote place to live—an area burglars rarely bothered to venture merely on the off-chance of a looting.

She locked the door and trudged wearily up to bed, not seeing those same yellow eyes appear outside the front window, and collapsing into the pillows she was asleep within seconds.

Downstairs, a claw, razor sharp and strong as iron, razed a hole in a glass window. The circular piece fell to the carpet with barely a tinkle and a paw reached in and opened the latch.

Carefully, quietly, a figure, human-shaped now for ease of movement, climbed through and alighted on the floor.

It crept through to the hall, up the stairs, stopped outside Isabel's bedroom. The door was open a crack and the figure pushed it farther, wincing in expectation of a creak, smiling as it realised the hinges were well-oiled. The intruder watched the sleeper for signs of mental disturbance, but Isabel was deeply asleep.

The intruder metamorphosed once again and became the wolf. It stepped, graceful despite its bulk, through the door and across the floor to stand by the bed.

For a moment it watched Isabel at peace. Then it slipped a hand over her neck and squeezed.

Isabel woke and screamed. "Jodhi, no!"

The wolf ignored her and applied pressure to the voicebox until all that emerged was a croak and a cough.

It lifted the body easily with the other hand and stood it up.

Isabel stared at the wolf in terror. It gently eased up on her voicebox, allowing faint speech.

"Jodhi?" Isabel said, doubtfully this time.

The wolf grinned grotesquely and in a single, swift movement, smashed Isabel's head against the wall, knocking her cold.

With an unconscious figure over its shoulder, the wolf left the way it had entered, retrieving the car keys hung on a hook in the hall as it went.

Once outside, the wolf unlocked Isabel's car and dropped the body on the back seat. Then it morphed again, back into human form.

Sansé hopped into the driver's seat, started the engine and drove off, chuckling to herself. "Time to meet the mad old witch again and show her the small alteration to my plan," she told the night.

***

Jodhi was sat cross-legged on a large cushion in the middle of one of the spare bedrooms—the easiest to clear of the chaos.

"So, why am I sat like a Buddhist and playing with a necklace?" she asked Menw politely.

"The pose is simply a general comforting, relaxing position. The necklace is a rosary, used by many Catholics while praying as an aid to assist them in focusing their mind. We will find your best way in time, but to begin with this will suffice."

Jodhi nodded. "Right. So I'm picturing a sea. Waves and stuff."

"You said that the sound and sight of gently breaking waves was soothing to you," Menw reminded her.

"It is, it is. So I'm picturing." She was silent for a second. "Do I get dolphins too?"

"If it assists, then you may picture dolphins."

She smiled widely. "How about a hot bikini-clad lifeguard?"

Menw opened his mouth to rebuke, but was interrupted by Lana in the corner who burst into laughter.

At his annoyed look, she forced herself to stop. "Sorry, Menw, but that was funny…"

"Hmmm," he grunted. "No lifeguard. The idea is to relax, not get overexcited."

Jodhi and Lana giggled again at Menw's dry attempt at humour.

"Sorry," Jodhi apologised. "Visualising, I promise."

Good, good. Now, concentrate on the waves. Lapping at the shore and moving gently away. In and away. Soft and smooth, in and away…in and away…in and away…"

He left her for a second, pleased at the peace which began to try and cross her face.

"Good, good. Now, those waves are not just waves. Imagine them as they slip to the shore, latching onto everything that bothers you. All the bad feelings. All that hate, anger, fear, all being covered by the waves. And as each wave retreats back out into the ocean it takes some of those bad feelings with it. Then the next wave, covering and taking…covering and removing…in goes wave, out goes bad…wave in, bad out…wave in, bad out…" He repeated his mantra over and over, getting slowly softer, quieter, until he was silent, he and Lana near trance themselves.

He watched peace and calm reform Jodhi's face into a picture of serenity and smiled to himself. *I think she'll be OK,* he thought.

Lana was thinking the same thing, and they shared a pleased glance.

After a few more minutes, they both stood; slowly, carefully, so as not to make any sound or movement that would rush Jodhi back from where she was. Quieter than mice, they left the room and softly closed the door.

***

Jodhi blinked and came back to earth. She looked around the room, a little surprised to find it empty. Then she shrugged, stood and stretched.

Inside her, the wolf whimpered a little, as if to say *Please don't do that again,* and she smiled to herself, realising she felt more at peace now than she could ever remember being; realising also that this was nothing to what could be, and needed to be.

She picked up the rosary and made her way downstairs where she greeted the others with a relaxed smile and seated herself casually on the floor which, she noted, had been swept clean of most of the debris.

The others smiled back at her.

"Feeling relaxed, then?" Lana asked with a pleased smile.

Jodhi nodded. "As chilly as a…um…"

"Billy?" Lana enquired.

"A what?" Cam asked.

"It's a book, dear, *Chilly Billy*. Never mind." Lana grinned at his befuddled expression, kissing his cheek and settling more comfortably against him.

"So, this is how you all do it, huh? How you stay so calm?" Jodhi asked.

Menw nodded. "Essentially, yes. Of course, while we work on the same basic principles, we will take it to a rather more advanced level where you are concerned—for obvious reasons."

Jodhi nodded. "And after I learn to keep it down when required, do you think I can learn to bring it up? As a proper wolf, instead of whatever it is I turn into now?"

Menw nodded heartily. "I believe so totally, you have a skill in this area— soon you will be able to call within yourself and bring out a sleek, well-turned wolf, advanced in all its natural traits and instincts, and complete with your mind, talents and instincts to boot."

"You sure? Because right now it's sort of crying, and what if—"

Menw stopped her. "Fear not. It will cry sometimes, it may scream sometimes, it may attempt to manipulate you, or scare you more. You must learn to ignore its tricks, even as you learn to control it enough to prevent them. That, of course, is why you must become its master before you can hope to control it as an equal being."

"How do I know when that is?"

"When it is no longer a separate part of you, but an integral, seamless addition to your very self."

"Okay. I won't ask how I know that, I'm pretty sure the answer will be that nobody knows and I must wait and find out. How often should I be meditating, though?"

"As often as you are able. There are more advanced, less time-consuming, easier ways for you to learn once you are fully proficient in this first."

Jodhi nodded once more. "I'll ask more another time then. For now, I'll just digest peacefully."

Menw smiled at his pupil. "Indeed."

"So when do we go?" Jodhi now asked. "I see it's daytime again. Everybody slept, right?"

Everybody nodded.

"We were waiting for you," Lana told her. "But now you're here, we'll just stuff some breakfast down then off we trot."

"I have orders from all but you, Jodhi," Menw added. "What would make you happy this morning?"

***

Once all had eaten, drank and showered, they all piled once again into Lana's car. Cam, this time, took a seat in the front with Lana, while Menw joined Jodhi in the back. Jodhi glanced at the two lovebirds, and then at Menw to share a pleased smile.

"To Depot E…hopefully," Lana said good-naturedly as she started the car and set off.

Jodhi had a sudden thought. "What if Depot E decides to take me and do…whatever they do to people like me?"

Menw shook his head reassuringly. "You came to us first, that makes you one of us whether they like it or not. We have a long-standing good-relationship agreement with them; in exchange for what we can do to help them, and the world, they leave us alone."

"Good, good. Just checking." Jodhi smiled a trifle nervously, but trusted the mage and settled back.

***

Isabel awoke in a strange room. It was soft, creamy coloured in the dim moonlight that filtered through the bars on a tiny window too far away to look through even if she was able to stand.

She moved her head and groaned as a stabbing pain shot through it, so she laid it back again on the leathery-padded floor and opened her eyes instead, to see a leathery-padded ceiling.

She rolled her eyeballs around as best she could, finding leathery-padded walls and a leathery-padded section that was probably a door with what looked like a small, rectangular hole close to the floor.

She was proved correct as that part of the padding flipped upward to reveal a rectangular slot, one just large enough to slide a tray through.

The tray clattered to the floor and the flap closed again, leaving silence.

Isabel lay where she was, willing her headache to subside at least enough to allow her to see, and hopefully ingest,what was placed on the wooden tray.

After an eternity, or perhaps two, it did. She rolled onto her side with only a painful, swimming sensation and a small retch, and looked.

Four chunks of bread with ham and cheese stuffed in-between. A dish of water. Three small aspirin-sized tablets.

The thought of actually eating made her stomach roll a warning, but she drank the water gratefully, sip-by-sip. The pills she ignored, but once the water remained in her stomach where it belonged, she picked up and began to nibble on the sandwiches.

After a time, when all but the pills were gone from the tray, the flap opened again.

"Tray," an indistinguishable voice commanded.

"Who are you?" Isabel croaked.

"Tray," repeated the voice.

"Where am I?"

"Tray."

"What do you want from me?!"

"Tray."

Isabel threw the tray towards the door and watched it disappear back through the flap. Once it closed, leaving her isolated once more, she gave a disgusted sigh and laid back, head still spinning.

"Help me…" she whispered, but her cry was absorbed by a powerful psychic field around the building, and Cam heard nothing.

Chapter 10

Cam had sent a call ahead to inform Department E of their impending arrival, so as they arrived they were greeted and escorted inside by a cocoa-skinned lady introducing herself to Jodhi as Morgan.

First-time visitor Jodhi stared around her as they entered, wondering why Depot E, though realising she knew only a little about it, looked just like any other bland, grey, boring office building.

The others noticed and smiled to themselves as they rounded identical corners and allowed themselves to be led down identical corridors.

Eventually they reached a blank, grey wall where Morgan stopped and winked at Jodhi who stared back, more confused than ever, and waited.

Morgan faced the wall and stepped close. A narrow beam slid out and scanned her face and a moment later the wall slid open, revealing another, entirely different, corridor.

Once they had all stepped inside, the wall slid closed and Morgan led them farther within this new, hidden part of the complex.

Jodhi stared around her in amazement. The walls were black, though not dull; they seemed to give off a comforting light and heat of their own. To the eye they looked soft, and when Jodhi cautiously reached out she found it did indeed give very slightly to her touch.

At intervals on the walls were small panels—a seemingly innocuous and pointless decoration.

Morgan saw her glance and explained, "The correct fingerprints will allow entry to whoever is authorised. Some are where our residents live, some offices, laboratories, things like that. We have a bit of everything here."

Jodhi nodded.

"I'll give you a tour later, if we get a chance."

"That'd be cool. Thanks." Jodhi smiled, easily warming to the lady with the typical office wear mode of dress and warm demeanour. "What do you do here?"

"Me specifically? I tend to oversee things. New talents, fresh arrivals, strange goings on in the outside world, one or two emergencies or projects.

That's me and Zeke and occasionally, when she's needed, his wife Maggie."

"Maggie?" Cam interrupted. "So the cure worked?"

Morgan nodded and allowed Cam to explain to Jodhi. "Maggie is an incredibly powerful empath, too powerful, it got so she went half-insane with it all and she could never shut it out. The Depot came up with a chip, an implant, which Maggie allowed them to put in her. It dulls the empathy enough for her to live, allows her to exercise some control and direction—give it some focus, if you like." He smiled pleasantly at Morgan. "I'm real glad it worked. Maggie and Zeke are two of the nicest people I've ever met."

Morgan nodded in agreement and pressed her thumb against one of the pads in the wall. A door unsealed itself and allowed them to enter before closing again. They were now in an office, neat and yet somehow homey. There was a large TV screen on one wall, in front of which sat a desk covered in complicated looking buttons. Morgan wheeled her chair out from behind this and signalled for the rest to take a seat, one of which had been provided for each of them.

"Cam, I received your messages. If you'd all be so kind as to just tell me your stories, explain what's been going on, what you need, I'll help you any way I'm able'"

Cam glanced at Jodhi who nodded and, hesitatingly at first, told her story; from the walk in the woods to Isabel's departure. One by one the entire group told their own version of recent events, each finishing up with the departure of Isabel and their decision to continue down to where they were now.

Once done, there was silence as Morgan thought for a while. "I think I can offer some help," she said. "First, Jodhi, something for you to consider, perhaps. We have been developing, over the past few years, a medication that, taken regularly, can repress and control your wolf. There are, of course, two sides to this. If you decide to use it you will need to remain in contact with us simply for refills—which you may either collect yourself, or ask us to deliver. The scientists would also ask occasionally for you to submit to testing, in attempts to understand and control the wolf better—of course you can always say no to them, but unfortunately that doesn't usually shut them up for too long. Also, the effects on those who forget to take or simply choose to cease the medication can be unstable, violent, unpredictable and usually dangerous. The other choice is to continue the meditations you have mentioned. It seems you are quite the little prodigal. We may be able to pass on a book or two, but Menw and Lana, I know, are more than capable teachers. I would personally recommend the continuation of your current course, but I felt I was obliged to at least offer you the other option—one which will, of course, remain open to you at all times. And should we ever manage to develop an emergency cure—for those times you unavoidably lose your control—I will see to it that you are given that choice also."

Jodhi considered carefully. The idea of just taking a pill and gaining what seemed to be an easy cure, appealed to her, despite the warnings. However, the knowledge that she perhaps possessed the ability to do it herself won over. "I'd rather keep doing it on my own. I know it'll take a while, and be hard and everything, but I want to do know I can do it. Anyway, if I can get control of my wolf, like Menw says, I can eventually make it my own—and use it to help."

Morgan smiled broadly. "I confess I am very glad to hear that reply."

Jodhi smiled back, relieved.

"As for Sansé," Morgan spoke again, "I will have our team find everything we have, and if you would accept our hospitality for a short time, we will pull everything together for you as fast as we possibly can."

Affirmative nods and thanks allowed her to move on quickly. "In the case of Isabel, I had no idea they were trying to pull her back, or that your request, Cam, was met with such a frosty refusal! I will do my best to correct this situation for you. But..." She pushed a button on her desk. A monitor and keyboard rose and she tapped some buttons and waited. Then she shook her head. "As I thought. Isabel escaped the attempt to bring her in, as you know, and she has been neither seen nor heard from since—excepting in name through Cam's contact with the telepaths." She looked at the worried faces. "I'll put out a call to locate her, just as soon as I persuade the bosses to allow her release into your discretional authority."

Cam nodded. "I'll help locate. I know her signal and where she lives, we can start from there."

"I was hoping you'd say that. I'll let you know as soon as we begin that, put you in charge of the team." Seeing Cam's pleased nod, she moved on. "Lana, I am truly sorry to hear about Mark. I've had occasion to work with him in the past and I liked and admired him greatly."

Lana gave a melancholy smile. "Thank you."

A phone tinkled. Morgan took one out of her pocket and held a short conversation, and then she turned back with a chuckle. "I presume the vampire outside is the one with you?"

Cam chuckled back. "Yes, sorry, I forgot to mention I had directed her here. May she be allowed in—on my 'discretional authority,' of course."

Morgan laughed. "Of course. I'll go and fetch her myself. If you'll excuse me." She pointed to a machine sunk into the far wall. "They've done some great improvements on that thing. Just use the touchscreen to tell it what you want and it'll send it along—it even has flavour now and everything. I'll be right back." She smiled and left the room.

They all took the opportunity to eat a quick snack. As they were finishing, the door slid open and Morgan returned with Alnthea in tow, looking mildly bemused.

"You sent me a nice dance," she accused with a faint smile. "What'd I miss?"

Cam caught her eye. "In quick form…" he murmured and closed his eyes.

A few moments later he opened them. Alnthea stood quiet for a minute longer, considering, digesting, then she nodded. "Got it."

Morgan smiled. "Great. Well, fortunately we always have our guestrooms prepared." She took a handful of keycards from her pocket. "Unfortunately they don't have thumbpads, but we do have these. I picked them up on the way out to get Alnthea. One each; the number on the card corresponds to your room number. Follow me over and I'll get you all settled in for now."

Once again they followed Morgan's lead and soon found themselves alone in a spacious room each. A bed, books, TV, DVDs, computer and a well-stocked kitchen had been provided for them. Alnthea was last into hers.

"I'll have some fresh blood brought for you, you must be starving and we only keep human food in the rooms," Morgan told her. "What's your preferred animal?"

Alnthea chuckled. "I usually have to put up with that offal the butchers palm off. If I can live—or perhaps I should say unlive—on that, I can probably survive on anything!"

They shared laughter and Morgan left the room, both still smiling.

***

Cam experimented, reaching for Lana with his mind. He found only a faint telepathic damper laid out, one that could monitor psychic activity, and be strengthened by the talented in the organisation if required.

Lana, feeling him announce his presence—almost a gentle knock on the outskirts of her mind—smiled and invited him inside.

"Can I come over?" he asked.

"Please do," she replied and pressed the button to open the door from the inside. A moment later Cam was there, closing it behind him.

"This place never fails to be unfathomably interesting to me," he declared.

"Yeah," Lana said, discouraging further conversation for the moment with a kiss.

***

Jodhi, pacing anxiously, slipped a hand into her pocket and felt her rosary. She pulled it out and looked at it for a moment. Then she sat, cross-legged, on the bed, closed her eyes and, using each bead as a focus, began to visualise her meditation of the sea.

***

Menw, restless as ever, exited his room and began aimlessly prowling the corridors. He saw the occasional person, who nodded to him amiably, but no-one he knew or wished to stop and speak with.

Eventually, he found his way out into the garden. It was as vast and blooming with colour as he remembered, fountains babbling gently in odd places. He strolled about more peaceably, nodding a greeting to the old gardener, Stan. A little later he encountered a young man digging a portion of flowerbed. Menw stopped and watched. He had never known Stan—or Department E—allow just anyone to take their place as gardener.

Presently the young man realised he was being watched and looked up, shyly. "Hi," he said.

Menw nodded to him. "Hello. I'm Menw. Just visiting for a short time."

The young man stood and removed his gloves, wiping sweaty palms on grimy overalls. "I'm James," he said and held out his hand for shaking.

Menw shook it warmly. "You must be one of the youngsters who saved us all from the bad guys not all that long ago!" James blushed and Menw smiled. "I'm sure I speak for everybody when I say thank you." James blushed even more and Menw took pity on him. "I'll let you to your gardening, James; looks like you're doing a good job around here."

James thanked him, still blushing, and turned hurriedly back to his flowers. Menw walked on, smiling to himself, finding peace.

***

Alnthea thanked the chisel-featured guard who brought her two sealed cups of blood. She placed one in the fridge, and popped open the other.

Taking a sip, she swilled it around her mouth thoughtfully. It was familiar, pig's blood she decided, but purer and cleaner than the usual guff the butchers pushed her way. She drank with some relish, feeling it enter and revitalise her body. She realised it had been almost two days since her last meal. Grief over Mark plus the long journey to find the others had left little time for thought of such trivialities as sustenance.

Now, feeling restored, she browsed the bookshelves, smiling at some of the titles—*Dracula, Necroscope*, and others about her kind. Eventually she picked up a detective story and settled down to read, at least until exhaustion and the knowledge of impending dawn caught up with her enough permit sleep.

***

Cam and Lana lay in bed, waiting for their minds to awaken to conversation, enjoying for now the glow of being together.

Eventually, Cam spoke, repeating his earlier observation. "This place never fails to interest me."

Lana nodded. "I know what you mean. Some parts, some people, like Morgan—they almost make it a decent place, probably could if given the chance. Others, like the ones who would take Jodhi for experiments if they could, the ones who want to bring poor Isabel back…"

"And the ones who took her to begin with," Cam added.

Lana nodded in agreement. "It's the usual story. A good idea that somehow lost its way a bit. You've still got the few good people in it, trying to do what was meant, but the rest…"

"The rest forget the idea of helping it in pursuit of controlling it, and somehow they always wind up outnumbering the good ones," Cam finished.

"Yeah. Do you really think Morgan can persuade them to take our word on Isabel?"

"I'd stake most things on Morgan and Zeke doing anything they say they will," Cam decided after considering. "There are not many here I would trust, people are easily corruptible even when they mean well. But those two—and Maggie—yes."

"That's kind of my thought too. So, what shall we do until they're got everything we need?"

Cam thought. "Well, I'm free until Morgan sets me to work helping locate Isabel…" He flashed a cheeky smile. "I'm sure we can find some way to entertain ourselves till then."

Lana grinned back. "Well, aren't we full of beans today?"

***

Morgan entered the boardroom, politely declined the chair she was offered, and took in the faces watching her. She had managed to speedily assemble most of those dealing with Isabel's case and attempted re-assimilation. At the head of the table sat the man who had officially requested her capture and Morgan spoke mostly to him. "I know we have been trying to bring Isabel, our invisible girl, back in to the Department. I know we made one attempt, which she escaped, and that since then she has physically disappeared off of our radar. I know that Camlaidh, a highly-skilled telepath and respected Shadow Walker—has since contacted you via our telepaths to inform you that Isabel had come under their sphere of protection and that he wished us to allow her freedom on his promise. I know that the reply he was given was for her to remain constantly with them, else we would consider her fair-game as, years ago, she originally came—unwillingly, I might add—under our experimental wing first. I also know that Cam and his group were planning to visit us regarding another, highly dangerous and important, matter. Isabel, upon finding this out, panicked and ran and has not been seen by them or us since."

Those sat around the table nodded impassively, feigning boredom even at information they had not previously known, or had no idea yet how Morgan knew.

She continued. "Cam's group—consisting of himself, Lana and Menw, who we know well; also with Alnthea, a good vampire, and Jodhi, an emotional werewolf whom they are assisting even as she works alongside them—are here now, as my guests.

"Cam has offered to assist in locating Isabel, in return for your agreement to allow her to go free. He will, of course, accept responsibility for this, as will all of them, should she prove to cause trouble.

"I believe firstly that they can be trusted. This has been many times proven in our encounters with the Shadow Walkers, and specifically with Cam, Lana and Menw. Secondly, I believe that Isabel is no threat to anyone or anything and we should never have attempted to force her to return to us in the first place, also that she may even help the Shadow Walkers, if she ever trusts them again after this—which in turn helps both us and the world at large. Thirdly, I think that the damage all of this has so far done to our relationship with the Shadow Walkers may be left irreparable if we continue to be pointlessly stubborn over this matter."

The man at the head of the table raised his hand. "I do not agree with you, Morgan. But, as we know, I rarely do; yet despite that you have never let me down or failed to prove me wrong. I shall, therefore, accept and trust your judgement once again. We will allow Isabel to go free; we shall never bother her again, so long as Camlaidh fulfils his promise of finding her and vouching for her presence in the outside world. The rest of this situation I leave, as ever, to your discretion."

Morgan smiled politely. "Thank you, Steven. As always, you have my word that you will not regret this." She gave a small bow and exited, allowing her triumphant grin to surface only once well out of sight of the door.

She walked to the guest rooms and buzzed the intercom on Cam's door. There was no answer. After buzzing twice more, she glanced at Lana's room and a knowing smile crossed her face. Almost apologetically, she buzzed Lana's intercom and was greeted by a female voice. "Hello?"

"Hi, Lana, it's Morgan…is Cam there, by any chance…?"

"Um, yeah, just a minute."

A few minutes later, the door opened and Cam stepped out, looking mildly sheepish, his shirt tucked in untidily.

"Didn't mean to interrupt." Morgan hid a sly smile.

Cam blushed.

"I spoke to the big guns. You find Isabel, we'll leave her alone."

"That is excellent news!" He grinned and gave her an impromptu hug. "Point me to your locators!"

"This way." Morgan hugged him back and started walking. "So…you and Lana?"

Cam blushed again, but couldn't keep down the large smile.

Morgan smiled back, remembering her one-time crush on the gentle telepath. "I'm happy for you both—very happy."

"So am I," he replied dreamily, and they walked on.

Chapter 11

This time, when the tray arrived, Isabel crawled from her corner and devoured the food without even tasting what was between the chunks of bread. As she chugged the water she realised there were no aspirin-shaped pills on this tray. Apparently they were quick to take a hint.

She sat back in her corner, as far from the door as possible, making sure that the tray was within easy reach of whoever it was that would collect it.

After a few moments, much faster than before, the flap opened and the tray was removed. Isabel heard a chuckle, but yawned sleepily and decided not to wonder what it may have meant.

She lay on her side, head resting on one arm, and closed her eyes to nap. Slowly, a dream came into view.

She was sitting peacefully on a bus, riding past dreary, samey houses and side roads. Every so often the bus would stop and somebody would climb on, pay the fare and sit down; or somebody would shuffle down to the front and climb off. Either way, the bus would move on as peacefully as before.

Isabel was hardly paying attention to the stops and starts until a bright flash of primary colour attracted her eye.

She looked over to see a clown, with orange wig, baggy trousers, enormous buttons on a bright red waistcoat and giant yellow shoes; the image completed by greasy white facepaint and a blood-red smile. The clown paid its fare and sat down, some seats behind her.

Isabel shook herself inwardly. "Only a clown. Nothing to be afraid of."

When the bus stopped again, she glanced up to see an identical clown board and sit a few seats ahead of her, giving no recognition to its twin.

When the bus stopped a third time, Isabel tensed and, sure enough, another identical clown hopped aboard. This one sat in the seat on the other side of the aisle, directly opposite Isabel, again paying no attention to the others.

Over and over the bus stopped and a clown came aboard until, Isabel realised, one sat on every double seat except for the one in front of her. More, she was the only non-clown left on the bus.

She looked out of the window and stifled a scream. The streets were full of clowns. Each one was standing still, staring at the bus. Each one was staring at her.

As the bus stopped again, Isabel's gaze was drawn to one particular clown, glaring at her malevolently. As she looked on, it opened its mouth in a grotesque smile, revealing sharp, white fangs.

She turned away quickly, swallowing another yelp, to see the clown that had just got on sitting on the seat in front of her, turning to face her with that same menacing glare, and that same pointed smile.

Now she did scream, and try to move. But she found herself bound to the seat by large, colourful handkerchiefs, and screamed louder.

Every clown on the bus was now looking at her with that greedy smile. As she stared around, she saw glints of silver; a gun, an axe, a dagger. In the hand of the clown in front of her was a vicious-looking hunting knife.

The clown moved the knife closer to her face. Isabel twisted and cried for help but the knife came steadily closer. She heard laughter and realised it was the deranged, psychotic sound of the clowns.

As the knife touched her flesh and she felt the cold steel begin to part her skin, she shrieked again…

…and found herself back in the padded room. Blood slid down her cheek and she touched it in disbelief as the clownish laughter echoed and then faded slowly.

There was a clatter and she jumped, but it was just another food tray being dropped through the flap.

As she reached for the food, she remembered the earlier chuckle and thought better of it. She left it untouched and curled up small in her corner, eyes wide and ears straining, perhaps catching the occasional strain of crazed clowny laughter.

***

Cam opened his eyes momentarily, glancing around the talented men and women who were seated in a circle.

The room was spacious and empty, the lighting purposely dimmed. Each of the telepaths and locators was deeply in the trance Cam had led them into. Now, able to draw on their strength, he closed his eyes once more and began to make his way to the place he had seen Isabel last: the library in Lana's ruined house. Hopefully he would be able to pick up her trail and simply follow it—the task of casting a net and narrowing it down was time-consuming and far more draining, if eventually just as accurate.

He studied the psychic signatures in the room, finding Isabel's easily—agitated, afraid and angry, but unmistakable. He followed it logically to the front door and through it, down the driveway and to the gate where he looked to the left and caught it again. Cam took hold of the lead and followed it at speed.

As expected, Isabel had returned to her house. She had wandered a little, eventually going to bed. A lower psychic signal showed that she had slept for a time.

Then there was a flash of panic and terror which led out of bed to hover in the air. And then, just as suddenly, a lower pattern than before—something deeper than sleep. Cam studied minutely, and found the exact moment where her trace signal shot out to hit the wall, before it dropped into unconsciousness.

He frowned and followed the signal, recognising beside it the muggy, unreadable aura he had sensed back at the house where Sansé had held Jodhi captive.

Sansé, then. She had taken Isabel. But to where?

In the driveway of Isabel's house, the trace was enveloped by the fog.

Cam cast around a moment, but the fog had faded—or been sliced off by Sansé—the moment it left the threshold.

Cam sighed and shifted a little, settling more comfortably. He would be forced to cast a net after all.

***

In the guest rooms, the Shadow Walkers waited impatiently. Lana paced, Jodhi meditated, Alnthea flipped restlessly through her book, Menw drew patterns in the air with colourful sparks from his fingers.

Morgan occupied herself by overseeing the compiling and cross-checking of any data they could find relating to Sansé. Whether there would be anything the Shadow Walkers didn't already know, she was doubtful, but it was surely worth the effort. Besides, having it all pulled together may at least be a useful reference—especially for the Shadow Walkers who had not been around during Sansé's last rampage. And at least it kept her from sitting around doing nothing. Somehow the concern these Shadow Walkers had for Isabel, and the fear they felt at Sansé's return, was infecting her.

"I can feel it too, from the other end of the complex," agreed a voice behind her.

Morgan turned with a smile. "Maggie. Anything wrong?"

"Not really, like I said, I can feel what's going on. Thought I'd see what it was, if I could help."

Morgan nodded gratefully. "Thanks, Maggie, I'll let you know if I can think of anything for you, but for now I think the Depot is in sidekick mode. Though I could perhaps do with Zeke, if he's around?"

"He's resting. Just finished up with that intensive training thing he was doing."

"Oh, with the shapeshifter? Well, let him be then. I'll fill the details in when he's feeling up to it—both of you, actually, in case we're needed again for anything later."

Maggie smiled and turned away. "Oh, Morgan," she turned back, "you may want a quick chat with the werewolf? She's doing her best to cope with everything that's going on, but I think she's new to it all and, with the stress, in severe danger of inconveniently-timed morphs."

"As ever, Maggie, what would I do without you? Thanks."

Maggie nodded again and strolled from the room.

Morgan turned back to watch the progress.

"Almost done," said the chief researcher, a stooped-over fellow with bifocals and a sallow expression that belied his usually cheerful, if shy, persona. "Just a few bits to check on; make sure we're fully written up on everything."

"Thank you, Vince, you're the greatest. Wire it all up to my office when it's done."

Vince nodded and flashed a pleased smile. "Will do."

Morgan left for her office. She would read the information and then assemble the Shadow Walkers once Cam's team reported back.

***

Cam frowned in annoyance.

He was unable to locate Isabel's signal anywhere. She was alive, of that he was sure if only because he had located no death trace either.

Even more annoyingly, his net was constantly, almost instinctively, being pointed to a small area. Finally, he gave up pulling away and began to examine it minutely. His frown only deepened as he found nothing at all. Not even a fly buzzing aimlessly around.

He pin-pointed the location and took a birds-eye view. Then he smiled grimly and opened his eyes to bring his team back to their senses.

After thanking them heartily, he scurried away and began to buzz urgently on the doors of his friends, before simply barking at them to follow him—almost at a run—to Morgan's office.

It was with a note of mild surprise that Morgan opened the door and saw them gathered. She invited everyone inside and looked at Cam, guessing that whatever he had discovered was the cause of the hurried, en masse invasion.

Cam explained how he had followed the signal to Sansé's tell-tale fog. How he had then cast the net over everything and simply ticked off and deleted, in clumps, clusters and finally one-by-one, every current signal not matching that of Isabel. He explained finding nothing, but being attracted to the one area, and after following up on this he had realised why. "There was nothing there. It was psychic empty space! Everywhere holds something, even if it's unoccupied at the time. Faint traces and echoes of people who've been there in the past, signals from a plane that whipped over, flies and wasps and butterflies even leave some form of trail. But this—this was like a place out of time. Nothing at all. Then suddenly, outside of this small area, whoosh! Everything back again. To follow something inside that perimeter is like hitting a wall of silence."

Morgan nodded her understanding. "You mean it's being shielded."

"Yes. And it's the only place I can't look for Isabel, but she's certainly nowhere else…"

"Which means that's where she is." Lana finished for him.

Cam nodded excitedly. "Exactly! I got the location, I can get us there. Means we're going back up north though."

Alnthea groaned and turned to Morgan. "When are you people going to invent something useful—like vampire sunscreen. Hmm?"

Morgan grinned. "Sorry Alnthea. I might be able to help though. How would you like a van with windows that are 100% UV proof?"

"Or my money back and a nice little urn for my ashes?" Alnthea asked politely, a corner of her mouth turned up in a smile.

Morgan smiled and tapped a few things into her computer then nodded in satisfaction. "Alright, one vamp-friendly van reserved and ready for your departure."

"Thank you." Alnthea smiled.

"No problem. Now, to the issue of Sansé," Morgan handed a folder to Menw, "this is everything we have—substantiated and not. If there's anything you didn't already know, great, if not it might come in handy for a quick reference anyway."

Menw took the folder with thanks. Looking at the others for confirmation, he spoke again "I believe we should be on our way now."

Nods of agreement came and Morgan stood. "Perhaps one day we'll manage a social call. It was good to see you all." Morgan embraced all but Jodhi. "May I beg a moment with you?" she asked.

Jodhi gave a shrug. "OK."

Morgan smiled reassuringly. "Your van is at the entrance, I'll walk Jodhi out shortly."

"Don't leave without me." Jodhi warned, only a little fearfully.

Cam ruffled her hair with an evil grin, chuckling as she growled playfully and set it straight again. "Don't keep her too long; we really do need to get going."

"I won't, I promise." Morgan ushered them out and sat Jodhi down, pulling a chair into a position opposite her and taking it for herself. "Don't look so afraid." She smiled warmly.

Jodhi, anxious now her protectors were gone and she was left in the presence of another—no matter how friendly and understanding this other seemed to be, shifted awkwardly and said nothing.

"Remember I mentioned Maggie—our empath?" Morgan asked and Jodhi nodded. "Well, she sensed the arrival of all of you, sensed big things, and came to see if she could help. Obviously there was not much she could do but she did mention you. She said you are having a hard time keeping controlled, what with all of this new and scary stuff you keep running into. She said that there is serious danger of you wolfing at the worst possible moment."

Jodhi looked at the floor and shrugged sadly. "It's all new. It frightens me."

"And that's to be expected. But somehow you need a way to control that fear and anger in a tight spot."

"Or I'll put everyone else in danger."

"Yes. Now, we're not going for that medication we already mentioned—we already agreed that's a bad idea. But there is another one, not fully tested yet, taken once a day, which is able to dampen the parts of the brain that control those emotions. You'll still have them and feel them, but with your talent for control and meditation, this should allow enough leeway for you to remain human in most circumstances—perhaps with the assistance of an anchor as you and Lana almost managed once before. Yes?"

Jodhi nodded. "I take these pills, and keep learning control, and then I might be able to not wolf? Then when I've got better control…"

"You can stop taking them entirely without side effects," Morgan promised.

Jodhi nodded. "OK. But you said they weren't properly tested yet?"

"I'll be honest with you, you'd be our first mood-wolf, and there's a danger of some initial side effects—tiredness, lack of concentration, that sort of thing—until they adjust properly. It's all up to you." Morgan held out a bottle. "In here are 200 doses. A lot, it meant special dispensation to get them for you. But, if you decide to take them then by the time they are gone— probably even before—you won't need them anymore. And if you do, you just have to let me know. And if you decide not to take them, then that's great too—drop them back in sometime when you're around."

Jodhi took the bottle. "Thank you."

Morgan smiled and stood. "The people you're with—Cam and Lana, Menw. Mark too, and other Shadow Walkers. They're my friends. That makes you my friend. And though some parts of the Depot are…unfortunately unpleasant, I do try my best when I can. Hope to see more of you, Jodhi, I have a feeling you've got a real warrior inside of you."

"Yeah, only it's being sat on by a bloody great wolf." Jodhi grinned.

Morgan walked Jodhi out to the van, black panelled with completely sun proof windows, and gave Jodhi a quick hug before she climbed in and shut the door.

"Take care," Morgan ordered them and waved as the van drove off.

"You alright?" Lana asked the thoughtful-looking Jodhi.

She smiled, nodded, and explained a little nervously about the pills.

Cam smiled. "Our Morgan, she always comes through somehow. don't worry, Jodhi, we might not trust most of that place, but Morgan is one we do trust with anything. Like she said, the choice is entirely yours."

Jodhi nodded, relieved, and put the pills away, as yet undecided whether to take them or not.

"So, where are we off to this time?" Lana asked, wanting to know which way to drive.

"Small, sort of out of the way place up the top of Scotland, called Fort William," Cam replied, reading the instructions for the GPS directional system installed in their new vehicle.

Chapter 12

Isabel came out of her fitful doze at the sound of a key rattling in a lock. Unsure whether to be relieved at a potential rescue, or afraid of whoever might be entering, she opted for the latter and cowered in her corner.

A woman entered, small and blonde. "Isabel, you haven't eaten your food." A grating voice emerged from the woman's mouth.

Isabel said nothing.

"Now, now, this is no way to act is it?" The woman grinned, a somehow hideous sight. "Perhaps if I introduce myself. I am Arlene." She moved closer. "There, now we're friends—so you can talk."

Isabel stared at her hypnotising grey eyes. She tried to look away, but found her gaze fixed.

"Talk to me, Isabel," Arlene commanded.

"The food was drugged," Isabel said lazily. "I fell asleep, I had a nightmare."

"Oh, you poor dear," said Arlene, the shattered sound of her voice belying the attempt at sympathy.

"Clowns. Lots of clowns. They hurt me." Isabel touched her cheek, feeling dried blood. "I'm afraid of clowns," she whispered.

The grey eyes blinked and she was able to look away at the floor.

"It wasn't the food, Isabel," said Arlene.

Isabel's eyes travelled slowly along the padded floor and came to rest on a pair of bright yellow shoes. "No…" she whimpered pathetically as the clown took a step closer. And another. Until it stood directly over her. With a swift movement its hunting knife descended on her arm, loosing blood that coursed down and onto the floor. Then the clown began to laugh. Horribly, high-pitched, maniacal.

Isabel clamped her hands over her ears but the laughter still grew louder. A small cry escaped her lips and soon she was screaming, screaming to drown out the crazy sound.

Suddenly she realised there was silence except for her own cries. Timidly, she let her hands drop, registering the ache in her bleeding bicep, and opened her eyes. The room was empty again; the door locked, the untouched food tray was lying where she had left it. Isabel covered her face as she pressed her sleeve to the bleeding, trying to stop the blood from trickling down her arm to join the small, red puddle by her thigh.

Once the bleeding had stopped and the clotting was well underway, Isabel curled up once more and sobbed quietly into her uninjured arm.

***

Arlene nodded enthusiastically. "Yep, scared her real good. Clowns. Haha. Clowns. What next? What next?"

Sansé held up a hand. "You may do whatever you please with that one, she is secure where she is—even if she gets out of the room, she will not get out of her head Have some fun if you wish, just as soon as you make sure everything else is prepared."

Arlene grinned. "Okay, yep, okay, I'll make sure Sansé. I'll make sure. Everything will be ready. All prepared," and she scurried off, interspersing her rapid shuffle with the occasional hop and skip.

Sansé leaned back in her comfortable armchair and smiled.

***

In the van, Cam was reading the file Morgan had given them on Sansé, passing on the highlights to the rest for the benefit of Jodhi and Alnthea, who knew of her only what they had so far encountered.

"Back in the 16th century, Sansé was been bitten by a werewolf. One of the lucky ones, she had been saved from the recriminations of her village by a daring rescue performed by Menw, already a legendary mage amongst his kind. Menw had taken Sansé under his wing and taught her, much as he now taught Jodhi, the art of control. She was less of a natural at it perhaps, but worked steadily and, after many years, assisted by her lover—Danieel, also a wolf—mastered it in triumph.

Sansé and Danieel formed a duo of their own and fought the dark side successfully for a long time.

Once, however, they were unlucky. A battle against a powerful, evil vampire left the vampire dead and Danieel wounded. He would in time become a vampire himself, but he was already a wolf, and such a mix is more dangerous than I care to imagine. Sansé did the only thing she could have done; she ended his misery with her sword.

95

For a while she had wandered aimlessly, other Shadow Walkers taking her into their band for a while until she drifted listlessly away.

The story of how she turned to the dark side is one only Sansé knows, but she did, wreaking havoc on any reminder of her past. Villages, Shadow Walkers, even the innocents she had once been the saviour of. Years later, Menw encountered her again, now a slathering beast of a wolf to show her evil.

But Menw's younger apprentice, myself, naive and impressionable, fell under the woman's spell. When I began to act on her behalf, Menw realised quickly and acted. In battle, he vanquished Sansé, who escaped and was not heard from again.

"Until now," Cam finished.

"Wow. What a bitch," Jodhi murmured and grinned as laughter exploded in the van.

"Couldn't've put it better myself," Lana chortled from the driver's seat.

"So, what're we going to do now?" Jodhi asked.

"We're going to go to this place that is shielded. We're going to walk right in, rescue Isabel, and capture—dead or alive—Sansé and her little slaves, the witch and her Cantor," Cam said. "In theory, at least. I find it best to be flexible and improvise with such things, myself." He handed Jodhi the file. "Here, there's some embellishment inside. Morgan left out the… the things that I did…but everything else is here."

Jodhi took it and began to read, shifting position to accommodate Alnthea. As the sun set, Lana turned to Alnthea. "Do you need to feed somewhere? Sorry, I should've thought about that before…"

Alnthea cast a glance at her rucksack, lying with the others at the back of the van. "Thanks Lana, but Morgan kindly got me stocked up as much as she could. I should be all right for a good few days yet."

Lana nodded. "OK, just make sure you let us know when you need a restock." She smiled into the rear-view mirror, concealing a yawn.

Alnthea stretched herself. "You know, night really is more my time than yours. Why don't I take over the drive—let you all get some rest?"

"You sure?" Lana asked and gave a grateful smile at Alnthea's nod.

They stopped the van and everyone except Alnthea curled up in the back for a rest.

"I'll wake you when we get close," Alnthea promised and was greeted by some tired murmurs. She smiled and set off into the darkening night, listening to the deepening of breath behind her and the occasional outbreak of snoring.

***

Isabel, no longer weeping, too exhausted to even shake with fear, drifted in and out of an unpleasant, though mercifully dreamless, sleep.

When the flap opened and a newly-stocked tray clattered to the floor, she dragged herself listlessly over and eyed the contents. It was what she had come to expect, though perhaps the glass of water was larger? She ate and drank anyway and watched as, with uncanny timing, the flap opened and the tray was removed.

Instead of closing immediately, however, the flap remained open just long enough for Isabel to start moving closer. Then something dropped through and hit the floor, making her jump back.

Now the flap closed, leaving her to study the object.

It was a doll. Plain, pink, naked. Its eyes were closed as it lay on its back. Its legs and joints were hinged. Isabel wondered if it spoke, too.

She watched it a while, refusing to trust its innocent, rosy-cheeked, chubby smiling face. When it continued to lie motionless, she began to relax.

For a while she dozed lightly, eyes snapping open constantly, always finding nothing changed, the doll still in its original position. Eventually, her eyes closed fully and she drifted into a restless sleep again. How long she slept did not know, but eventually reality washed over her again and she reluctantly opened her eyes. Immediately she saw the doll and screamed in shock. It was now sitting upright, staring directly at her with its fixed smile and cold, pale blue eyes.

"Somebody moved you," she told it. "I slept deeper than I thought and somebody came in and moved you, that's all."

The doll made no reply.

Slowly, cautiously, ready to snatch back, Isabel crawled forwards, one hand outstretched. With the tip of a trembling finger she touched doll and jerked back. It wobbled slightly, stilled, carried on staring.

She moved closer and touched its head with the flat of her hand. It remained still.

Braver now, Isabel grasped it by the torso and picked it up. "You're not so scary are you," she taunted.

The doll stared at her for a moment longer. Then its cold, pale blue eyes blinked and its tiny plastic hand gripped hers like a vice. "Yes I am," it said.

Isabel screamed and tried to pull her hand away but the doll hung on. She shook it and hit it against the padding but it held, relentless. She stopped, sobbing, feeling the bones in her wrist grate and crack under its hand. "Please…" she begged.

The doll let go and landed on the floor, feet-first. It tottered a few steps away and turned to face her. "Hi, I'm Chucky, and I wanna be your friend," it said in a perfect Good Guys doll voice and then, head thrown back, tiny feet stamping on the floor, fists clenched, it began to cackle. It was the insane call of the clowns, only coming from that mouth it was somehow even worse.

Isabel crouched in a corner, covered her ears, closed her eyes and sobbed. When the cackling finally stopped the void of silence made her eyes jerk wide open.

The doll lay in its first position—face-up, on the floor, by the flap. Except now its eyes were open, head turned towards her, smile malicious.

Her wrenching sobs went unheard as it held her eyes and took her down into the cold blue of it's own.

As the haze cleared, Isabel found herself walking around what looked like Toytown. Tiny children rode their tricycles down the road, one perhaps proud to have finally gotten rid of its training wheels, parents watching anxiously, one running to kiss better a graze sustained in a clumsy fall. Dinky cars drove by, drivers stopping with a grumble at a red light or a wave at a zebra crossing, nodding to those they passed and recognised. Some to-and-froing for work, some with a boot full of shopping or a back seat full of children being noisily happy. Perhaps one was a husband or wife on the way to a secret assignation. Small bells tinkled occasionally as people entered and exited small shops, perhaps pleased with their purchases, or annoyed by the price. Here and there a door slammed shut from a gust of wind or a forcibly ended argument. Dolls scurried or strolled, hurried or leisured, ignoring Isabel's alien presence.

The doll from the cell tapped Isabel's leg and she jumped. It grinned evilly. "Cute, huh?"

Isabel nodded.

"Wanna see what the Valley of the Dolls really looks like?"

Isabel shook her head.

The doll laughed and held her gaze again. When she opened her eyes this time, she saw a very different scene.

Children cried as their tricycles toppled them to the ground or were stolen from under them by sour-faced dolls. A parent scowled as her child fell from its saddle and ran crying to her with a bruised knee, leaving its tricycle to be taken along with the rest. Dinky cars, black with dirt, stripped of paint, wheels, windows, riddled with bullet holes and knife wounds lined the edges of the road and the odd still-usable vehicle crept through cautiously, driver watching fearfully, waiting for it to be his turn to be attacked. One or two cars came through confidently; they were clean and well-groomed with tinted windows and rock-faced drivers. Houses and shops were barred at window and door. As Isabel watched, a doll scurried up and rung a shop doorbell, but was carried away by a gang of ruffians in biker jackets, flashing silver knives, before the door was opened by a shopkeeper who, on seeing no customer, closed the door firmly and cowered back inside.

The decor was no longer bright, airy, welcoming and fun. The buildings were grey, the street was grey, the sky was grey, even the few people daring the streets; or those prowling for victims; were grey. The only colour existed in cruelly flashing blue eyes, silver knives and the strange, orangey-red rust that seemed to cover everything.

With an intake of breath, Isabel realised that the rust was no rust, but old, dried streaks of blood. She turned to the doll who was smiling up at her. "Why?"

"Why what? Why this? Or why show you this?"

"Both?"

The doll grinned evilly, shrugged and scurried off into an alley Isabel's eyes could barely register as more than a crack in a wall. She watched it go with despair. Her only connection to her own world, gone down a hole even Alice might have trouble with; and there was no bottle inviting her to "Drink Me" there to provide an easy solution.

She stood where she was for a moment. Until, from the corner of her eye, she saw movement and whipped around just in time to see a figure vanish.

"Great," she muttered and started moving forwards. At least her stride was bigger and, if it came to that, so was her fist.

She moved through small streets, sticking to the middle of the road to avoid any small people or objects that might accidentally slip underfoot. All around her she sensed more than saw the threatening presence of murderous dolls.

She scolded herself. "They're dolls! Just stupid dolls!" But her wrist throbbed badly, swollen and bruising, reminding her that these were more than just your average dolls—that one doll had done more injury with its tiny hand than a large clown complete with a knife.

Turning down streets at random, her only plan to keep moving, Isabel soon knew she was lost, and soon knew she didn't care. There was no way to

leave this freaky place, whether she was back where she started or anywhere
else. As panic overtook her, she began to run. No longer caring if she trod on
something or not, she took small corners at a bound, passing through street
after identical street until, rounding a corner, in her fright seeing nothing,
she bowled into a dead-end wall and flew over, landing head-first on
something soft and leathery.

She leapt to her feet and saw she was back in the padded room. A quick survey revealed no dolls, no clowns, not a thing. Exhausted, panicked, frightened, she curled in her corner once more and vowed not to move a single muscle, not for anything.

***

As promised, Alnthea disturbed the sleepers in the back of the van once the small village of Fort William, last stop before John O'Groats, read on the GPS system as just a few miles away. She left them to wake properly and kept quietly to her route until Cam climbed over and into the front seat. "How you doing?" he asked, glancing at the remaining distance.

Alnthea smiled, her eyes almost luminous in the dark. "Good. Everybody rested?"

Cam looked back and smiled. "A bit cramped, by the looks of it, but they'll be glad of the rest later. Thanks for that."

Alnthea shrugged and kept on driving. "So, where exactly are we going to?"

Cam turned so all the sleepy faces in the back could hear him talk. "Fort William is only a small town compared to many we know. We don't need most of the history, but there is one part that even historians don't really know about. The Fort William Hospital for the Criminally Insane."

Lana took over. "The Hospital housed some of the worst, most depraved people the justice system had—still has—ever seen. The cases even the bloodthirsty don't wish to hear; some of the cases still remain officially unsolved, because the culprit could never stand trial. Think of Jack the Ripper, and you may get a small glimpse of the nicer side of these people. The powers that be, for reasons best known to them, decided that Fort William would make a perfect place to house these men. So, they built the most secure place they could possibly build in those days. Barred windows, too small for even a tiny child to squeeze through. Padded walls, floor and even ceiling. Doors triple reinforced with an advanced blend of iron—sort of a pre-cursor to steel today. No way could anybody escape, not even those with what seemed to be preternatural abilities—strength, jumping, and the like. Of course, as you can probably guess, things were never going to be simple.

"To keep the compound secure, the government also chose the most ruthless Governor they could find to run the place—a man as black as the people he was supposed to be guarding. Then they 'forgot' it existed, and left him to it. In turn, instead of employing a proper staff, he hand-picked inmates and set them to work, usually in a position that complimented their crime. A poisoner might be allowed to work in the kitchen. The physically cruel might be guards. Let the job fit the crime was entirely his motto, and anybody who disagreed could be easily punished by his thugs. And if they caused too much trouble, the kitchen staff would be glad to oblige; or perhaps the torturers, for those who especially riled their Governor. After all, nobody cared, nobody asked, nobody even knew the place existed. Obviously this couldn't remain a working system. The psychotically, sociopathically, evilly insane presided over by their fellow inmates and a chief as bad as any one of them?

"The Fort William residents had a measure of awareness about the place and early on began to spy on it, and the more the snoopers built up year-by-year, added to by the odd mysterious disappearance of one of the curious, angered more and more those who saw and understood.

"Finally, faced with one disappearance to many; a teenage boy, last seen going on an information gathering mission close to the Hospital, the village gathered together. Letters to Government were ignored, ditto spokesmen dispatched to MPs, and to London. They tried all they could, but a denial was all they received. Letters to the compound were returned with 'Address Unknown' scribbled on. Officially, the Hospital did not exist.

"Angry, frustrated, they gathered again. Thwarted by the proper channels, they came up with only one solution. They must destroy the building, and all within.

"They worked together, some creating sticks of gunpowder, some planning routes inside to plant it, some arranging a perimeter around to prevent escapes.

"We will never know exactly what happened, but they did attack the place. Most of it was blown apart and, so far as we know, nobody escaped. There was no recrimination as the place had never existed to begin with, and it has been left there in ruins ever since for the same reason. It is mostly a ruin, but there are some parts of it that still stand—though word is they house ghosts."

"Or a clever werewolf," Jodhi said.

"And that's where Isabel is?" Alnthea asked.

"Yes," Cam said.

"No, I mean that's where Isabel is." She stopped the van and pointed. All eyes took it in and for a long moment, nobody made a sound.

"Why?" Jodhi asked.

"I have no idea," Cam replied, honestly.

***

Sat in her corner, knees clamped to her chin by two white-knuckled hands, Isabel fought a mental battle with the exhaustive sleep that desperately tried to take over. Her head drooped time and time again, and time and time again she jerked it up with a gasp, all the while knowing that she could not defeat it altogether, but vowing still not to move from that spot, whatever may show itself to her next. Better a speedy death where she sat than a torturous, drawn out one playing their game. Whoever They were—right now she had no idea, right now she couldn't even remember one face from the next.

Her head dropped once more, shot halfway back up, but settled again.

A sudden sloshing sound forced her bloodshot eyes open again. Suddenly there was no support for her back and, shoving herself forwards in fright, she almost fell forwards onto—into—the floor. The floor which was now wet. More than wet; it exuded a smell of freshness and salt as it lapped at her shoes. Isabel swore.

Looking up she saw no sign of land, no sign of birds. She saw a blue sky with whispers of cloud and a hot, bright sun. She looked behind her; saw her wall replaced with more oceanic expanse. She was crouched on a small square of padded floor, with nothing to hold her up except herself.

Time passed. Whether in reality or artificially she could not say, and did not care; but the sun set and the clouds rolled over the moon and stars, heavy and black, leaving not even the faint reflection of the sea upon itself to give relief.

Shivering, muscles tight and cramped from her position, Isabel stared into darkness and listened to the gentle lapping of waves.

"This isn't so bad," she thought, vaguely, and began to doze. As she did, the waves began to move closer, further. Little-by-little, each lap rose higher up her now-sodden shoes. When the first freezing cold lick touched her ankle she jumped awake, startled, and toppled backwards into the unseen water.

Gagging on the cold, salty wetness that filled her mouth she took a panicked breath and started choking. Her feet kicked and her hands grabbed as her lungs cried for air. She hit something with one hand and held on tight with both, pulling her face out of the water and gulping oxygen. She realised she was holding her piece of floor and attempted to pull herself upwards onto it, but her strength failed and she remained clutched to it instead, shivering as the water cooled the blood in her veins to what felt like ice.

Slowly she began to lose feeling all over and knew she would not be able to hold on. She sobbed, adding her own salty tears to the invisible expanse before her. She put her head down on her numb arms and closed her eyes, waiting to die.

Time passed and she became aware of a pain in her legs, in her arms, all over. Pins and needles, her body waking up. She started, almost letting go her perch and realised with a mixture of relief and muted, terrified expectation that the water was now warm. Pleasantly so. Also, she saw the sun had risen again. There was still no land, but there was light and warmth.

A burst of energy, and Isabel was sat on her square of floor again, dangling her legs in the water and letting the sun dry and warm her until she fell, again, into a doze—this one more pleasant than the last.

She woke up to a new sensation in her legs. A pulling and burning. A look at the water revealed rising steam and she tried to pull her legs up in panic. The pulling sensation resisted any strength she possessed and kept her legs where they were, beneath the slowly heating water.

The heat and pain increased so steadily Isabel hardly knew when to scream. She gritted her teeth and clenched her fists, threw back her head and wailed to the sky but still her legs remained imprisoned and the water grew hotter.

Isabel felt nothing but scalding pain but as she glanced downwards, taking a breath to force her hoarse throat to keep screaming, she froze and watched as a piece of her thigh, well-boiled by now, simply loosed itself and began to float away.

Suddenly past screaming, brain blocking the pain in favour of numb shock, Isabel watched with horror as her skin slowly peeled, bobbed to the surface, and slipped gently away on the tide.

When the water hurriedly became chilly again, Isabel had only a second to register the change before the salt hit her open wounds. She opened her mouth, managing only a squeak as she saw a shark's fin coming closer, smelling the blood which clouded the water around her.

Closing her eyes, she willed herself to somehow return to the padded cell. When she felt firmness beneath her again she opened her eyes to find herself curled up in the very spot she had vowed not to leave.

"Ha..." she muttered weakly, feeling her trousers scrape against her fleshless legs. "Take that."

"Indeed," said a familiar, awful voice.

Isabel peeked and saw plain, black shoes. Assured this was no clown, she looked Arlene in the face.

Arlene gave her an indulgent smile. "Is it you who just controlled it? Or is it really just controlling you?"

Isabel shrugged pathetically.

Arlene smiled, clapped and left, closing the door once more with a firm thud.

Chapter 13

The Shadow Walkers slept the day away in the quaint little B&B they had stumbled across at last. Surprised and pleased, the lonely landlady had them breakfasted and tucked up between fresh sheets before the sun had risen.

Alnthea slept the easiest, daytime being her usual time of rest, but all fell fairly speedily into corpse-like slumber, any lumps in their old mattresses ignored by the level of exhaustion.

Cam had requested a wake-up call just before sundown, and the landlady sat on her sofa now, watching the clock and pretending to read a book; all the while idly wondering what this strange band of travellers were about.

As promised, just as the sun began to dip, she roused them room by room with the promise of hot food and coffee.

Alnthea politely declined food, claiming a sensitive stomach, and once the others had backed her up the landlady retreated and left them to it.

Cam spoke directly into their heads. "We know She's listening, so keep an open mind and I'll let us all hear each other."

There were murmurs of assent in his head.

"When we are done eating, we are going to check out, get into the van and drive close. We go in, we find Isabel, and we walk straight back out again."

More agreements.

"Great. So eat up, we likely have a long night ahead."

They ate gladly enough and politely offered to assist with the chores. With a smile, though, the landlady declined and wished them a pleasant journey; whatever it was they were up to. Thanking her heartily then, they piled into the van, taking themselves away from her curious gaze.

Cam directed Lana to the building and spoke to them all on the final approach. "There is little point in hiding. Park up outside the perimeter, get in, get out—fast as we can. I want the van there so we can get away fast, we can't run if we have to carry Isabel and we have no idea what state she'll be in. Everybody okay?" He got their nods and looked forward again. "Another hundred yards, then park up and turn the van about."

Lana obeyed and secured the keys firmly in a pocket.

"Keep together. If you get separated, call me; once we are inside the perimeter that should be possible. Then, stay put and we will come and get you. Ready all?"

All made as enthusiastic an affirmative as they were individually capable of and Cam led the group out of the van and beyond the first ruin of walls. As he crossed the blank perimeter he winced and then smiled; as he thought, the psychic atmosphere inside was no more than mildly muggy. He took the first step, a half-pace ahead of everybody else, but he stopped and transmitted a thought. "Perhaps somebody with a better sense of direction than me ought to choose the way?"

Lana took his arm. "I'm not very good at choosing, but I can at least remember the way once you've done so," she said.

Cam took her hand gratefully and they faced forward again, at each step expecting…something. He listened carefully; the mindsmog prevented him from properly locating Isabel but if she made a sound, he would hear her. Unwilling to call to her without a location, however, for now all he could do was walk onwards, deeper into this place that still, after all these years, seemed to seep evil through its walls; seemed to remain standing despite attacks and time and be held together simply by an evil that sent an icy finger down his spine and infected the group with every breath, soaking through their clothes and into their very skin.

"Shh." Cam stopped dead and listened. He had heard a faint cry with a familiar signal. Straining, he heard it again. "It's her!" he whispered and set off at a loping run, leaving his companions to follow. After taking a few turns, he looked back and saw his line staggered. Stopping, he let them catch up before setting off again at a slightly friendlier pace, tracking the faint mumblings to their source.

Soon they stood outside a locked door. Menw stepped forward and rattled the lock to the floor without breaking a sweat. The door opened and they saw Isabel. She was huddled in her corner; eyes squeezed tightly shut, hands over her ears, whimpering.

Lana stepped inside the room. "Jodhi, come with me," she said and moved slowly closer to Isabel.

Halfway there, she realised Jodhi was not following. "Jodhi!" she hissed and looked back to find confused and afraid faces; but no Jodhi.

"Fuck," she hissed and thought quickly. "Cam, we'll get Isabel to the van. Rest of you, find Jodhi."

106

"But if Jodhi calls for help—" Cam protested.

Alnthea stepped forward. "I'll help with Isabel."

"Find Jodhi," Lana ordered the rest through clenched teeth. Cam blew her a kiss and led them away at a striding pace back to the place they had begun to separate out.

Lana moved closer to Isabel. Alnthea followed a step or two behind, aware she was a stranger and not wanting to give Isabel more cause for panic. Lana halted within reach of Isabel and held out her hand. "Isabel, honey, it's Lana. How you doin'? Can you talk to me darlin'?"

Isabel moaned and shifted, curling further into herself.

Lana saw blood on her t-shirt, black trousers stuck to her legs, pale skin and eyes that looked directly at her, and yet through her to some place far away. "Oh—oh Isabel, honey, we're gonna get you out of here, okay? Me and Alnthea. You remember, I'm your friend, and so is she, OK? We came all the way up here to help you."

"Not real," Isabel muttered, but allowed them both to move close enough to touch her.

"Legs're injured," Lana murmured.

"But lighter. It'll take a lot of pain for the poor thing, but get them resting on your arms, in the crook of your elbows; that'll make them easier for you to carry and less painful for her in the long run. I'll take the torso."

Lana saw her vampiric eyes flash and knew which one of them was the stronger. Carefully, wincing at the stiffness of dried blood, the pained cries from Isabel and the thought of what lay underneath, she cradled them as gently as she could in her arms.

Alnthea received a nod of readiness and worked her arms gently beneath the unresponsive, gently whimpering body. A count of three and Isabel was lifted.

"Right, can you do this all the way out?" she asked.

Lana nodded. "I think so. I hope so."

"You need to stop and drop; you let me know, OK?"

Lana nodded again and they set off walking. They moved awkwardly at first, finding a match for their separate paces, Alnthea facing forwards to direct them around obstacles her eyes could see better than Lana's; Lana directing from the map in her memory.

Watching, Alnthea saw Lana become more and more strained with the dead weight she carried until, on the final run, she stumbled.

Alnthea stopped. "Lana, give me the legs. Run, open the van. Now. Go."

Lana obeyed the command without question and forced her shaking legs into a half-sprint. She opened the panel door of the van and collapsed inside, looking back to see how far behind the vampire was. Surprised, she saw Alnthea only a few paces away, grunting with effort. In another moment, Isabel lay in the van.

Alnthea smiled faintly at the sight of Isabel breathing heavily. "Looks like you're catching breath for both of us." She smiled and sat beside Isabel. "What do we have in the way of things to assist this poor creature?"

"Normal first aid kits. Menw, when he comes back."

"No time for waiting, who knows where Jodhi got to? Isabel needs him now. you'll be all right here with her? I'll find Menw, send him out and help with the hunt."

Lana nodded. "Hurry. And, please. Find Jodhi. And tell Cam—tell him I…" she trailed off.

Alnthea nodded. "I think he knows, and I'm not much of a messenger I'm afraid, but I promise you I'll not walk out of that building without Jodhi or a way to get to Jodhi." Alnthea leapt from the van and flew swiftly back into the building.

Lana placed a hand on Isabel's neck and felt the irregular pulse. Needing to do something, feeling nauseous at the thought of peeling back her shirt or trousers to find whatever lay underneath, Lana rested Isabel's head on her lap, stroking the untidy hair and wondering where the mind contained within might be, and how damaged it was.

***

The rest of the group backtracked to where Cam had set off at a run and found nothing. No trace of Jodhi, no sign that somewhere along the way she had been snatched from them. Cautiously, Cam listening intently, they began to explore the rest of the building.

As they did, Alnthea raced up to them and stopped so suddenly that they all jumped. "Menw," she said. "Isabel needs serious medical aid. Lana's with her. I'll help here. Go."

For once even Menw took no time to consider or even contest. He simply took to his heels and moved as fast as he was able.

Moving deeper inside the building, Alnthea took the lead, where her night vision was most useful. All of them looked, listened, and found nothing.

***

Isabel had no knowledge of her rescue. No knowledge that she lay in a van with her hair being stroked soothingly. Her physical body was something apart, something other, something that had no place where her mind had been taken.

She sat in a dungeon of fears. Her own and those of others which soon became her own. A museum of fears, all finely crafted and on display for her and her alone.

Physically away from the padded cell, these phantasms possessed no more influence over her body, but one-by-one each took hold of her mind and led her into a place of terror to play itself out.

All the while, Isabel, unable to resist; helpless to prevent; simply stared through space and back into her own mind.

***

Jodhi had lost the group as they pelted after Cam. She had seen a door they had all missed, and it opened for her. She knew it was meant for her and her alone, and that was why the others had not seen. The golden light blinded her gently and beckoned. Jodhi took a look towards her friends, but was already under its thrall. Without a further thought, she stepped inside.

The golden light surrounded her, warm and soft, and gently urged her to walk forwards. As she walked she strained to see what she moved towards. Soon she could make out shadows and fixed on them as she moved closer, watching as they became clearer until, suddenly, like stepping from behind a golden curtain, she emerged into a garden.

There was grass and trees and colourful, blooming flowers. The sky was bright blue and a warm breeze caressed her hair gently. Looking behind. she saw the golden light still there. Jodhi tried to step back into it, but was pushed away.

"Hey!" she protested, and then stood still as a sound reached her ears. Somewhere, a child was crying.

Turning back, thoughts of returning forgotten for the moment, she scanned the garden more carefully. In front of her stood a fountain, and on its edge sat a child. The fountain was black marble, shining as if freshly polished. The figure in the centre, a cloaked man holding an urn from which water trickled, looked down upon her benevolently. As Jodhi came near the child stopped crying and raised its tear-stained face to her. It was a small boy with sandy hair and black eyes.

For a long moment they just looked at each other. Then he broke into a teary smile. "You came."

Jodhi said nothing.

"I was told someone would come. Someone nice. Like you."

"I-I don't know if—" Jodhi faltered before his innocent gaze. "Yeah. I came. What's your name?"

"Bian," he said sweetly. "Shall we go home now?"

"Home…?" Jodhi looked around and saw an impressive-looking building to the left of the garden. *How'd I miss that?* she thought vaguely. "That's home?"

Bian nodded. "It is now that there's somebody to live there with me."

"Oh, Bian, I can't—I mean, I—" Jodhi frowned. She knew there was something else she should be doing…but, as recollection escaped her she found she had already entered the house.

From the outside it was warm and friendly-looking; whitewashed walls, Victorian style roof, hanging baskets and the sun glinting off the chimney.

Inside was different. Odd. Plush and luxurious, certainly, yet somehow disconcerting. "Looks smaller when you're not inside," she murmured.

Bian smiled. "It's a special house. Been waiting just for you and me to come inside."

"Waiting to do what?"

Bian shrugged and bounced up the stairs. "I wanna see my bedroom!" he yelled over his shoulder, masking slightly the sound of the front door closing.

Jodhi almost went to reopen it, but the house called to her. She found herself climbing the stairs, wanting to see her bedroom too.

She passed Bian's without a thought and pushed open the door to her own with a gasp. It was huge. An oak four-poster bed caught the eye and pointed it to matching wardrobe, drawers and writing desk. The walls and carpet were a gentle peach and the carpet, too, looked as if it would caress the bare foot that walked upon it.

There was a door set into the wall on the right and she walked carefully to it. Behind the door was an ensuite bathroom in matching colours, its floor tiles showing a gleaming, distorted reflection of her figure.

Utterly bewitched, Jodhi closed the door and began to draw herself a bath.

***

Finished in the bath and wrapped in an enormous towel, Jodhi padded into the bedroom again. On the pristinely-made bed lay the clothes she was obviously meant to wear. Hesitating, thinking of her comfortable and comforting old jeans, she examined the cream dress with curiosity. It was long and backless, with a slit up to one thigh. Holding it against herself by the straps, Jodhi opened the wardrobe to reveal more fabulous clothing and studied herself in the full-length mirror.

"Jodhi? You there?" Bian asked a while later, knocking on the bedroom door.

Jodhi opened her mouth to reply, and then paused. *When did I tell him my name?* Then the thought was gone and she drew a brush through her shining hair one last time. "Coming," she called, taking a second to test her simple-but-elegant white, kitten-heeled shoes and opened the door.

Bian grinned and applauded, looking immaculately adorable in a suit of his own. "Time for food," he said and bounded along the landing and down the stairs.

"Food?" she repeated. "From where? By who?"

"C'mon, it'll get cold!" Bian yelled.

"Okay, okay," she yelled back and walked carefully down the stairs and towards the voice, trying to remember everything about holding her head up, her back straight and gracefully placing one foot directly in front of the other for that special movie-star wiggle.

The dining room she entered looked like the one from every big-budget film featuring rich people—enormous! With a table almost as long as the room. A wooden floor, oil paintings adorning three walls, the fourth left blank to save damage from the steam which rose from freshly cooked food placed along a side table. Overhead crystal chandeliers, hanging from a minutely-sculpted ceiling, offered a cosy, intimate light and well-placed wall-lamps chased away any remaining shadows.

From a chair towards the middle of the table, Bian waved. "It's good!" he promised through a mouthful of food, try it!"

Jodhi took a plate and piled it with tasty-looking and smelling morsels and poured herself a large glass of wine before claiming the seat opposite Bian and tucking in.

"Good, see." He grinned as the last bite disappeared from his plate.

"Good," she agreed. "I wish I had three stomachs just so I could keep eating."

Bian laughed. "Funny. Come on, food done. Let's play."

"Play what?" Jodhi forked another mouthful and followed him into another room. This seemed to be the living room—or perhaps, in a house like this, the games room.

There was a pool table in the centre, with an orange-shaded lamp hanging above. A piano by the French windows, a green table for cards or board games, a sofa, an overflowing bookshelf and a crackling fire giving the room pleasant, glowing warmth.

"Play." Bian pointed to the piano.

"Oh, oh I wish I could."

Bian tutted and sat before the instrument himself. He tinkled a few notes cautiously then smiled. "Song then?" he begged.

"I'm not very good at that either…but I can try. For sure I'll give it a go!" she finished hurriedly, seeing his face begin to crumple.

He broke into a beaming smile and clapped. "Get some music."

Jodhi looked at the bookshelf and took a sheet of music at random. "Minnie the Moocher?" she read, doubtfully.

"Okay, that's good. I'll play, you sing," and without so much as a glance at the staff Bian began to play, leaving Jodhi to find her own way around the words.

***

"There is nothing more I can do," Menw said, sadly. "Physically, she is as good as new. But I cannot cure whatever has been done to her mind."

Lana, cradling Isabel in her arms, felt herself grow hot with anger. Controlling her voice, knowing it was not Menw's fault, she spoke through gritted teeth. "Nothing? All your magic and nothing?"

"They took her to a place other than here. A place where her fears, and everybody else's, come to life over and over and over. With whatever she has been through before and what she has been through more recently because of us…" he trailed off with a helpless shrug. "I cannot simply snap my fingers and cure this. Believe me, my dear, when I say I wish I could'"

"I know. I believe you," Lana replied with a sigh. "Then what can we do?"

Menw turned to leave. "Just keep her body comfortable and safe. Her mind…I do not know. I must return to hunt for Jodhi. I shall give you a shield for protection," and hopping from the van he paused long enough to enclose it in a protective bubble, and then walked across the perimeter of the psychic blackout and called quietly for directions from Cam.

***

"How is she?" was the first question Cam asked once Menw had found Alnthea and himself.

"Physically she has never been better. What they did to her brain, however, even you could not fix. She resides now in the Realm of Fears."

"Oh no…" Cam breathed, "oh Isabel, poor Isabel."

"Is that where Jodhi is?" Alnthea asked, timidly.

"I wish I could say." Menw sighed.

"One thing is for sure," Cam said, "she is in no place where I am able to hear her."

"Not a good sign," Alnthea voiced their thoughts. "But, voila, a door. Shall we?" Without waiting for a reply she pushed it open and walked through.

"Alnthea?" Cam called and looked at Menw incredulously. "Did she just walk straight through the wall?"

Menw nodded. "Indeed, I believe she did."

Cam swore under his breath.

"Quite," the mage agreed, attempting to blast straight through the wall and failing admirably. "Which of our missing friends would you like to look for first?"

Cam shot him an evil glare. "Why don't you keep working on that wall, see if you can find our fine, photophobic friend. I will continue hunting for our pet wolf." With that he tramped away.

"Nothing like a spot of badly-timed humour," Menw said to himself angrily and turned to face the blank wall with a cowering stare that had absolutely no effect. In fact, even his most withering of stares caused not even a ripple. Each blast he sent to it was simply absorbed, creating neither a crack nor even a momentary distortion. Menw leaned against the opposite wall, frustrated and tired.

***

Alnthea stepped through the door and onto an empty beach. As the sun hit her eyes she cried out and turned to run back through the door. The door was gone. "No!" she cried and fell to her knees; in her mind she was already aflame.

Slowly, though, she realised the heat on her back was the sun itself—and it didn't burn. Standing, turning, the vampire faced the sun and looked directly into its glare as her pale skin soaked up its warmth.

"This is wrong," she told the sun. "This. Is. Wrong. I wish to leave."

"You wish to live in my light," the sun seemed to reply. "As a human you loved me. As a vampire you long for me still."

"So what am I? Human? Vampire?" Alnthea grew her eye-teeth and felt her eyes flare yellow. "A vampire that can stand in the sun?"

"Indeed," was the reply. "All the advantages the Undead have over Humans, and yet with fewer of the weaknesses that prevent your demonic soul from fulfilling the destiny it longs for."

"My 'demonic soul,' nice oxymoron by the way, longs for a peaceful life amongst Humans and has no destiny to fulfil but the protection of those who cannot protect themselves."

"Your demonic soul wishes to taste of their pulsing life-blood, wishes to command them, to rule them, weak as they are."

"Their weaknesses match mine."

"How? They are feeble, naïve, unseeing. They—"

"And a vampire burns in the sun, can be stopped or killed in many different ways. A vampire fights its blood-brother out of sheer arrogance, for supremacy over itself. A vampire's ego says it will never conquer anything even as it attempts to conquer everything. Less ways to kill me than a human, and yet my species is so much fewer, and in hiding. How so if we possess such superiority?"

"This is why you—a vampire without ego, who can walk during the day—this is why you could—should—take the lead. You are stronger, faster, and more intelligent. You possess more stamina, require less fuel and rest…the list goes on but it all ends the same. You, Alnthea, you can be the beginning of a new breed. A whole new world."

"And if I refuse?"

The sun said no more but Alnthea felt a prickling pain on her cheek. Touching it with her hand, she felt a spot of scorched skin and understood.

"Decide," the sun ordered, "for I will not wait forever."

"Nothing like a fair and balanced set of options," Alnthea spat and turned her back on the sun, who simply laughed and kept on shining.

***

"What?" Cam said aloud, spinning around to find who had spoken. There was nobody. He switched to telepathy and probed for an echo, something that might tell him who it was—for somebody had said his name, of that at least he was sure.

He found a glimmer, something faint, and followed it into a solid wall. "No. Not solid. Solid to me, but not always…Jodhi! Alnthea!" He hit the wall with his fist, succeeding only in the removal of a layer of skin. "Somehow…" He thought hard, followed the line until it dissolved and fell apart. "Some—somewhere? Somewhere! That's it!" He paced, reaching for Menw through the muggy ether. "Menw. Could they have been taken elsewhere?" Speaking with pictures he gave a clear explanation of his thoughts and Menw almost punched the air.

"Yes!" he returned. "Yes, of course! I should not be trying to break the wall, only dissolve it into the door to whatever plane it goes to. Yet that is hard magic, Cam, and for a younger man than I."

"Then use my strength!" Cam set off at a run to rejoin Menw. "We are bound," he explained as he arrived. "This makes the strength you can draw from me even more potent than it would be otherwise. Take from me what you need, even unto my own death—I would have you do so!"

"Death will not be necessary. But between us, we will have the strength. The power, however—"

"You have the power," Cam encouraged. "You are the most powerful mage the Shadow Walkers have ever known. Especially when friends lie in danger."

Menw set his face proud and strong. "Then join me!" He took Cam's hands. "Meditate; take yourself away so I may draw on you."

Cam sat himself cross-legged on the floor and let the cold pass through him, focusing on it, disappearing into it, becoming the chill until it warmed and carried him to a place outside of both time and space.

Menw watched his face grow calm and vacant, gave him some extra time to be sure, then, meditating himself, he grasped a corner of Cam's floating aura and attached it to his own. Both flowed with strength until Menw felt they would burst, but he remained steady and calm, fighting for the control he needed to be able to harness and direct it the way he wished for it to go.

***

Alnthea turned to face the sun again.

"I said answer me. Now. Say yes now or you will burn. Become a miserable pile of ashes as your entire race become. Or take it, take what I offer. Take the world."

Alnthea looked into its dizzyingly bright centre, squared her shoulders and replied. "Yes. Yes. Give me what you promise. For I would rule."

The sun laughed. "I knew you would see the truth, given a little encouragement."

Alnthea smiled. "What else is there to do? I know my strengths, I know the truth. I've wasted my time saving these Humans when I could be ruling them. If they could run their own planet, then fine, but look at them! They have no idea."

"Good g—"

An explosion sent Alnthea sprawling face-first in the sand.

"Alnthea!" Menw shouted and grabbed her hand. The wall had reappeared and he was stretching out, holding firmly onto the part that remained intact.

Alnthea used him to drag herself towards the hole in the scenery.

"Remember," called the sun. "Remember…"

Back in the gloomy corridor, Alnthea looked around to find the wall was intact, and the door had disappeared.

Cam returned from his trance and the three of them leaned against the undisturbed wall.

"Remember what?" Menw asked once his breath had returned.

Alnthea hesitated then shrugged. "I don't remember."

Cam looked at her carefully, vaguely suspicious, aware a vampire was difficult to read but sure she was hiding something.

Alnthea closed her eyes tight. To be out in the sun, to be more powerful than any other. But to hurt those she loved. Could she? Would she? Vampires were supposed to have no love, no scruples, no thought for others—but she was not the sort of vampire so easily portrayed.

Sighing, she opened her eyes again. Time would tell.

***

Jodhi stepped out of the bath and wrapped herself in a towel. Where she was, days had already passed. She felt at home, had forgotten everything but the house, the garden, and Bian.

She turned and saw the boy standing by the door and started. Had she forgotten to lock herself in? No, the thumblock was still turned.

Bian smiled innocently.

"How did you get in?" she asked sternly. "It's not nice to watch people like that."

Bian kept smiling.

"This isn't funny, Bian," she scolded, rubbing her arms, goose-pimpled both with cold and apprehension. "Please leave."

Bian took a step forwards, still smiling.

Jodhi took a step back, grating her heel on the bath. "Bian...?"

Bian's smile changed to a malicious grin.

Jodhi pulled her towel about her, suddenly remembering something. "Lana..." she whispered, "Cam, help..."

There was no reply.

Digging within, she found her wolf cowering, refusing to protect her. She swore at it, trying to feel anger, but it simply quivered and was still.

"Who are you?" she asked timidly.

Bian still said nothing. Instead he grew.

In a moment Jodhi's innocent boy was gone. In his place, 7 feet tall, stood a creature of darkness. Dark grey scales covered its skin, pearly teeth protruded from its grinning jaws, its eyes danced with emerald green fire.

A powerful grey hand reached out and grabbed her arm, pulling her to him.

Jodhi struggled and gave a small whimper as his other hand tore the towel from around her. It pushed her against the wall, laced its hands vice-like around her waist, and lifted her off the ground.

Jodhi fought uselessly, crushing her bare feet against solid armour, bruising her hands against its rough hide. When she felt a hard presence between her legs she froze. Until the pain started. Then she screamed until her throat closed and her lungs ached. The searing hot and cold seemed to touch her heart until it bled, giving up everything before the eyes that bore deep into her own. She sank down into a void of nothing and felt no more.

Until she awoke, shivering; dried blood making her thighs crackle, a physical ache between her clenched legs, and another ache deep within, somewhere no amount of medicine could ever reach.

She gave a dry sob that convulsed her chest and ejected bile from her mouth, the trickle of greenish-yellow fluid sliding down one cheek until it pooled on the floor beside her desperately dull, blank eyes.

Jodhi lay unmoving on the cool tile of the bathroom floor and did not even realise she was weeping.

Chapter 14

Cam looked around uneasily. "I may be wrong, but this could be the place. It feels…like the place Alnthea disappeared. It feels off, somehow, unreal." He ran one hand along each wall in turn, stopped and came back to a point on the second. "Yes. Here. Something not quite right."

"Between us, do we have the strength?" Menw asked.

Cam shook his head. "I don't know."

"Between the three of us, we must," Alnthea said. "Use me."

"It will not be as easy to use you, but I am able." The mage nodded. "Very well. Find a comfortable position."

Cam and Alnthea settled on the grimy floor, the vampire taking hold of the telepath's hand.

Though unable to read her thoughts, he understood and squeezed reassuringly. "Won't hurt a bit." he whispered.

For the sake of Alnthea, Menw took them both into a deep trance before drawing their force out of them to mingle with his own. He concentrated and aimed on the spot Cam had indicated. With a thrust of thought he powered a bolt of magic into the wall and sent himself after it to get Jodhi and pull her out.

But his bolt threw itself back at him and he hit the wall behind with a heavy thud. Unconscious, Menw slid to the floor, dripping warm blood from the back of his head to his neck and down his spine.

Beside him, Cam and Alnthea remained in their trance, their auras lingering in the air around them.

Arlene walked around the corner and stood in front of them, rubbing her hands, chuckling and giving a few gleeful hops.

***

In the van Lana was half-dozing, Isabel's head on her lap. She jerked awake and looked around for the cause of her disturbance.

Out of the open side-panel she could see a door, standing upright yet connected to nothing. The faint sunlight cast a shadow and a glint of metal revealed a handle. On the door was a gold plate, unreadable.

Lana looked away, told herself it was a trick, and looked back. The door remained as solid-looking as any door she had ever seen.

She gently moved Isabel's head from her lap and rested it on a pillow. Eyes fixed firmly on the door; she stepped out of the van and towards it.

The door stayed where it was, standing solidly on the ground. It had hinges, she saw, and a snugly-closed handle, all attached to a frame.

Moving closer, Lana stepped to the left side. The door remained still as she sidled cautiously around to the other side. As she did so the door disappeared. It didn't bother to fade and slide into nothing, it was there and then it was gone.

Lana moved her head back a fraction to the right and grunted to herself as the door flipped back into existence. "Dark Tower here we come..." she mumbled, half-looking around for lobstrosities.

She moved all the way around the back and looked through clear air at the sleeping Isabel then, completing her circuit, faced the front once more. The gold plate caught her eye and she read the small, engraved text.

THE BEARER OF THE KEY IS WELCOME

"What key?" she asked aloud and was startled to see the text fade and be replaced by:

THE BLOOD OF THE LUPINE MUST BE MIXED WITH DEATH

"The Lupine? Jodhi?" Lana asked.

The writing remained fixed.

"Sansé, then?"

Still nothing. Lana reached out and touched the doorknob. It was cool and solid and would not turn. There was no keyhole.

"Well give me something," she begged.

The writing changed again to a warning:

FIRST SAVE YOUR FRIENDS

"Save my friends?" Lana repeated and backed away. Then, with a cry, she bolted into the ruin calling Cam's name in her head.

***

Menw came back to consciousness with a groaning headache. He opened his eyes and closed them again, seeing stars.

Concentrating his other senses, he gave himself a sketchy picture. He was lying on something hard—wooden. There were straps holding his arms, legs and torso down. He could faintly hear two people breathing—the link between himself and Cam told him he was close, it must be him and Alnthea. Their breathing was calm but shallow; they were out of their trance. He could smell damp, moss and stone, dried blood which he presumed to be his own. The air tasted fresh and wet in his mouth and there was a slight breeze to cool his aching head. So they were outside, somewhere.

Gritting his teeth, willing his magic to begin the healing process, Menw opened his eyes again. A flare of agonising sparks exploded in his vision and he bit back a scream and waited for them to clear.

When they did he found himself looking at the sky, now clearing and revealing the sun. As he prepared to move his head sideways, there was a cackle and a figure shot across the sky, pluming smoke from its tail. He watched as the figure formed shapes, letters, the words "SURRENDER SHADOW WALKERS"

"How droll," Cam spoke from somewhere to Menw's left.

Menw turned to him, letting loose a short growl as the pain bolted through his head once more.

He spotted Cam a few feet away, strapped to a wooden table of his own. Cam saw Menw was awake and grinned. "Mornin'. Sleep well? How's the head?"

Menw grunted.

Alnthea spoke now from his right. "They really let the Emerald City go to shit, huh? By the way, if it's any help, your head doesn't actually look the size of a beach ball, probably only feels that way."

With an effort Menw looked at her. "Thank you, I was wondering."

"So now what?" Alnthea asked.

"I don't believe I've ever been in quite a situation like this," Cam mused. "Although the last time I was strapped to a table there was also a tiresomely stereotypical movie bad guy involved and he had a large circular saw making it's way up towards a rather sensitive area.

"When will they learn that if the James Bond villains themselves never win, a bad copy has no chance?" Alnthea tutted. "How'd you get out of that one?"

"I wasn't tied up next to him," Menw replied.

"Ah. That may cause a slight problem then."

Cam began to speak but was interrupted.

"None of you will be escaping this time."

Al three captives turned to face the new voice. Sansé greeted them with a gruesomely smug smile. "But before I kill you all, Alnthea do tell me your trick for being out in the sun and yet still remaining so...so not a pile of ashes."

Alnthea struggled with her bonds, suddenly realising the truth of that statement, painfully aware Menw and Cam were suddenly wondering the same thing.

Sansé chuckled. "I do believe you made a deal with the friendly Mr Sun you met on the beach. Shall you tell or shall I?"

Alnthea spat in Sansé's general direction. "The sun told me it would take away my weakness to itself if I would follow my true vampire self and begin to conquer Humans."

Sansé looked at Menw and Cam. They were both expressionless.

Alnthea continued. "I said yes. To save myself I said yes. And okay, for a second I maybe even considered it, but I helped you!" She looked at Menw and Cam pleadingly. "Didn't I give you life force to try and free Jodhi?"

"No," Sansé answered, "you are a vampire. You gave him the essence of death."

Menw chortled. "It was not that which caused my injury. If that is what you are about to suggest."

Sansé shrugged. "Does it matter anyway? She made a deal. She broke a deal. Now, I believe, I shall remove the immunity...slowly. Like putting a frog into cold water and boiling it ever-so-slowly." She smiled. "Now then, if I am correct then the wizard's death will be the death of you." She looked at Cam. "Which is a shame, because I would have liked to save you until last, take my time...but still, it is a good plan. And I do enjoy a good evil plan."

"Me too," said Lana, coming up from behind and landing a powerful blow on the back of her neck; a chunk of rock merely adding to the damage caused.

Sansé crumpled to the floor and Lana stepped purposefully over her. "Need a hand?" she enquired politely.

Alnthea whimpered, looking slightly flustered as the immunity began to wear off and the sun started to tan her skin painfully. "Sunscreen?"

Without bothering to ask for explanation, Lana bolted to her, unbuckled the straps and helped her into the shade of a half-ruined wall.

"Thank you." Alnthea nodded, breathing heavily and touching her blistered skin gingerly. "Guess my agreement got well and truly broken, then."

As Lana freed the other two and assisted Menw, healing slowly, to their shade Alnthea told them of her conversation with the sun. By the time she finished, the four of them were resting in a small huddle.

"I did think about it," Alnthea admitted. "At first I agreed just to stay alive, but then I did consider it...and I'm sorry, I'm so sorry—I—"

Lana touched her arm gently and offered a caring smile. "Sounds like a bad trip to me. I think anyone would have considered that, Alnthea. Absolute power, removal of personal weaknesses, superiority...I know I would have thought about it."

Cam nodded. "For sure you did better than I did, once upon a time..."

"So it's alright? I mean, I didn't do anything, and—"

"If we were all held accountable for everything we thought or considered, there would be no hope for any of us," Menw said. "We are safe now. Sansé is secured." As he spoke, Sansé was raised by an unseen hand and buckled to one of her own tables. "The only question remaining, I believe, is where Lana appeared from?"

Feeling oddly foolish, Lana described the door and her headlong dash through the ruin with Cam quietly guiding her steps.

"The Lupine, hmm?" Cam repeated at the end of the story. "Jodhi or Sansé?"

Lana shook her head. "It wouldn't tell me."

Alnthea looked at Sansé. "Well, we have a Lupine. She contains blood. Say we try her first?"

"How?" Cam asked. "Do we just cut her throat? Here or by the door? Or does the door need to blood to touch it? Either way—how much blood? And what if it isn't Sansé?"

"Trial and error," Menw said simply. "Take Sansé to the door and give it her blood. What else can we do?" He touched the back of his head and winced slightly, but it felt much better, and he could at least move without pain. Soon he would be healed.

The table wheels being broken, Menw was forced to loosen the straps and bind Sansé magically before levitating her off the ground. So hovering, Cam and Alnthea took their turn pushing her through the air while Lana backtracked through her mental map, leading them back to the van.

When the van was in sight, the door a growing smudge, Alnthea halted. "It's still daytime. I'll be out as soon as I can." She gave Sansé a last shove and watched them walk on, glancing at the sun to gauge remaining daylight.

Upon reaching the van, their first act was to leave Sansé hanging by the door and check on Isabel. She was still soundly asleep, no signs that she was beginning to stir but also, thankfully, no more physical manifestations of her nightmare world.

Satisfied, the three turned back to Sansé and the door.

The writing on the plate had changed once more, now reading:

GO AHEAD. TRY IT.

"Well, there we go." Cam sighed. "Not ones to back down from a challenge are we."

"Sure," Lana agreed. "But who gets to—I mean who's going to—"

"I am," Cam said, stepping into the van and removing a hunting knife from a side pocket of his bag.

Lana took a quick step back and Cam looked shameful. "I have to," he said. "All that she did, all that I did because of her. Who else can do this?"

"I can," Menw said, dashing the knife from Cam's hesitating hand. "With magic."

"Wait!" Lana said. "Mixed with death," she reminded him. "The Lupine, Sansé's blood. Alnthea, a vampire…?"

Cam understood. "Alnthea has to drink from Sansé."

Menw made a noise. "The old man almost acted rashly. So I suppose we simply wait for Alnthea to be able to make it outside?"

"I'll go in and talk to her," Cam said. "But basically yes, we need her to be here." He walked back beyond the perimeter where Alnthea, waiting patiently in the shade, watched.

"Problem?" she guessed.

Cam nodded and sighed. "The riddle—mix the blood of the lupine with death. That door, it's cheeky actually, but seems to be trying to help us. We think what it means is not to kill Sansé, but mix her blood with another kind of death…" He let Alnthea work the rest out on her own.

"You want me to taste that thing's blood," she spat. "I haven't supped on a human for a long time, Cam, and you want me to start with a half-human monster? Oh, and when I say that I'm not talking about the wolf in her, I just mean she's an inhuman bitch."

Cam bowed his head. "I know. I thought if I came and told you about it you could have time to think about it, while you wait for the sun to fall. It's up to you, and I think we would all understand if you say no. And we will find another way, if we that's what it takes. Don't worry about that." He smiled gently. "Take your time, we'll be over there when the sun goes down, I give you my word nobody will try and make you do something you do not wish to do."

Alnthea watched him walk back, saw he and Lana sit down together, saw Menw glance at her and then turn back to continue guarding Sansé. Sitting back she closed her eyes and remembered the taste and texture of human blood. Everyone slightly different, sometimes you could taste their diets, sometimes their drugs, alcohol or cigarettes. Sometimes you could taste that their humanity was not total—there was part of another in there, a wolf, a demon, something more than the person you saw on the surface. She remembered the thrill—the chase and capture, then in later years the more refined seductive courting dance. The look on their face as they realised, the smell of their fear and sweat, the way they cried out and then lost themselves in a private, shameful ecstasy. The choice: to kill, to let them live, to make them one of her own; to play God. How she remembered the surge of energy, the rush of power. How she had loved to watch the aftermath, even as it changed with the years; how she had loved to watch a family as, one by one, each person they loved was taken from them.

She shook her head, opened her eyes and realised the sun had receded to create the gloomy dusk that signalled a gloomy night. Alnthea stood, sighed, and made her way to the van, her friends, the door, Sansé, and the small fire Cam had roasted their food over.

Sansé raised her head as she approached. Thanks to Menw she was unable to move or speak, but her eyes said it all. Alnthea ignored her and sat down beside Menw.

Nobody asked for her answer. They were all waiting for her to volunteer it. Eventually she did.

"I'll do it. But you have to watch me carefully for a while afterwards." Her eyes flared. "There's a reason human blood drives a vampire wild, why one taste can change a good vampire straight into a bad one. If I look to be doing that, you've got to cold turkey me again. Or kill me."

"Don't worry," Lana promised. "You look like turning even a tiny bit evil—we'll hogtie you and throw you in the van to sweat it out."

Alnthea smiled, her eye teeth gleaming faintly in the light of the fire. "I'm counting on it." She stood and faced Sansé.

Menw left his food and stood beside her.

"How much blood?"

He shrugged. "We do not know." He looked at the door. "How much? Are you able to tell us?"

The door gave no indication.

Alnthea nodded. "Then I shall take only a little to begin with. The less I am able to drink the better for us all," she grimaced. "But you should probably finish eating first."

The three of them ate in silence. They had found no way to feed Isabel, who lay motionless as ever in the van; soon, they hoped, they would be away and able to find proper help. If not, they would think of something.

When they were done and Menw had wiped the plates clean with his magic, Alnthea turned back to face her victim.

Sansé wriggled and groaned as well as she could, but Menw's bonds held her fast. Alnthea motioned to her wrist and Menw freed it enough for her to raise it to her growing teeth. She nipped gently and Sansé yelped then was silent as Alnthea took a few sips of blood.

She paused for a moment, then grasped the door handle and tried to turn it.

The handle fizzled and threw her onto the ground.

Alnthea shook her head and sat up with a growl. "Dammit."

She stood and grabbed Sansé's hand again. Using the same two wounds, she pulled a few mouthfuls of blood and tried the handle and was thrown backwards again, though with less force.

"Getting there," she growled and bent her head again to the bleeding wrist, drinking deeply this time, until Sansé's skin turned white. Alnthea stopped as she felt the heartbeat begin to slow and wiped her mouth with the back of her hand.

A tad gun-shy now, Alnthea cringed as she gripped the handle and tried it again, jumping back as another shock surged through her.

She turned to tell the others it was working, the shocks were less, and saw Cam and Menw nodding in understanding. But Lana, at the back, was being held at knifepoint by a madly grinning witch.

Seeing the vampire's smile collapse and flee, Cam and Menw turned to see.

"Lana!" Cam cried and took a step forwards. Arlene cackled and made sawing motions with the knife she held against Lana's neck. He stopped dead and his eyes brimmed with tears. "Let her go."

Alnthea scoffed. "A knife? Some witch."

Menw placed a hand on Cam's arm and drew him back. "That is a sacrificial knife," he said. "See the handle, and the blade."

The handle was carved and shaped beneath Arlene's hand, and the firelight flashed on engraved symbols on the blade.

Arlene nodded. "Yeah. Yeah. And I'm gonna sacrifice her. Yeah. Yeah. Let Sansé go. Might let your girlfriend live." She leered at Cam who started forwards again, to be pulled back by Menw.

"We will not let Sansé go," Menw told her.

Cam turned on him. "What! The door's almost open! Let the miserable witch have her wolf back."

"You know that's not how it works, Cam," Alnthea murmured. "Better we die to keep her in a place where she can't harm anyone else, than we live and let her go free."

Cam spoke directly into their heads. "Menw? Magic?"

Cam read his sad reply. "If I bind one I have to bind both and Arlene can still use her knife. If I cast anything at Arlene, I will hit Lana too."

"But that won't kill her," Cam insisted.

"The hit won't, but if the knife slips…"

Cam groaned. "Well think of something!"

"Why do you want to sacrifice her?" Alnthea asked, sounding curious.

"Power. Lots of power."

"In her?" The vampire laughed. "She's a glorified librarian! Where's the power?"

Arlene faltered. "Power in, um, just power, there's power in people, all people. Like power."

Alnthea shook her head. "Dear, oh dear. You have me, Cam and Menw all standing here—and you pick the one with the least power. Oh well, enjoy."

"Wait. No." Arlene screwed her face up. "He wants his girlfriend. Gimme one of you. And Sansé. Then can have girlfriend."

Alnthea shrugged and walked towards her. "Great. Give Cam his girlfriend. Take me. I'm just stuffed full of power."

"Alnthea!" Cam started after her but Menw held him back again. "What?!"

"Shut up," Menw told him quietly. "Watch."

Alnthea halted just out of reach. "Let her go now."

Arlene hesitated, eyes flicking all around, looking for a trap but seeing none.

Alnthea took another step closer and repeated. "Let her go."

In a swift movement, Arlene released Lana and grabbed Alnthea.

Lana ran to Cam and looked back, tearful.

Menw spoke quietly to them both. "Don't move. Just watch."

"Now, Sansé," Arlene said, knife pressed firmly to Alnthea's throat.

"No," Menw told her.

"I'll sacrifice your friend," Arlene threatened.

Alnthea locked eyes with him and nodded slightly.

"Go ahead." Menw shrugged.

Arlene looked at him suspiciously. Then looked at Cam and Lana who, trustingly obeying their instructions, shrugged and looked nonchalant.

Arlene shrugged along with them and, holding Alnthea facing away from her raised her arm and plunged the knife down into her heart.

She dropped Alnthea and staggered backwards, cackling. But slowly her face showed confusion and then terror as Alnthea, still standing, smilingly pulled the knife from her heart and approached the witch with her teeth bared and the knife raised. "You really are just an idiot, aren't you? I. Am. A. Vampire." Alnthea looked at the knife. "So unless it's got some some silver in it, or been smeared with garlic or something…I would highly recommend not stabbing me with it. Wanna guess why?"

Arlene staggered backwards some more, pale-faced, shaking her head.

"Because it pisses me off!" Alnthea tossed the knife to Menw, who caught it deftly, and lunged.

Arlene ran a few steps before stumbling and falling, allowing Alnthea to grab her by the scruff of her neck and haul her up again. "So. Your mistress is hanging in mid-air half-drained of blood. You've lost the only weapon you seem to have brought. And you're being held by the angry vampire you just stabbed with a big knife." Alnthea clicked her teeth close to the witch's ear. "Waddya gonna do now?"

Arlene trembled. "Please don't let her kill me," she appealed to Cam.

Cam laughed. "Last refuge of the cowardly—begging for mercy."

"What possesses you to think we care what our friend does to you?" Lana asked, rubbing the part of her neck that still felt the steel of the knife pressing against it.

Arlene sobbed. "Because I'm really, really sorry."

Cam laughed. "Liar. You want us to think you're weak, and apologetic, and pathetic, and sorry. Then the second we relax, you can get us. isn't that right? The knife isn't your only weapon, is it Arlene. You might be a mad witch, but you're also a rather talented one. Aren't you."

In a flash, the weeping face was replaced by a cold, calculating look. "You see too much, thought stealer."

Cam gave her a smug smile and said nothing.

Sansé mumbled something and Menw clicked his fingers, allowing her to speak.

"Kill the miserable bitch," she snapped.

Menw shut her up again. "Well there you have it. Even your beloved mistress sees no reason to spare your life. Why, therefore, should we?"

"I-I'll be g-good?" Arlene suggested, showing real fear now even her protector had deserted her.

Alnthea laughed heartily, keeping her grip on the witch as firm as ever. "I think we've all heard that one before," she snarled.

"And only a very few actually mean it," Cam added.

Arlene whimpered.

"Bind her," Cam suggested and in a flash Arlene was bound by Menw's magical cords and floating in the air beside Sansé.

"Now, where were we?" Lana nodded to Alnthea who gave a bloodthirsty smile.

"Just a little more should do it," she said, bending her head again to the wrist and breaking open the tentative clots that had begun to form to take more of the willingly flowing blood.

This time she drank until Sansé turned grey and her head lolled back on her shoulders before pulling away with a grunt of effort.

Pausing to give herself time to savour the taste and lick the red from her lips and teeth with relish, she faced the door. When ready, she took hold of the handle and turned, wincing in anticipation of the shock.

The handle turned and the door clicked open.

For a few seconds the vampire stood where she was, surprised, and then leapt to one side as the sunlight shone through and hit her full in the face, scorching her photophobic skin.

A collective gasp came from Cam, Menw and Lana as, through the frame, they saw another world revealed.

It was a bright, fresh and enormous garden. Grass, trees and flowers grew on either side of a brilliantly smooth, white path which led to a gleaming black-marble fountain upon which a figure stood, though from this distance, they could not quite discern what was depicted.

Leaving the view for now, they moved their attentions to Alnthea who lay on the ground, holding her hands over her face and making small weeping sounds.

Menw knelt beside her and gently removed her hands to reveal a face of burnt flesh.

"Look at me," he said softly and her eyes, tearful with pain, rose to meet his. "Will you let me help?" he asked.

Alnthea nodded.

"You are a vampire, so immune to many of my powers; including that of healing. But of course, as a vampire, you will heal yourself in a short amount of time. I can stop the pain while that happens."

Alnthea nodded again. "Please," she whispered through cracked lips.

Menw held his hands close to her face, feeling the heat from the burns, and a soft glow passed from them and covered the roasted flesh. A few minutes later he lowered his hands.

Alnthea smiled gratefully. "Better," she said.

Menw stood and offered his hand to help her up, noting that the flesh already showed signs of drying. She took it and stood by him.

"So," Menw said, "do we wait and presume that this new place has such a thing as night, or head right on in?"

"Leave me here, with them." Alnthea nodded to their prisoners. "You go. If it gets to daylight here I can take them with me into shade, if it goes dark there I can come and find you."

"It would save us a lot of bother in taking them with us," Cam agreed. "But what if they find a way to cause trouble?"

"It's a risk. Live a little," Alnthea told him. "Go."

Cam nodded. "I'll go through first and see if I can return, and if you are able to speak to me telepathically from this side." Without waiting for a reply he stepped through the doorway and into the garden. Stopping to admire the view for only a second, he turned and stepped back again with ease. "Question one answered," he said and stepped back to the other side again.

Alnthea transmitted a thought to him and he nodded. "It is strange. I am unable to read you, but when you send a thought to me it seems to humanise and allow me to hear. Even over here, wherever this is."

"Well, off you go then." Alnthea ushered Menw and Lana towards the door.

They stepped over the threshold and gave her a wave before following the path to the centre and the figure on the fountain that seemed to beckon them.

Alnthea pushed the door a little more closed so as to avoid the sunshine, and sat by the fire, head back to watch the stars.

Chapter 15

The road was wide enough for them to walk three abreast and so they did, Cam and Lana close together, hands entwined, Menw slightly apart as he always was. All three stared around them at the rich greenness and the colourful flowerings, they breathed in the scent of the air but their eyes and thoughts were drawn helplessly, over and over, to the fountain that came slowly closer.

Despite straining their eyes, they saw only that the figure was human-shaped, and stood proudly with its back to them. As they moved closer, it seemed to tower over them, and its back became an insult, a rude assumption of their harmlessness, of their smallness.

Cam touched the side of the fountain as soon as he was close enough. The marble felt cool to his palm, yet the sensation of something burning within caused him to frown and squeeze Lana's hand before letting go and walking around to the front where he stopped and stared, a gasp escaping his gaping mouth.

Menw and Lana joined him and looked at the figure they had followed to the centre of this garden.

He wore a toga, delicately positioned over his body to reveal and yet hide his figure. Water trickled from an urn tucked casually under an arm that rested on one hip. The other hand hung by his side. His face seemed to move; somehow beautiful and somehow not. The smile that flickered, was it amused or cruel? The life that seemed to flicker behind the eyes, was it deep and full, or shallow and mocking? The very cut of his face was somehow both benevolent and malicious.

The three of them stared, unable or unwilling to tear their eyes away as it spoke to each of them in their minds, words for nobody else to hear, words they longed for, promises of those things that burned deep within. One by one they knelt before this stone figure, heads bowed.

The voice spoke to them again and each rose. Two turned to face a different direction, and walked from the path to find the place they had been ordered to. The third remained.

***

Lana walked over the soft grass, avoiding stepping on the flowers that grew all around, eyes fixed on the crest of a hill in the distance. With the gentle voice whispering in her head, she walked until her feet were sore and her legs ached.

Reaching the top of the hill, she stopped and took in the view. More grass, more flowers, an endless bouquet of summery scents. And there, directly ahead, a building. Lana set off walking again, grimacing at the pain in her calves, but obeying the voice, and her own curiosity.

As the building grew larger, she saw it was a sturdy, wooden cottage, with a thatched roof. Though seemingly without windows, there was a door with a wooden handle, and she set her sights on it as she approached.

At first she kept her distance still, circling the small building, studying it, her suspicions being soothed away by the voice in her head. Eventually she reached the door again and stood with her hand on the handle, unsure.

The voice in her head spoke encouragement, promised her all would be well, reminded her that it loved her, that all it wanted was to make her truest dreams become real.

She took a deep breath, closed her eyes, opened the door and stepped through.

Behind her the door swung closed, making her jump and open her eyes.

She stood in an enormous room lit by candles. The walls stretched farther than her eyes could see and were filled top to bottom with books.

The voice spoke to her again. They were hers, all of them. Every book she had ever read, every book she had lost to Sansé's claws, every book she could ever read; every book that had ever existed, each new publication being added as it came into print. All for her. All she had to do was love Him.

***

Cam walked in his direction, across the never-ending lush green field until he came across a giant oak, where the voice in his head told him to stop and rest.

Cam sat under the tree and leaned back, closing his eyes and allowing himself to soak up the sun and the peaceful atmosphere.

After a while the voice spoke to him again. "I know the one thing you desire," It said. "Only love me, and you shall receive it."

Cam cracked open one sleepy eye. "What is the thing I most desire?"

"Forgiveness," breathed the voice.

"And you can gain this for me? How?"

A shadow obstructed Cam's sun and he frowned, sat up and opened both eyes. He saw a teenage boy, bright-eyed, ruffle-haired, and standing in front of him.

The boy smiled sadly. "It wasn't your fault. I don't blame you."

Cam pulled himself shakily to his feet and studied the boy. "Y-you...you're...you're dead."

"For a long time now, yes. And I know you blame yourself for it. But don't. It wasn't you who did the things you did, not really."

Cam looked away. "You're not real."

The voice in his head sighed. "You are given what you need and yet, you refuse it."

Cam looked back and saw the spot where the boy had stood was now empty, only a fading imprint of his feet remaining in the grass. "It isn't real," he said. "It can't be."

"There are more things in heaven and earth, Cam."

Cam shook his head. "No."

"I will leave you, then. Do as you wish. Only call me if you decide to accept my gift." The voice moved away with the whispering breeze, leaving Cam alone, empty, and still longing for the forgiveness he had craved for lifetimes.

***

Menw stood where he was for what seemed an age, looking at the fountain, at the figure mounted upon it, waiting to hear it speak to him once more.

At long last, it did. "I know what you most secretly desire, Menw. And I can give it to you."

Menw said nothing for a moment. "Then tell me. What do I most secretly desire?"

"The one thing that even you, with all your powers, has no real control over. The power of life and death."

"I can heal. I can kill. Is this not power of life over death?"

"You can do those things when you are able. But when you are too late, or your healing powers are inadequate? When your enemies outnumber you and grow? I can give you the power to breathe life back into somebody, to remove life from somebody else with a snap of your fingers. I can give you the power to live forever, if you wish it, and the power to grant the same to others you deem worthy."

"You wish to grant me the power to 'Play God'?"

"If you wish to call it that, then yes."

"I have lived for such a long time already, taken responsibility for my own actions and those of others until it sits on me like the weight of a world. Why should I wish for more?"

"Because you wish for life for your friends. For yourself. You have lived long and well, and lost many. Even now, with all your power and gifts of extra life granted you by some you have helped, you will not live to see the next century approach. Your hair is white and thinning, your muscles ache and your bones creak and your brain works slower than it used to. Who will help the good or the needy as only you can, if you are no longer around to do so?"

"To be able to breathe life back into the fallen innocent would be a good thing; this is true and cannot be denied. And yet, nobody is supposed to live forever, not myself, nor anyone else—we are born to live, and then to die. Who am I to judge whether somebody's time has come or not? Who am I to judge who has the right to life or death? I am but a man myself."

"But no ordinary man. And I offer you the chance to be a God."

"I do not wish to be a God. I wish to be a good man, to live and to die in pursuit of those who threaten others."

"And when you die? Who then to hold back the things you do? Who is there to take your place?"

"No human has the right to live forever, or to choose such a thing for his fellows." Menw folded his arms and turned his back on the marble figure.

"Then this is your decision. All the good you can do, you will not because your own scruples are more important than what you claim your life's mission to be?"

Menw opened his mouth and faltered in speech.

The voice spoke softly now. "Think a while. I will leave you. Only know that the water behind you contains the power I have promised. It is yours for the taking. Just one sip, and all I have promised will be yours."

Menw sat on the ground, leaned against the fountain and closed his eyes to think.

***

Lana stared at the rows upon rows of books—an infinite eternity of bound and printed words. Her mind refused to accept the enormity and her head swam with trying.

The voice returned to her. "Choose one," it said, understanding. "Choose one and hold it in your hand. Read it, smell it, turn the pages. Choose one, any one, and give it life."

Lana closed her eyes and walked until her hand rested on a spine. She drew it carefully away from its brethren and read the cover.

It was a book she had never heard of, by a name that rang no bells.

She stroked the cover, opened it gently and flicked through the pages, breathing in the scent of paper and ink. Then she sat down, her back against more books, and let her eyes skim the words, let her mind bring them to life.

Bian left her, smiling. She would love him. But the others, the mind-reader and the wizard, they sensed his true nature, he was sure. Somehow their age and their talents allowed them the smallest pinprick of a glimpse into his unfathomable being. That was why they resisted him, resisted their own desires.

He would leave them a while longer. For now, he had another game to play.

For Bian was going to be a father.

***

Jodhi rocked herself. Back and forth, side to side, around in circles. In the centre of that black room she could have been in the deepest, darkest depths of space if not for the ground she sat on and the shackles chained around her raw and bleeding ankles. So she sat and wept silently, unaware there were no tears, unaware even that she sobbed. She was aware only of the thing that grew within her, stretching and distending her stomach until the pain first made her faint, then woke her again. The thing was swelling inside her until her flesh split, showing smiling red lips to the dark. Somehow it held her womb intact, repairing the tears and pummelling it into elasticity so its protective shell would stretch until she seemed to be more dome than person.

Bian came to her as he always did now. Gently, chastely, proudly. Stroking her, wiping away the blood with a soft cloth and a soothing touch. But Jodhi remembered the hardness, the icy fire, the pain, the emptiness and the loneliness that followed. And she understood that the thing inside her was what had come of that union. And so, deep within the recesses of her shattered mind she shuddered, cringed and screamed even as her ravaged, reshaped body rocked, betraying its owner with each second it refused to rebel against the thing that tended to it so tortuously.

Bian closed the new flesh wounds and cleaned the dried blood from her body and the floor around her. He cared not for her, this human female he had been given by those who served him by believing he served them. He cared for his child, wanted it to be well, healthy, born into a place carefully cleaned of this human's offal.

He sat for a while and wondered. What would it look like? Boy or girl? Would it kill her by birthing itself? When would it choose to be born? And as what? Human? Demon? What mixture of the two would be contained within?

He shifted, impatient with the wait, and left to visit his other victims.

Lana was where he had left her, unmoving except for her eyes as they devoured the words that cluttered the pages, jostling for her attention, cramming themselves into her eager vision.

Cam, pacing under his tree, felt the presence return and spoke to it, broken by his painful longing. "Give me forgiveness," he begged.

"You will love me?"

"Yes. Please."

Bian smiled to himself and plucked an image effortlessly from Cam's mind, placing it in front of him and commanding it to speak any words the man needed to hear.

"I will return," the demon promised, and left him to it.

Menw was sat on the edge of the fountain now, examining the water. Bian smelled the mortality on him and knew he had not touched it.

"Have you thought?" he asked softly, knowing that there was little point in trying to force this man with centuries of stubbornness behind him into a decision.

Menw nodded. "I have."

"And?"

"Return my friends to me, forget whatever promise you tempted from them, and allow us to leave."

"Without Jodhi?" Bian hissed.

"I included Jodhi when I spoke the words 'my friends,'" Menw said, sighing at the prospect of another word game.

"Your friends belong to me. Pledged and promised," Bian lied effortlessly.

"Liar," Menw accused.

"Very well. Cam belongs to me. Lana will the moment she draws herself away from her books. And Jodhi…Jodhi carries my child."

"Give me back Lana and Jodhi," Menw ordered.

"No. Lana is mine unless she rejects me—in which case I will simply feed her to the child I am not going to hand over to you with the body of your other friend."

"You will not keep them," Menw stood, "and you will not keep me. I know your desire, demon. You are locked here, and you need us to escape. Well you shall go wanting. I will be back for my friends." Menw began strolling back towards the door. "Good day," and with seemingly practiced ease, he booted the demon from his head and locked the doors. But still, so long as he remained in this world, he kept his thoughts unformed and foggy, concentrating solely on the door and stepping back through it.

***

Alnthea jumped and leapt to her feet as the door opened.

"Blimey, that was fast! She said, seeing Menw step through. Then, seeing his grave face and lack of companionship. "What happened?"

"How long have I been gone?" he asked in return.

"I barely had chance to sit down and get comfy," came the reply, then a repetition. "What happened?"

"Time moves faster there." He seemed to be talking to himself as he closed the door and entered the light of the fire. "Very bad. That is very bad indeed."

Alnthea touched his arm. "Menw…"

He seemed to remember her again. "Alnthea."

She nodded.

He turned to their prisoners. "They're still—"

The vampire nodded again.

"And…" He looked towards the prone figure in the van.

Patiently, Alnthea nodded once more. "She's fine. You were only gone a few seconds. Menw, what happened?"

"It's a demon prison." He looked at the door. "He's trapped. He needs worshippers, believers, souls—whatever part of a person it is that goes to whichever thing you pledge your true, undying love to. He needs it to make him strong, so he can escape. He has Cam. Whatever Cam's desire was he

136

gave it to him, or made Cam believe he did. He almost has Lana. And Jodhi…"

"Jodhi?" Alnthea pushed gently.

"Jodhi is to give birth to his child."

Alnthea breathed in sharply. "Oh Jodhi…How did you escape?"

Menw shrugged. "I always was a stubborn old fool. I think he needs the three of us—or three people, any people. And now we opened the door for him, I don't know what he can do. For all I know he may be able to let others in at will. And I didn't even find out his name, I can't stop him."

Alnthea dug into her small store of magical knowledge. "No name, no power over him."

Menw nodded.

They halted their conversation, puzzled, as an odd noise reached their ears.

Sansé was laughing. Despite the magic that held her mouth closed, despite being bound and hovering and half-drained of blood, she was laughing.

Menw removed the bond around her mouth and returned her speech. "What do you know that makes you laugh?" he demanded.

Sansé said nothing, only chuckled more.

Menw sent a bolt that slapped her across the face and she laughed harder. "You're all fools," she told him between giggles.

Abandoning magic, Menw walked up to her and slapped her, again and again, but she said no more until, eventually, Alnthea cried his name.

"Stop it. Please," she begged.

Menw relented angrily and replaced the magical gag.

"She isn't going to talk," Alnthea told him, "and you're wasting time! Time that moves faster over there—remember?"

She saw his face soften into apology.

"I can't go into that world," Alnthea reminded him sadly, "and every second we waste here…" She shrugged the remainder of the sentence into the air and let it hang.

"I have to find them," Menw said. "Find them and pull them back, somehow."

"I'll be here." Alnthea sighed helplessly.

"Try to make them talk," Menw suggested. "I'll check back when I can, or when I have somebody to drop off."

Alnthea nodded and bared her teeth at a trembling witch and a pale-but-chuckling werewolf.

Menw stepped back through the door into the demon's world and tried to remember if he knew which direction Lana had left in. It seemed he remembered her standing to his right as he stood at the fountain, facing back towards the door.

Trusting his instinctive memory, having no other choice, he turned to his left and began to walk towards the distant, grassy knoll.

***

Alnthea watched her two captives carefully before mentally discarding the witch. She was weak, Sansé obviously cared nothing for her, and it was quite obvious which of the two was in charge.

No, Alnthea decided. The witch would be a waste of time. Still, just in case Sansé really did refuse to talk, it may behove the witch to watch.

With a wicked smile, Alnthea allowed her vampire instincts, freshly awoken with the recent blood-letting, to surface, and then reining them in, her goal firmly in mind; she grinned at Sansé and went to the van to fetch her bag.

***

It was soon now, Bian could feel it, feel the connection between him and his son—for yes, he was certain of its sex now—strengthen and toughen.

He left Cam and his line of those he had wronged, or believed he had wronged; left Lana still devouring her book. He sat by Jodhi, soothing her brow with a damp cloth, placing his hand on her painfully swollen stomach to feel the movement within; a nightmarish parody of a loving couple, waiting to welcome into the world the newest addition to complete their happy home.

As the time neared, Jodhi edged back to reality, her mothering instinct awoken through, even despite, the fear, disgust and loathing. Whatever thing this was, it was still hers. Her body had nourished it, protected it (though for however long or short a time, her warped conception could not tell). So as she felt its time draw near, she returned to everything. To the demon father, to the pain and horror, to the wolf that still cowered pitifully even as she stole what strength it had to keep her mind from snapping completely. At least for now.

***

Menw crested the hill and narrowed his eyes to squint ahead of him. There was something there, definitely something.

138

He set off walking again at the speediest pace his tired legs would allow, feeling his way over the grass with his feet, never taking his eyes from the growing speck he moved towards lest through some trick it disappear.

It was a wooden box, he saw eventually. A cottage-shaped box with a thatched straw roof. It was a box because it lacked windows of any form. It was a box not made to let in light. Menw remembered the demon's passing mention of books and understood: a place of books where no sunlight could enter to fade them. Reasoning suggested that Lana had probably entered the box, which meant that somewhere there was a door.

Menw scanned the side he raced and smiled as his gaze lighted on a door-handle. Expecting it to be locked, he tried it anyway and sighed, for once disappointed to be proved correct.

A few spells later and the door was still locked, the box intact and the thatch smouldering slightly from its brush with a blazing inferno.

Menw walked around the box, thinking. Though he was unable to enter, perhaps there was a way to force Lana out.

A simple summoning fizzled out. A spell to command her attention had no visible effect. Levitating and floating her out was equally unsuccessful.

Menw grunted. A box that was impervious to magic. The perfect defence against a man whose only strength was wizardry.

But was that really his only strength? Perhaps not. Even without his spells he was still possessed of a brain—an old, learned one at that. One that, in its time, had solved many an insurmountable problem.

Menw threw up his hands in frustration. Whatever solution he could come up with, without his magic he could do nothing by himself. He needed Cam.

Dejected, he lowered his head and plodded in the direction his connection to Cam's life-force took him.

***

Inside the box, Lana raised her head and shifted uncomfortably. There were tinglings in her head and stomach. Not unpleasant; strange, like sherbet placed on the tongue to fizz.

She closed her book and looked around, slightly disoriented. The massive number of books tried to invade her mind again, but she blocked and concentrated on finding the door. There was one, she had used it, and she remembered entering through it. But the wall that should have been there was not. Perhaps she had moved farther to pick up the book than she had thought. A lot farther. She could see no end to the stacks on either side.

Checking her panic before it could rise, Lana forced her mind to logical thought. There was an exit somewhere. She had entered through it; therefore, it existed, and when she found it she would be able to step back outside.

Admittedly the place seemed infinitely bigger within than it did without, but that meant nothing. A trick of the mind, or of the eyes. There were any number of explanations and none mattered right now. What mattered was finding her way back to the fountain where she had left Cam and Menw. Finding them, finding Jodhi, and then returning to her own world.

The first required step, then, was to find the door. It sounded easy enough. Lana stood, turned back in the direction she had entered from, and started walking, eyes glued to the spot where, instead of land meeting sky, books met books in a vertical line that was dizzying in its impossible height.

***

Tearfully, Cam thanked the young boy that stood in front of him. The boy smiled, waved and vanished.

"No more." Cam begged the empty space to remain unfilled and, as it did, he collapsed, exhausted, onto the ground against the tree. His eyes were puffy and swollen with tears, his throat on fire, and his chest tight. Forgiveness, it seemed, was harder on the forgiven than the forgiver. To receive compassion for the wrongs he had done was somehow more difficult than holding onto the guilt. Cam closed his eyes and fell into an exhausted sleep.

Bian, scanning over the world from his protective position at the impending birth of his child, frowned. Lana tried to find an exit? Cam rested peaceably? Menw, with his walled mind, roamed unchecked?

Bian shrugged. None of it would matter once his child was born. He would be freed, and together they could tear apart any world they pleased.

He put thoughts of the humans out of his mind and concentrated on talking to his boy, willing him to be born, telling him all the wonderful things they would do, as father and son—a team.

Jodhi had achieved a balance. Enough of her in the black room to push and give birth. The rest locked away someplace beyond pain, beyond terror, beyond all the horrors, merely watching with idle curiosity. Something of her demon boy had entered her, it seemed, and it was that which would give her the strength and will to have her child.

***

Menw tapped Cam's shoulder and jumped back as he woke with a start.

Cam stared at him for a moment then spoke with a croak in his aching throat. "Menw? You forgive me too?"

Menw frowned. "What?"

Cam smiled at him. "You forgive me. For everything."

A lightbulb flashed in Menw's head. *Cam's desire,* he realised, *of course.* After a second he spoke softly to him. "Cam, I forgave you for anything you may have done a long time ago. I showed this by giving you life, by being your friend. If I had known how much you desired forgiveness…oh Cam, you pledged yourself to a demon."

Cam squinted up at Menw. "Wait. What?"

"Cam…you promised your love to a demon in exchange for pretence of forgiveness for everything you think you did wrong."

Cam thought carefully and then nodded slowly. "Yes. I did do that."

"It's not real, Cam. I'm real, you're real, Lana stuck in a box somewhere is real; Jodhi giving birth to a demon is real. Alnthea, Sansé, Arlene and Isabel. That, all of that is real. Not this. Only you can give yourself the forgiveness you need. And only when you choose to realise that, weighed against all the good you have chosen to do, the mistakes mean nothing. You'll have no peace until you realise this and give yourself that gift. Nobody else can do that for you. And certainly no demon."

Cam sat up and rubbed his temples. "Oh—what have I done?"

"It's okay. We will find a way to release you, but first—Lana and Jodhi. We must help them, and fast."

Cam stood a trifle shakily. "Tell me."

Menw told Cam all he had missed, explaining the box as best he could.

Cam nodded understanding and, testing his legs tentatively, began to walk, allowing Menw's hand to rest on his arm and give him strength. They walked at their best speed back to where Menw had found the box, half expecting it to no longer be there.

It was as Menw had left it, right down to the singed straw along the edge of the roof.

Cam concentrated, feeling the box telepathically. "There's no shield," he muttered, "nothing inside. No, there's nobody, but there's something else." *Something familiar,* he thought idly, casting around to find whatever it was. "Got it!" he gasped. "Oh dear."

Menw waited.

"The door. Our door. That door." He pointed in the direction of the door that led back into their world. "It's like that, kind of. Different yet similar. Lana's in there? Are you sure? It's muddled, I can't quite get through. I might be able to feel her but that could be wishful thinking."

Menw shook his head. "I did not see her enter, if that is the proof you need. But I am certain."

"Good enough for me. Now, we need to—" He stopped, trembled, let out a groan and collapsed to the floor in a way Menw recognised all too well. A vision. Nothing to do but be sure he did not injure himself until it stopped, leaving the usual cracking headache behind it.

When it passed, Cam lay prone and still, pale and sweating, the new exhaustion almost too much on top of everything else.

Menw dulled what pain he could and gave him a small jolt of energy, sitting himself cross-legged on the grass and affecting patience.

Eventually Cam roused himself to sluggish speech. "Jodhi. Baby. Demon. It'll let him get loose. Somehow. His name...ah I can't quite get his name! there's a B. That's all." He bowed his head, trying to coax more, knowing it was useless but trying anyway.

"Jodhi's having the baby now?" Menw asked.

"Not now. Soon," Cam told him. "And it'll be able to get Daddy Demon out. I don't know how. Together, their strength perhaps. But if it does..." He shook his head.

"Cam?" Menw placed a hand on his shoulder. "What?"

Cam raised a grey, stunned face. "Fire. Blood. Dead. Everything. Everyone. Everywhere. All gone." He blinked bright blue eyes that were filled with pain and the knowledge of responsibility. "If we don't stop them, Menw, there'll be nothing left."

Menw looked at the ground. "I don't know where Jodhi is."

"We have to get Lana. We're here. There's a way. It's not happened yet, there's still time, there has to be a way." Cam looked at the box, trying to reach for his loved one, catching only a trace that squirmed and slipped constantly away.

Chapter 16

Lana stopped walking and looked around. It seemed as if somebody was nudging her, trying to get her attention, but there was nobody else here. She shrugged and continued walking, attempting to convince herself that she was getting somewhere.

It came again and she recognised it—not a physical nudge at all, a mental tap. "Cam?" she said. "Cam, is that you? Where are you?" She felt her words fall flat and tried again, projecting her thoughts like an arrow the way he had taught her in the past. *Cam! Cam, hear me!*

She felt a return probe to her mind, and then an arrow bolted through her. *Lana!*

Cam! I'm here, I'm stuck. Help me! she returned.

Don't move, I've got you. I'm going to try and use this connection to allow Menw's magic through. Don't! Move!

Lana stood bolt still, fists clenched, breath held, eyes closed. When she felt a warm breeze on her face, she opened them and saw Cam.

"It worked!" He grinned and threw his arms around her, sweeping her off the ground and kissing her.

Menw, feeling like a stern old schoolmaster, cleared his throat. "Please, you two. Jodhi."

"Jodhi?" Lana asked as soon as she was put down, not letting go of Cam's arm.

"Speedy version," Menw told her. "Jodhi's giving birth to the child of the demon that put you in there. If she does, we are all going to die."

Lana stared at him, speechless for a moment, then the obvious question: "Can we stop it?"

"We were hoping you might know," Cam said. "All the knowledge you have—is there a way to stop this demon being born, or to keep it from its dad?"

"If it's that close to birth, nothing can stop it—even if its host died it would survive—slightly weaker, of course, but still too strong. Can we get Jodhi back to our world—where his dad can't go? Do we even know where she is?"

143

Menw and Cam shook their heads sadly.

"I tried scanning for her, but I can't find her. We hoped you might have a clue, somewhere in your head." Cam brushed Lana's cheek.

She thought hard. "Demon birthing. Yes, I know a bit about that. But what sort of a demon is this? They're different!"

"His name begins with a B…" Cam said, uselessly.

"Cam, contact Alnthea, see if she had a chance to pull anything from Sansé or Arlene yet," Menw ordered.

Cam sent a thought out, instinctively recoiling at the vampiric mind he knocked on. He could sense nothing, but hoped his tap would get Alnthea's attention. It did, the vampire slithered away and Alnthea's human-shaped thought came back at him. "Cam, how are you?"

"No time. Did you get anything yet?"

"Nothing. Well, nothing useful. Sansé thinks the demon serves her. They know nothing about the child."

"Okay. Thanks anyway," Cam said, withdrawing dejectedly and shaking his head. "Nothing from them. And all I remember is a dark place."

Lana jumped on that statement with an almost audible thud. "Dark place? You had a vision? What do you remember about the place?"

"It was dark…" Cam searched his memories. "Dry, clean, big. that's all."

Lana paced up and down. "Well if that's where they are, that's where they'll stay. It's up to us to find them. Can you feel anything, Cam?"

He shook his head. "I can't find Jodhi anywhere. And the demon is everywhere."

"There must be an epicentre, somewhere the demon is currently concentrated—he'll be still, can't you try it? Or-or look for not Jodhi, but something she might be feeling. Or maybe find the baby demon somehow, something waiting to emerge into this world. There has to be something, a trace, somewhere!"

"And what if I do find Jodhi? How do we fight a demon? Two, if we're too late!"

Suddenly, Cam was thrown to the ground as if hit by a bolt of lightning. "Too late!" he gasped. "It's coming."

***

Jodhi watched from the secret place in her head while the woman screamed; a sound to curdle the blood. The demon baby was clawing at her

144

insides, searching for escape. But he wanted his host, his protector, his mother, to live. So instead of tearing her flesh, pushing himself out fully formed and revelling in the gore that surrounded him, he moulded his shape as well as he could into something smooth and long, something that could push its way out and leave her—mostly—intact. He did not know whether he needed her, but he wanted her still.

So against her resisting bone and screaming agony, he pushed, pummelled, felt something crack as he shoved his way into life.

Jodhi's physical self felt its pelvis splinter and, through the pain, realised its unwelcome guest had departed. With a sigh of relief, it began to die. But the part of the demon that had infected it had also infected the wolf who, suddenly finding the will to live, fought back.

The demon's eyes, adjusting themselves to night vision for the first time, watched the wolf attempt to take control, howling in pain as it did, its ability to heal faster simply not fast enough.

In her secret place, the observer closed her eyes, took a deep breath, hauled the wolf back and re-entered her own body.

The demon saw the wolf vanish, replaced by the real human who, for a second, looked merely surprised. Then she began to scream.

The boy demon saw a figure shift and reach for his mother, sensed malice in its intent and dove forwards, a snarl on his lips.

Bian left the human for a moment and looked at his son.

There could be little doubt of his parentage. One of Bian's green eyes flamed in his face, which was softly scaled in light grey, the other eye was the soft brown of his mother's. A nose grew where Bian had but a stump, and a human mouth let out his growl. His teeth, Bian saw, were still razor sharp, the boy's tongue was forked, his nails long and pointed where his grey-scaled hands rose to defend Bian's intended prey. The boy did not speak but his intention was clear "Do not hurt my mother."

Bian moved back and raised his hands, palm out. "I will let her live, if you wish it."

The boy nodded and stood, straight and noble. He was taller than a human, 8 feet, Bian guessed, and still a bit to grow yet. His skin was less rigid than his father's, revealing a powerful, if slightly more vulnerable, frame. Yet he boasted a long, strongly-barbed tail and his father's loins.

"I am your father," Bian told him.

The boy nodded dismissively and tuned to care for his mother. He stroked her sweat-soaked hair until the rough and restless sleep the pain and exhaustion had brought calmed a little and her breathing was merely tearing and serrated instead of gasped and broken. Then he turned to his father and motioned to her wounds and shattered bones, miming pain.

"I cannot fix them son. That is a power I do not have."

The son growled and stamped, their connection again making his comments clear despite his grunted attempts at speech. "Find someone who can!"

"There is a wizard," Bian said, "who can heal. But he will kill us if he can."

The son hesitated a moment and then scooped Jodhi up in his arms, nodding goodbye to Bian before leaping out of sight. Bian let him go with a sigh, it may be his prison but it was still his world and all that happened within he could watch and follow.

He saw Cam stemming a nosebleed while Lana, kneeling by his side, exchanged panicked words with an angry Menw. He saw his son heading towards them with unnerving speed and accuracy.

Suddenly Cam's head jerked up and, nosebleed forgotten, he was on his feet, yelling something and shoving the other two towards the door that would take them from this world.

Bian decided to wait, watch, and see what happened. After all, once his son was happy, they could concentrate on what really mattered. So, resignedly, he sat back and attempted to enjoy the show.

***

"Go! Just go!" Cam yelled as Menw protested. "Door! Through! Fast! Now!"

Lana, unquestioning, grabbed Menw's arm and dragged him along until he broke into a run that matched her speed.

Cam cast glance after glance behind him, waiting to see the demon he felt hunting for them. Eventually he did, a speck on the horizon growing closer by the second. Looking forward, he saw they were almost at the door. Another few seconds and he nearly threw Menw and Lana through before diving for safety himself, only to hit an invisible wall and be thrown back to the ground in a daze, nosebleed beginning afresh.

"Cam!" Lana reached back through the door and grabbed his arm, but the wall still prevented him from following her, no matter how much she tugged.

"He pledged to Bian," Menw realised, stepping forward. "He pledged to the demon, and now he is stuck in his world."

Cam glanced around and saw demon was close now. Close enough to see his sickly coloured skin. Close enough to realise what he held in his arms.

The Thing slowed to a stop a few paces from Cam, towering over the telepath even as he stood, the motionless figure merely a doll in his arms. It held out Jodhi and nodded for Cam to take her.

On the other side, Lana cried for him to step back. Instead he took a step towards the demon and took Jodhi in his own arms, feeling her frailness.

The demon bowed its head for a second. Then it growled, the truce over, and galloped away.

Alnthea, watching as well as she could from her vantage point away from the sun's glare, her skin still crisped from the previous encounter, saw Lana reach back through the door, saw her reappear carrying Jodhi.

Menw took her and Alnthea hurried to his side, stoking the fire as the unconscious girl was placed gently beside its warming glow for Menw to examine the limp and broken body.

"Cam..." Lana stepped back through the door, bewildered from watching his movements; so fast over there, everything moved so fast.

He kissed her tenderly, tears spilling onto his cheeks and mingling with her own. "I'm sorry. He offered forgiveness, I...I couldn't..."

Lana stroked his tears away. "We'll find a way. I promise," she told him. "And we can still talk. That still works," she reminded him.

He nodded. "And while I'm here I can explore. If I find anything, I can tell you." He smiled sadly.

She matched his mournful smile. "Yes."

"I love you." He kissed her again.

She kissed him back with lingering pressure. "I love you."

He waved, but she had already stepped back into her own world, her own timeline, and the wave was little more than a blur.

***

Menw concentrated hard, his hands on Jodhi's splintered bones, a faint healing glow transferring between them. She moaned, shifted, moaned again.

"She is neither in pain nor danger. Her wolf will do the rest," Menw said eventually, covering her with a blanket.

Alnthea nodded to Lana. "What about—"

Menw sighed. "Cam pledged himself to the demon who offered him the

147

one thing he desired. He is trapped there now, until we find a way to release him."

"Surely unless the demon is released, nothing in that world is free!" Alnthea growled. "Fool, does he not know, has he never learned in all his years? Demons promise all and give nothing."

"Of course he knows," Lana snapped, "but if you were offered the one thing, that burning desire, that thing you have needed for 200 years, how well would you resist? He almost had me too; will you call me a fool? And what of you and the sun?"

"Cam's life was not threatened. Mine was," Alnthea snapped back. "And you, Menw. Did he have you?"

"He offered me immortality and the power to heal and raise the dead," Menw said quietly. "He lied."

"Well, at least one of you possesses some form of intelligence." Alnthea's eyes flashed ferally.

"Alnthea," Menw scolded gently, looking at their captives; pale, bloodless, barely alive. "I think perhaps your vampire speaks, not you."

Alnthea snarled and turned away. "A vampire is a demon too, remember? I pay no more attention to it than you."

Jodhi groaned, interrupting the oncoming flood. Her eyes were open, unfocused, and cloudy with pain and fear. Lana knelt at her side. "Jodhi, sweetheart, are you okay? Stupid question. Can you hear me?"

Jodhi rolled her head and reached out a grasping hand. Lana took it in hers. "Good girl. You know me, don't you?" The hand squeezed a yes. "You're back in your own world now. There's me, and Alnthea, and Menw all here."

A noise came from Sansé. Alnthea shut her up with a crunching blow to the face, ignoring the angry glance Menw gave her for it.

Jodhi closed her eyes again and slept. Lana kept her hand warm and looked at Menw. "What do we do now?"

Menw shook his head. "Sleep, if we can. A mind loses its ability to think unless it can also rest and process. Alnthea, wake one of us when you must escape the dawn."

Alnthea nodded, looking towards the captives with a flickering smile.

"And...don't drink any more. Of them. Please," Lana asked.

The vampire's lip curled slightly, but she held her tongue and merely nodded.

Lana and Menw carried Jodhi to the van and laid her down by Isabel.

"We're building quite a collection," Lana noted. "Maybe we're not as helpful to the Good of the world as we've been telling ourselves."

TO TAME THE WOLF

Menw said nothing, simply settled his weary bones down to sleep.

Lana looked at the two unconscious girls they were supposed to be protecting and helping and shook a sad and heavy head. "I'm sorry. We will fix this. Or die trying," she promised, kissing their foreheads; Isabel's cool and dry, Jodhi's warm and slightly fevered, before curling herself up close to them and closing her eyes.

Alnthea watched her captives carefully, eyeing their pulsing necks with a lusty gaze. The vampire spoke to her but she banished it, content to relish the tang that remained on her tongue.

Chapter 17

From the distant hills, two dark eyes watched the small group. Though even through the powerful binoculars the figures were small, almost indistinguishable from each other, his heart clenched as their emotions came at him in waves.

As Lana and Menw put Jodhi in the van and remained there to rest. As Alnthea poked the fire, throwing some more wood on though, as a vampire, she needed neither the warmth nor the light, merely the distraction from her captives and the juice that flowed inside them. Julio carefully placed his spyglasses back in their case and, wearing as many layers of clothing as he could fit, wriggled into his sleeping bag and shivered himself into a disturbed, uneasy doze.

After his fight with Menw, Julio had stormed out of the house and down the road at a clip sure to relieve his stress, if only by giving him a burning stitch in his side.

He walked so hard, staring moodily at the ground, relaying the argument furiously in his head, that when the figure materialised behind him out of thin air, he blocked his empathy without so much as a thought of who was there.

The figure straightened from his hunched, ready-to-fight position. From inside of him stepped two identical figures. Each wore a long, hooded brown robe and tough hide boots. They were young, smooth-shaven and dark-eyed. The single difference between the three was the rope tied around the waist of their cassock. The first figure wore black, his familiars deep crimson and dull green.

At the last second, Julio's talent screamed loud enough for him to hear. As he turned, he caught a glimpse of his attackers before they grabbed him. A moment later, everything was dark.

Julio sat up, rubbing his cheek in a nervous gesture. As he strained to see, the dark faded in slow increments to be replaced by a soft yellow haze. Through this he could see shadowy figures which, turning quickly, he soon realised had him surrounded.

His eyes settled instinctively on one shape, taller and broader than the rest. It spoke to him in a distorted voice.

"We are sorry for the inconvenience, young Julio. We trust you were unharmed."

Julio shrugged. "I'm fine. Who are you gente extraña?" he asked, slipping back into Mexican Spanish a little as was his habit under duress.

"We are the Council of the Shadow Walkers."

"Council? I've never heard of a Council, compañero."

"We help in small ways, when we can. Rarely do we introduce ourselves to anyone. Menw knows of us, you and he are of a small and select few."

"I'm honoured." Julio folded his arms. "If, that is, I decide to believe you."

The figure raised its hands. "Look," it bade Julio as a crescent of white light engulfed him.

He saw a scene he well remembered: Los Angeles at night. He saw himself emerging from the house carrying a trash bag, heading for the bins. He saw himself stop and look around, sensing the vampire that then emerged from the shadows and attacked.

"I remember that," Julio agreed, softening a little, "but what does it have to do with you?"

"Look again," the voice bade him.

Julio looked, saw the vampire attack, and saw himself fighting.

Then the angle changed to reveal a shape standing in the shadows across the street. Its face was hidden by a cowl, but it gestured and chanted.

The vision faded and the figure spoke again. "Do you understand?"

"You—somebody, anyway—helped me to fight that thing and live."

The figure nodded. "And because of what you had seen, fought and survived, you left home. You became a Shadow Walker, as we had hoped you would."

"You sent that thing after me?"

"We pointed it in your direction. You were never in real danger—we would not have allowed you to be harmed."

Julio fought down his anger. "You manipulated me. Why?"

"Your talent is strong and rare. Our spotters found you and we wanted, needed, you to join us. To bind to our cause. How better to convince you than to show you what we fight against?"

"And now? What? You can't just manipulate me into doing whatever it is you obviously want me to do?"

"Normally we would try," the voice said matter-of-factly, "but circumstances dictated otherwise. We encouraged your argument with

Menw, perhaps encouraged your reaction. The rest is for you alone to decide."

"Why?"

"The Council answers not questions of that nature. Simply hear, understand, and choose the course you will."

"What if I choose the opposite to what you want?"

"Then your choice will be accepted. We encourage, nudge, we do not force. But be wary, for your choice affects all."

"I'm listening."

And so they had told him a story. Then they had told him his options, and the consequences and possible consequences of both. They explained the one they hoped for him to choose and why. Julio found himself understanding, agreeing, pledging himself to do what they asked of him.

He was placed, gently this time, back on the road, a mere pace away from the slightly scuffed footprints of himself and his captors.

The Council had shown him the shadows they were able to see of the future, shadows that were changeable, open to misinterpretation, and they had shown him the possibilities that stemmed from each. Since then he had followed the small group at a distance. Locking onto and following their emotions, always far enough away to remain unseen and, he hoped, unsensed even by Cam. He was ordered not to simply rejoin them, for his task was a betrayal that would give him pause, perhaps even change his heart were he to find their company again. Now here, in this place, at this time, was where the shadows, vague and shifting always, had become muddy and unclear. Here was where he was required.

Julio awoke from his fretful sleep just as dawn began to brighten the gloomy sky. Wriggling out of his dew-shimmered sleeping bag, using the damp to slick back his hair, he looked through his binoculars again.

The vampire, the one he did not know, had gone inside the van to sleep away the sun. Lana stood at the open door, talking to whoever was on the other side. *Cam*, he thought, *it must be Cam.*

There was no point in his wondering what had happened, no way for him to find out. Not, at least, until he had completed his duty and was allowed to return to his friends. Though whether he would be allowed to return in order to assist in the trouble he was first to cause, he was doubtful.

Sighing deeply, he scanned his planned route again. Provided they remained where they were, he could pick his way down there today. With Cam in what Julio guessed was the Demon's world, and hopefully unable to

152

sense him, plus his own small talent for masking and rather larger talent for stealth, the only hope he had was to get close, remain unnoticed, and hope for a chance to strike.

***

"So tell me again why you didn't say anything before?" Lana asked, looking mildly annoyed.

"It didn't feel malicious; I don't think whoever it is means us any harm. Only, now I seem to be stuck here, now I cannot feel it, I thought you ought to know. In case he—yes, I think it a he—should make himself known."

"That's not what I'm asking! I can't believe you kept this a secret from me!" Lana threw her hands up in frustration.

Menw peered sleepily out of the van. "Problem?"

Cam looked pleadingly at Lana and sent her a thought. "Please, he'll only cast a spell to pull him in and I don't think he should. I'm sorry, I'm truly sorry, but please don't."

Lana turned to Menw and shook her head. "Nothing, Menw. You get back to sleep awhile."

Menw eyed her carefully, but nodded amiably and disappeared. *Lover's tiff,* he thought vaguely, shifting his bones into a more comfortable position with a creak. He was asleep again in seconds.

Lana turned away from Cam, still hurt by being kept in the dark; even if she understood his reasons.

"I'm sorry," he said, "I thought it was best. Perhaps I was wrong. I'm sorry."

She turned back to him. "I know. I forgive you. This watcher, does he intend to show himself? You said he seems harmless."

"I said I didn't think he wished to harm us," Cam corrected her. "He is shielded somewhat, and I did not want to probe further. If he follows, if he hides, he obviously has no wish to be seen. I feared that if I probed, and he sensed me, he would leave."

Lana nodded, his reasoning was as sound as she had expected.

"Please, do not tell Menw," he pleaded again. "Not yet. He will act rashly in his wariness."

"But what if…" she trailed off, unable to say it.

"What if I'm wrong?" Cam said it for her. "He means us no harm, about that I will not doubt myself. As to leaving him alone…I am sure we must. It feels as something else directs me in this." He shrugged helplessly.

Lana understood. Sometimes she felt as if she were being directed or urged to something. A course of action, the correct path to the information she needed. She had thought it merely her more conscious recognition of instinct or, perhaps, collective unconsciousness. Now she wondered if others, more than she and Cam, felt these directives. And what the consequences were of disobeying them. She shivered slightly, the thought that her actions were not her own made her flesh want to creep and shrivel.

***

Julio felt his flesh shrivel for other reasons as he crept stealthily, slowly, closer to the makeshift camp. His shivering flesh goose-bumped and sweated with fear and the damp cold the highland hills provided so well. He allowed his shield to slip a little, praying he was right that Cam could not sense him from the other plane, soaking up the emotions that rushed towards him.

Three sleeping figures. Two recognisable and a third he did not know; this one hardly there at all. Lana he watched and felt her agitation, nerves, confusion, expectation. Yet no fear. That came in nauseating waves off of one of the prisoners. From the other he felt only anticipation, cruelty, anger—and a wolf. Sansé, then, with her frightened witch by her side.

He had been told to free Sansé and do with the other whatever he wished. At that he had risen up and said he would free the witch, if only to free her in turn from Sansé. But the stench of fear—it was not the musk of a brave woman, facing what she was afraid of. Nor even a deer, frozen in headlights, too shocked to move. It was the dirty, muddy odour of the woodlouse that curls up into a tiny ball and rolls itself into the darkest corner it can find, hoping to be forgotten or overlooked long enough to die just as it lived—in hiding.

Julio's lip curled angrily. This was not even a noble fear. This witch was not afraid of justice, of punishment, of a righteous judgement against her misdeeds. She was afraid of being kept, or killed; of being unable to perform them any longer—be they of her own accord or, worse, at the bidding of another.

He shook it off like water from a dog and raised his shields some more, he could afford no distractions. Especially as he moved closer to the prisoners, his mind must be focused on his task—to free Sansé and escape without notice, back to a safe watching distance.

As the day wore on Menw emerged, stiff but refreshed, from the van to relieve Lana, by now yawning and pacing to keep alert.

Julio watched, now close enough to see the lines on the old man's face—his gift for stealth, heightened by a small boost from the Council, had dared him close. Yet not close enough.

Menw and Cam spoke in low voices. Julio strained to hear but caught only a vague sense of annoyance and impatience from the mage, whose calm composure hid a desire for constant motion, activity of some kind around him. Be it battle, palaver, or even so little as somebody else using their skills on behalf of whatever thing he was involved in. And, of course, he was always involved in something.

Julio recalled reading the Sherlock Holmes stories. Holmes, outwardly composed when around others, excitable and agitated in his mind. Holmes with a break between cases, injecting heroine into his arm as the only alternative, or perhaps the antithesis, to his craved form of action. His real addiction.

It was perhaps, Julio mused, this concealment, this gap between what Menw showed, and what Julio felt, that caused so many rifts between them. The empath cannot be fooled by a false exterior, perhaps must learn to accept and understand the reasons behind it.

All that, however, was for another time. The important thing was to never underestimate Menw; Julio had seen it done, and learned his lessons well. Similarly with Cam. Lana and the vampire, on the other hand, were wildcards to him. The researcher he knew for her knowledge, anything beyond and she was as much as mystery to him as the night-walker. Something told him that knowing Menw's weaknesses was his only strength in this task.

As he watched, Menw stepped back and slid the door to, shutting out Cam and all but a chink of sunlight from beyond. Julio wondered why, but shrugged it away. All that mattered was that this cleared Cam from the equation. Assuming, of course, that he remained undiscovered. That the two had not developed some form of plot to trap him. He had seen—participated in—that sort of thing with them before.

He shook his head slightly to remove the creeping doubts. What would be would be, if he were trapped then so be it. He would deal with that scenario when—if—it arose. Unless such a thing happened, he must act as if he were utterly unknown to them, and pick his time carefully.

I wish I had Menw's magic, Julio thought unhappily. *How much easier would that be!*

***

Menw strolled over to the prisoners and chuckled as Arlene wriggled, trying to escape his gaze. He moved his attentions to Sansé, her eyes blazing with hatred as they fixed on his. "So, little wolf, how are we feeling today?"

The little wolf growled in the back of her throat.

Menw nodded amiably and kept his tone light. "That demon of yours played you for a fool. You have realised this, have you not?" He saw she had and smiled indulgently. "It is such an awful feeling when people you trust betray you." He sighed theatrically.

"Menw," Lana called from the van.

He turned around. "You should be resting," he scolded gently.

"I was," she nodded, "then Jodhi woke up."

Menw was inside the van in a flash, kneeling beside the girl. "Jodhi?" he called softly, and then smiled as her eyes flickered open, searched, and then fixed on his with recognition. Her mouth moved in the shape of his name and he nodded. "Good girl, good girl."

"Is there anything you can do to help her?" Lana asked.

Menw considered. "Her wolf heals her now. If I interfere he may grow angry."

Jodhi shook her head and tried to speak. Menw moved his ear to her mouth and strained to hear.

"Wolf…mine…"

He sat up and smiled again. "She has gained control of her wolf. I can help her along."

Lana grinned then nodded outside. "What about those two?"

Menw shrugged "They are secure enough for a few moments."

***

Julio watched Menw enter the van. He waited a minute. Two. Three. The mage remained in the van with the rest of them. Cautiously, silently, Julio crept from his hiding place. He moved in a semi-circle, away from the van and around the back of the door. For a moment he stopped to stare at the empty space where it had stood, and then snapped out of existence. He shook himself mentally and continued. Low and fast, he crept close enough to touch Sansé before she gave a start and looked at him.

He avoided her eyes and removed a small vial of powder from his pocket.

It had been given to him by the Council with the instruction to sprinkle a small amount over the captive.

This he did, releasing the bonds. "Go, or die," he told her, suddenly realising that she could kill him this very second. Crush him like a bug and leave his corpse for his friends to find, to think he had betrayed them.

But then, as Sansé looked at him, confused, before morphing and loping into the hills at high speed, he realised that was exactly what he had done.

He turned to the witch. If she remained, she could tell all. With an inward cry he freed her and watched as she scurried away after the wolf.

Before guilt could overpower him he turned and, speedily covering his tracks, began the journey back to his hiding place—his safe distance from the friends who would surely kill him if they knew, if they caught him.

***

Jodhi sat up and blinked, testing her limbs, senses, memory. Avoiding the more recent memories she had no wish to remember. Being successful, for now at least.

Then she studied her surroundings for a moment before loosing the waiting tears. She was pulled into the comforting circle of Lana's arms where she lay, sobbing.

Menw remained for a few moments and then, at a glance from Lana, took his cue and left them.

Seconds later the van shook with the force of his cry.

Lana and Jodhi leapt out, the latter's tears stopped in their tracks.

Alnthea yelped as she made it halfway out of the van, discovered the sunlight, and then retreated slightly, eyes glowing in anger.

Lana's eyes swivelled to the spot Menw was staring at and her sharp intake of breath caused Jodhi to glance at her and follow the shocked gaze.

Alnthea was the first to speak. "How did they escape? Who was watching them? They were magically bound!"

"I was watching them," Menw said, shamed. "I entered the van to assist Jodhi's recovery and I left them unguarded. Too impatient. Too arrogant."

"Stop it," Alnthea scolded. "We can all line up and slap you later. Next questions: Who set them free? How? Why?"

Menw shook his head. "I do not know. It would take magic to break those bonds. Stronger magic than mine."

"Of which there's not much," Lana finished.

"As to the why," Menw continued, "I fear that will only be answered once the rest is clear."

"Where's Cam?" Lana asked, looking at the door, still only chinked open.

"He went to hunt, investigate, and find things," Menw said.

Lana called to him with her mind but felt her thoughts go nowhere. "Well, he's found something at least. He's in a place where he can't hear me."

"He's of no use to us stuck behind that door anyway," Alnthea pointed out, "not for this. He saw nothing, he knows nothing. he'll be back when he's ready—leave him to it."

Lana wondered, however. Would she be betraying him to tell? Before this, yes. But if it was that watcher, if he was involved somehow, or the culprit? She opened her mouth to speak. All listened to what little she knew—what little Cam knew—with grave faces.

Again, Alnthea was the first to break the silence that followed. "Such teamwork, I tell you, it's touching."

Lana frowned at her, knowing she spoke the truth, wanting to argue despite that. Instead her face crumpled into guilty grief. "I know. I'm sorry."

Alnthea shrugged. "That's okay. We can all line up and slap you and Cam as well. After we fix this. Sound good?"

Lana smiled gratefully and nodded.

"Can we track them?" Jodhi asked, suddenly.

Alnthea grinned. "And when we're done with those three—we can all line up and give you a big hug! I can trail Sansé and Arlene anywhere. I've tasted their blood, following their scent is like walking towards a light at the end of a long tunnel."

"Then as soon as you are able, you and I shall follow them," Menw said. "There are ways to track the other also, but the most important thing is to have Sansé and her witch back under our control."

Alnthea nodded. "Especially because I have an idea that one of them might be useful in rescuing Cam and closing that door for good." Her eyes blazed as she looked up at the sky, willing the sun to descend.

***

Cam had watched Menw pull the door to before turning to survey the scene before him.

Directly in front of him was the fountain. To the left of that was the direction Lana had been taken. To the right had been his journey. Ahead, much farther away, was where the demon had come from, carrying Jodhi tenderly to return her to them.

He shrugged. There was a path; logic would suggest it ought to lead somewhere. Cam began striding down it, feeling at last as if he had a purpose in all of this, even if it was possibly to prove a false one.

He walked, feeling the sun on his back, watching the path ahead recede endlessly into the unchanging horizon.

As he did, he found a song rolling around his head, timing his paces.

(I would walk 500 miles)

Or were his paces timing to it?

(I would walk 500 more)

Cam shrugged, trying to place the song.

(Just to be the man was walked 1000)

Some Scottish band, he thought.

(Miles to fall down at your door)

The Proclaimers. That was it.

(...500 miles...)

Why it was there he failed to even begin guessing.

(...500 more...)

But he let it flow through his tired legs, moving his feet inexorably onwards towards

(...be the man who walked...)

whatever he suddenly felt was awaiting him down the path.

(...fall down at...)

Because there was something…Cam stopped, squinting, trying to see through the shimmer of heat that obscured the road ahead. There was definitely something. A shape he could not yet make out, but it was there, and he would walk until he reached it.

Ignoring the vague feeling that he was cutting himself off from his friends, Cam let the song return to pick up his feet to draw him forwards once more.

Cam left his legs to do the work and fixed his eyes on the object ahead, willing it to become clearer. At first it seemed to mock him, remaining out of focus, almost slipping in and then turning his eye away so he must return and force it to concentrate and define what he saw. Eventually, though, he caught a shape. Lost it, and then caught it again. He held it, wavering in his vision, allowing it to become clear on its own.

Slowly he pieced together a gothic castle in black stone. Spires towers adorned each corner, parapets jutted from the centre, one flying a plain black flag. The walls were protected by menacing iron spikes. A massive double door, studded with iron bolts. Small slits for windows, and few enough of them. Suddenly he was close enough to mark even the door-knocker. A huge brass teardrop almost the size of his head.

Now within reach, though barely seeming to move, Cam grasped the knocker, knowing it would not budge under his paltry human touch. When it rose easily, he leapt back in surprise and let out a cry as it dropped back against the door with a resounding thud, the echo of which could have been enough to level a mountain.

Apparently failing to sense his sudden horrible lack of curiosity, the doors cracked open. Enough for him to slip through, not enough to see what may await him on the other side. This was beyond anything even he had ever seen. Foolish he, strolling off to unravel the mysteries of this demon world with a spring in his step and a song in his heart—and head. Of course he could. Of course he would. He was working for the Good Guys!

Him, knowing better than most that the Good Guys were sometimes Bad Guys in disguise. And more—that even the real Good Guys did not always win through with a torn shirt, a bleeding bicep and cheek, sheen of sweat on their brow and a girl to kiss as the credits rolled.

Yet, he reminded himself, even a losing battle can be fought to the bitter end. And was not that what the Good Guys did? Their motto, their creed—not some Hollywood fakery. Was not their aim simply to try? To try and climb the impossible mountain? To fight no matter what the odds, with a battle cry and as pure a heart as one could muster? Because sometimes trying was enough, sometimes that was all you could do, and sometimes—just sometimes, you really could win through, kiss the girl and know the innocents were safe to live and be free. At least until the sequel.

With his personal pep talk complete Cam walked forward, poker-faced, head up, showing none of the fear and doubt that wanted to spill his steaming bile onto the ground beneath his feet.

Closing his eyes as he passed through the door, he felt the sun retreat and shrink away like a plastic bag touched by naked flame. He felt the breeze pull at him as the massive doors swung shut, braced himself in expectation of the obligatory slam, and winced for his ears and head as he was not disappointed.

Then he opened his eyes.

The room he stood in—the entrance hall—was gloomy, lit only by faint shards of light filtered through the arrow loops on either side of the door. Dust motes bounced idly within them, placing the musty smell that accosted his nostrils. Must and something else. Something he could almost place. The demon, he decided. Its scent had infected the place as any home will take on its owner and hold it close, even in absentia, often for generations. Smell—the not-quite-ghost of a building with a memory.

He felt tile beneath his feet and looked down. He could sketch pictures of some kind, a mural. Of what however, the dark prevented him from seeing.

Cam let his eyes trail the floor until they found a wall. Dark, blank, refusing to arrest his roaming eyes until they settled upon the suit of armour, standing sentry, a spear held in one stiff arm, masked face pointed towards him. Cam probed for a sign of life, found it wanting and moved on.

Next stop—stairs. The balustrade was dark, made of what material he could not see, but crowned on each side with a snarling gargoyle.

Continuing his journey, Cam let his head turn to the other wall, probing a second sentry, finding nothing, seeing nothing but a blank wall except for what could be merely a large alcove, or a corridor running parallel with the stairs.

Top to bottom or bottom to top, he wondered, his perfunctory sweep complete. *Note for the future: buy a torch.*

As if his thought had triggered it, light flickered on. Cam saw flame torches adorning the walls, candle chandeliers hanging overhead. He squinted against the light, lowering his head a little to block the glare. As he did, his eyes found the mural and began once more to try and define its shape. There were swirls and pictures, scenes that were there and then not. As Cam watched, they formed and crystallised into letters. Then words. One of the words was his name—Camlaidh.

When the movement had finished, Cam read the letter—for that was all he could call it—with growing apprehension.

> *Camlaidh,*
> *Read the words of your master. You have entered my house, my domain. I know you seek freedom and information. I will give you both of these things—save the knowledge that would destroy me—and do so gladly.*
> *If you can find me, reach me, and look me in the eye,*
> *Play well, Camlaidh, for your challenge is begun.*

As he reached the end of the note, eyes now looking at the tips of his toes, Cam heard a metallic grinding, creaking sound from either side of him.

He looked up, somehow unsurprised to see the two suits of armour raising their spears and edging clumsily towards him. "Stylishly predictable," he told them amiably, side-stepping the thrust of the first with ease.

He grabbed the spear with both hands and kicked the carrier away. Turning to the second, he relished the sound of the empty suit hitting the floor and disintegrating. "Although the spears are a nice touch," he told the second, swinging his around in a high ark that removed the other's head, before stepping back to avoid any impending blow. "Axes are so passé."

He need not have bothered. The suit froze, arm drawn partway back, ready to thrust forwards and impale Cam through the stomach. Instead, the suit crumbled into dust and was gone.

"Convenient." Cam nodded approvingly. "Though the cleaner may be a little miffed."

He faced the grimacing gargoyles, spear raised, waiting for them to wake, climb or fly from their perches and attack. As they remained deathly still, he shrugged and took a step forwards. "Going to get me when I try to pass, eh boys?" He nodded as if they had replied in the affirmative. "Must be guarding something, then. Well, claws at the ready—here I come." He walked slowly to just out of arms reach and tapped one with the tip of his spear, feeling the metal click on stone. He prodded harder and grinned as the creature gave a little at its base.

"Boy, I hope you're all this easy," he chortled, toppling them one-by-one to the floor and hearing the satisfying crunch as they smashed themselves into oblivion. "Yes, it would be very nice if you were," he repeated, doubting his bluff even as he said it.

Cam mounted the stairs carefully, testing each with a tentative foot before slowly allowing his weight to rest upon one as he moved just as carefully to the next. At the top he looked left and right. Both directions were identical and empty. With no pointer to guide him, Cam instinctively followed the direction of his dominant hand—as people usually will—and turned left.

As he walked, he soon realised his initial survey had been wrong—though understandably so. From the walls on each side emerged faces, feet, hands, all screaming, all trying to grab him. A bony hand on the end of one long arm grabbed a handful of hair and pulled.

Caught off balance, Cam stumbled into the wall where he was immediately pinned by more flailing hands. His spear was stolen, splintered and cast aside. His clothing tore and his hair ripped out in bloody, agonising clumps as he fought to escape without finding himself caught in the throng reaching for him from the opposite wall.

Inch by inch, scratched, bleeding, bruised; he edged along the wall, gaining fervour as the grabbing hands lessened.

Finally he escaped the last with a roar and fell to his knees, gasping and straining to pull air into his bruised and swollen throat. As a final disgrace, a foot stretched just far enough to kick his behind and he collapsed to the floor, hearing a sickening crunch that could only be his jaw breaking.

Cam used his fingers to drag his bulk further from those body parts, dragged until the faces had stopped screaming and his fingernails were torn, bloody and in some cases missing entirely, left behind. Probably he was even lying on them right now. His mind created princess and the pea feelings of sharp, ragged nails pressing into his chest and stomach.

In a concerted effort to banish this and all other pain for a while, Cam passed out on the cold, stone floor even as it hungrily drank the blood still oozing from his wounds.

***

Bian felt the blood enter him through his castle and relished the surge of power that accompanied it.

His son watched, wordless, feeling the power it also fed to him—linked to the castle via his father.

"This, my son, is how we escape," the demon roared. "The blood of this one is strong and old. Ancient talents run through every atom of his being. He is the key!"

The boy cocked his head in a question.

"With the strength he will give, you can escape this world and find me more, until I, too am strong enough to break free of my unjust prison. And then, when I am finally free…oh, the things we will do…"

The boy demon nodded eagerly, smiling and ready. Yet still the images flashed through his mind. Mother and her friends. So like him—or he them—and yet not. Their rejection angered him. Even though he had never given them the chance to do so, even though it was merely a perceived rejection, it angered him because it hurt him, and his father knew well how to pour salt into such wounds. He would kill them all and do so gladly.

Chapter 18

Alnthea stepped into the lengthening shadows with impatience. "Go, damn you!" she growled at the sun, unwilling to risk it peeping from behind a cloud to catch the barely healed flesh of her face.

Menw nodded in agreement, buzzing inside despite his relaxed, half-dozing posture.

Jodhi was watching Isabel sadly. "She looks so peaceful," she said to Lana, "are you sure she—"

Lana nodded her head. "A doctor would test her to be comatose, or almost so. That's only because they don't have the right tests. She's in a place that…doesn't bear even imagining. A place that probably can't be imagined, except by the doomed that are sent there."

"Will she ever be okay?"

"After this, as soon as we can leave here, we'll take her to Depot E. I know, I know, they're not all good, but they're not all bad either. I don't think anyone else has a chance of pulling her back. If even Cam can't do anything, they're the only hope she has."

"So much for helping people," Jodhi said miserably.

Lana said nothing, only bowed her head and sighed in agreement.

"Finally!" Alnthea cried, seeing the shadows complete their merge into night. "Get up, old bones! We got us some bad guys to sniff out!"

"Are you sure you do not require a leash, my dear?" Menw asked, rising calmly. "Trackers often have a habit of racing ahead…"

Alnthea flicked her tongue out between pointed teeth and flashed her feral eyes at him. "Then move faster, Grandad. That way!" She slowed to match his speed despite her comments, and goodbyes were both sent and received on the move as the vampire and the mage vanished into the twilight.

"Now what?" Jodhi asked.

"Now we get to wait," Lana replied, "and hope nothing too bad happens."

"That's it?"

"Unless you have a better idea?"

"I could wolf and try to trace the other guy."

"You can do that?"

"Sure I can! Me and the wolf got kind of…acquainted when I was—when we were—" Jodhi stopped, her eyes haunted and pained.

"Try it," Lana suggested softly.

Jodhi snapped to with an effort, hopped out of the van and, shedding her clothing hurriedly, in a moment became a wolf.

Lana, still expecting the slathering beast of before, gasped in astonishment. The wolf now sniffing around the camp was big, yes, far larger than a normal wolf, but sleek. Its fur was the dusky gold of Jodhi's own hair and the eyes, as it turned and padded back to her, were identical. Even the satisfied grin it wore was nothing but a toothier version of Jodhi's own.

"Found it?" Lana asked, already knowing the answer, averting her eyes so Jodhi could become human enough to speak.

Jodhi rose and morphed to her usual shape with a small shiver as the night air hit her bare skin, Lana thoughtfully turned her face away slightly to save the other's embarrassment. "Found it. And I know it, too. Somehow. I can't quite place it, though."

"You're still a beginner, remember. Though I doubt it'll be long before you're teaching the master-class! What do you want to do?"

"Follow it." Jodhi bounced on the balls of her feet, eyes shining. "I won't get into trouble—I promise! Let me find him, at least!"

"It could be quite a help. Go, but carefully, we don't want you to do anything silly and wind up hurt." From the corner of her eye Lana watched Jodhi wolf and leap off after the scent, muscles rippling beneath her glossy fur. "I sound like an indulgent mother," she reflected, amused. Then, looking at the door. "I hope I did the right thing. I'm no use against a demon and his kid. Not on my own."

Shivering, she stepped back into the van and rummaged in her bag for a jumper which she put on, wishing suddenly that she at least had a symbolic form of protection. Something to hold like a gun, a knife, or even a club.

Remembering, she grabbed Cam's rucksack and rummaged in the side pocket where, she hoped, his wicked-looking hunter's knife would still be. Her hand grasped the ivory handle and pulled it out, still in its metal sheath. Metal because the knife would make short work of any lesser material. Even the metal needed regular replacement, she knew, else the blade would make slightly longer yet still just as effective work of that, too.

With the blade on her knee, one hand on the grip ready to pull it out at any time, Lana huddled in the van, facing the open panel—facing the door to another dimension—with every inch of her physical and mental being tensed in expectation of…something. Of whatever would happen next.

***

Cam awoke feeling the coldness of stone seeping into the depths of his bones. Every one of which ached, along with every muscle and inch of flesh.

At first there was nothing, and then every memory rushed back to him, clear as day, making him scramble to his feet. He swayed, stumbled, and crashed into the wall. With a cry he jumped away, expecting hands to reach out for him once more. None did, but still he preferred to struggle on his feet, just in case.

Slowly he tested each limb, feeling cuts, bruises, a deep gash or two. His head; scabby and bald where patches of hair had been yanked free, finger-shaped welts on his neck and a painful grate in his swollen jaw.

"Umph," he grumbled and started walking, little more than a stagger in his current state. *I can't fight anything else in this state,* was the one clear thought in his addled mind. *I'll be killed in a second!*

Defeated, he sat himself clumsily in the centre of the corridor. If ever his and Menw's strengths needed testing, it was now. Cut off telepathically he may be, but he could still feel the link, the line that connected him and Menw life-to-life. If he could touch it, if he could tug it, or feed through it, something…

Concentrating on the only hope he had, Cam isolated each ache and pain, one-by-one blocking them off. Then, carefully, almost timidly, he visualised the line, a string of energy, flowing back and forth between the two of them. From his heart to Menw's and vice-versa. He saw each detail, each strand that linked them solidify in his mind. Felt it push and pull like the tide as the force passed in and out of him on its journey. Carefully, like a man reaching out to touch a fence that may be electrified, he reached out and placed the tip of one finger on it. He felt a buzz zipping through his body, a powerful, healing sensation, and he grasped it with his whole hand. He gave it a gentle tug…two…three and waited.

***

Menw stopped in his tracks, uttering a surprised grunt, one hand flying to his chest.

166

Alnthea stopped and turned. "Menw, what's wrong?"

He grunted again and looked at his chest. Faintly, he thought, he could see a faint shimmer.

"Menw?" Alnthea reached to place a hand on his arm, but he shook her away urgently. She stood back, looking concerned, and waited.

Menw turned back towards the camp and followed the shimmer as far as he was able. *Cam?* he thought, and felt his call go nowhere. Fixing on the shimmer, he visualised as Cam had. To him, the string was filled with colour and magic, atoms pulsing and flowing at high speed between them. It was not a string he could grab, but he thought a reply was unnecessary. Instinct ordered him to act now and save his questions for later, so instead, he concentrated on the atoms flying into him, willing them to reverse, to take his healing power and what strength he did not need and return them to Cam, hoping it would be enough.

As he grew light-headed, as his knees began to wobble, the colours faded and the string became invisible once again. Now he allowed Alnthea to take his arm and sit him down. From a pocket he produced an energy bar, unwrapped it and ate hungrily. Once he had eaten it, she looked gravely into his dull eyes. "You can't go on, not now."

"Give me a moment," he said, closing his eyes, using that given to him by the energy bar to pull back his own energy from the ether that provided him with his powers. "Mere bodily tiredness is nothing," he said, standing. "Not to the likes of me."

"What happened?" Alnthea enquired.

"A story for later, I think," Menw replied. "A time when we have no witches and wolves to be catching."

Alnthea turned away to hide an annoyed frown. "Let's go then, if you're sure you're okay."

Menw gave her a playful push. "Lead on."

***

Cam opened his eyes, feeling refreshed. He was not truly healed, that was a task for time or magic to perform, but the energy had lessened the pain and knitted together his cuts and broken bones allowing him, now, to stand up, strong and unswaying. He took a few steps forward, watching his dank surroundings carefully. Ahead of him he saw the corridor end in a door, a smaller version of the main entranceway made of dark wood, studded menacingly with iron. It lacked the brass knocker, instead sporting a black handle for turning. Cam approached, looking to either side, seeing the corridor really did end here—no side passageways. *Whoever built this place ought to be shot,* he mused. *Sure, it has that nicely gothic demon-esque atmosphere that's all the rage nowadays, but it's hardly well designed for proper use.* He shut up his internal rambling and tried the handle. Only half to his pleasure, the door creaked open a few inches to his push, then swung open the rest of the way on its own.

He stared at the scene with his mouth open as far as his still-injured jaw would allow. It was Bluebeard's room of wives. Some hung from the walls on hooks, some from the ceiling by noose, some lay in pieces on the floor, gathered around a bloody axe. Each one had Lana's face. The walls, floor and even ceiling were stained with arcs of blood, dried yet somehow fresh, the coppery taste filling his nostrils. As he stood, frozen, each Lana opened her eyes to look at him, even those whose heads no longer met their necks. Just for a second, they simply looked at him blankly, and then each eye filled with a cold hatred and each mouth opened. In unison each voice dripping with bitterness, they spoke. "You killed us," they said.

Cam shook his head in horror. "No…"

"You killed us!" they repeated emphatically, some of the heads even nodding in emphasis.

"No!" Cam cried, reaching forward, without taking a single step inside, stretching for the handle and wrenching the door towards him.

As it slammed shut, he stumbled backwards, hands over his face, trying to shut out the pictures now burned into his brain. "Not real," he told himself. "Not real! It's a fake. It's a room that plays on fear. Stop being a baby and get over it."

Fully scolded, he turned back to face the way he had come. "Next task. Get past this lot again. Possibly twice, if they're on the other side too." He braced himself for a run. "Heck, I'm a Shadow Walker. Achieving the unachievable is practically the job description!"

He rocked back on one heel, steadied, shifted his weight forwards and gathered himself into as small a target as possible and, ignoring the screams of pain from his abused body, sprinted down the corridor. Hands and feet slapped at him but gained no purchase, save ripping his already battered shirt into more rags. Reaching safety at the top of the stairs, he ground to a halt, hands on his knees, panting. Looking ahead he saw no sign of what might await him on that side. Were he to assume a general symmetry—as suggested by the suits of armour and the gargoyles—he should expect more body parts, therefore he ought to be moving at high speed. If, however, he were to assume wrong and wind up running into, falling down or otherwise finding another nasty surprise, that would be very little use to anybody. The demon was clever, more so than his current challenges might suggest at first sight.

Crouched in his runner's posture, Cam began to edge forwards, ready to run at the first inkling of something attacking him from either wall yet for now moving slowly, able to examine his steps before taking them. As he moved farther along and nothing came from the walls, he had to force himself not to relax—not yet—just in case. He need not have worried. Halfway down the corridor he stopped before a gaping hole that, in this light, seemed to lead nowhere.

There was a 2-inch thick piece of corridor left around each side for Cam to edge across, back pushed firmly up against the wall, eyes closed, bracing himself to the slip and fall he felt would come at any moment.

Instead, he felt his toes meet solidity and he leapt as far away from the hole as he could, throwing a quick glance back at it before looking forwards to find the door he was expecting. Not to disappoint, the door was there. It was identical to the other, but, Cam hoped, of more use.

He grasped the handle and pushed. The door swung open without so much as a creak, revealing another—identical—door behind it. Cam grasped the handle on the second door and pushed again. The second door opened just as easily, revealing a third door, also identical. Grunting his amusement, Cam pulled open the third door, then a fourth, a fifth, a sixth. At the seventh he stopped, considering something. At the sixth door, he had instinctively ducked his head under a frame which descended too close to his head for comfort. He moved backwards through it, and forwards again, then opened the seventh door and, keeping his head up, stepped through.

The top of the frame brushed the hair on his head, just enough to be noticeable, and definitely not something the previous six had done.

The eighth door opened just as easily and Cam ducked a little, stepped directly under it, and stood upright. The crown of his head touched the cold stone.

Cam walked through more doors, ducking more and having to minimise his bulk as each door grew smaller and smaller.

Finally, Cam sat on his haunches, looking at the smallest door yet. The last had fit him through on all fours—just. This was the next step down. Almost expecting to be accosted by a white rabbit, Cam opened the door, took a deep breath and began to wriggle his way through. The stone scraped his shoulders as he forced forwards, only to be held fast by his hips. He threw a curse at the doorway and heaved, grazing the heels of his hands as he prevented his chin from hitting the floor again as his hips popped free and propelled him forwards.

Cam lifted his head and saw the main entrance hall. "Wha-?" he mumbled, spinning his head around to look behind. The endless collection of doors was gone, replaced by the two enormous double doors he had entered through. Looking to the front again, he noted that the gargoyles were still gone, as were the suits of armour.

"That was a stunning waste of time," Cam grumbled, standing and brushing himself down. "Whoever made this castle was having a very bad day. The inside doesn't even match the outside." He stopped speaking, aware that he was being uselessly catty, and looked at the corridor to the right, by the staircase; the only other obvious place to go. He ambled over cautiously, studying the shadows that sprang up on every side.

They seemed to gather around him, behind him, urging him onwards, yet clouding his vision until he progressed at a cautious snails' pace. Once he glanced back over his shoulder, only to find his back-route blocked.

He was being guided towards a light, seeping from around the sides of a door, which opened as he drew near, leading him into what could only be the Great Hall—or whatever a false castle like this may call it.

As he stepped across the threshold, the door slammed shut, seeming to blow out all the light, leaving him trapped in the shadows. These seemed to breathe and shift around him, fluttering past, brushing his face with a faint, small movement of air or a fragile wing. Cam brushed his face absently, making contact with a small, furry body. "Yaaah!" He leapt backwards, crashing into the door.

"What. The. Hell!" he grimaced and struggled not to bolt as more bodies brushed by him. One settled on his hair and he slapped it off with a cry, stumbling away from the wall, almost losing his balance and completely losing his sense of direction.

Cam forced himself to stand still and calm. He cleared his mind and felt the air around him. Hundreds, perhaps thousands, of tiny, buzzing little minds zipped to and fro on every side. "Moths." He breathed a sigh of relief. Unpleasant, but harmless. He reached up to rub his face and found something that felt like cobwebs. It pulled away in a clump, and the moths resting on him took flight in a hurry. He found more cobwebs on his clothing and pulled them all free, only to feel what had been on his face being replaced. He reached out a blind hand to swat the moths away, but they simply swerved and came back for more.

Cam closed his eyes again, concentrating, finding one of the tiny buzzing minds, isolating it, watching it, then his hand came out in a flash and caught it. "Gotcha," he told it and felt tiny pinpricks in his hand. He let go in shock. "Bit me," he said. "Bit me? It's a moth! Moths don't bite people!" But as he felt more pinpricks, on his neck, his head, his arms, his legs, everywhere, he began to change his mind. Not only did these moths bite, they shot something into him that made his limbs go weak, his muscles collapse, and the world fade from his vision.

***

Jodhi moved swiftly in wolf-form, following the scent she could almost place. It was somebody she knew, or had encountered, she was sure. Her first thoughts were of Department E, could one of them have followed them and set their prisoners free? Why would they do such a thing?

Her wolf riled at these excessive thought processes, wishing for peace so the scent could be followed faster. Seeing the sense in this, Jodhi allowed the predator to take more control.

She loped on, nose swinging back and forth in an arc, never losing the scent, never missing a stride, growing excitable as the trail grew stronger and fresher. Suddenly she rounded a hillock and stopped. Ahead she could see an unmoving figure, surrounded by objects she could barely make out. He was hunched up, what could only be binoculars held up to his face.

Jodhi crept closer, knowing each step brought her closer to breaking her promise, but needing to see who this tantalisingly familiar scent belonged to. He moved and Jodhi froze, ducking low in the heather for concealment, willing him to turn her way.

He lowered the binoculars and reached for a nearby flask, drinking a deep draught.

Still Jodhi repeated in her head *turnthiswayturnthisway...* pushing the thought out to him with all her might, *turnthiswayturnthiswayturn—*

As if finally receiving her thought, the figure looked in her direction, scanning the hills.

Jodhi's jaw dropped, a sliver of drool sliding down her sharp teeth and into the grass. Suddenly the scent made sense. She felt her hackles rise and reigned in the wolf, putting all the strength from her anger into holding it back.

Julio sat back, leaning on his gloved hands, and looked at the sky.

Jodhi watched him for a few moments and then began creeping backwards. Once out of sight, she turned tail and galloped back to camp, resisting the primal, wolfish urge to return and tear him apart, or at the very least howl her anger, hurt and frustration to the moon.

As soon as she found herself within the perimeter of the camp she changed into human form and called breathlessly for Lana who bounded from the van a second later, blanket in hand. "Jodhi! What is it?!"

"It's Julio!" Jodhi spat, covered herself and collapsed, panting, by the made, though yet unlit, fire.

"Julio? What? He's the—he set…"

Jodhi nodded, ill-concealed fury mounting behind her troubled eyes.

"Are you sure? I mean, Julio, he—"

"I'm sure," Jodhi confirmed. "I followed the trail—remember I said it was familiar? I followed it to him then got close enough to see. He was watching the camp through binoculars. He put them down, drank something, and then looked in my direction. He didn't see me, he looked right past. But I saw him. I saw him well. Julio."

"Maybe, I don't know, maybe it's just…" Lana shrugged helplessly.

"I knew that scent," Jodhi said. "As soon as I saw him, they both fit together. Like Cam with telepathic signals, or Alnthea with blood. It was Julio sitting there. It was Julio who came here and let Sansé and Arlene loose."

Lana sat by her, absently playing a match over the kindling.

"So, what do we do?" Jodhi asked, helping the fire catch.

"I still can't get in touch with Cam. Alnthea and Menw are tracking the ones Julio set free—you could go and fetch them, I suppose, but why? He still seems to mean us no malicious harm. Hard as it is to leave it, he really is the least of our problems."

"So we just sit here and wait some more?"

"Unless you have another bright idea, it's all we can do'"

Jodhi growled quietly and jabbed the fire angrily. "Fine," she grumbled and entered the van to redress.

***

Alnthea looked at Menw. The mage had stopped, out of breath but trying to look fresh.

"Can we rest for a minute?" the vampire asked. "The trail's strong, but I'm a bit out of shape."

He looked at her appraisingly, guessing she could go on for a good many hours yet without so much as a twinge. Grateful for the opportunity to rest without being forced to stop and admit his need, Menw nodded and sat heavily.

"At this rate I'll be too done in to be any use when we do catch up with them," she commented, dropping easily beside him.

Menw grunted. "You'll be fine."

Alnthea left him to retrieve some energy in his own special way. She guessed it could never be a permanent solution, but then, come daylight she would be forced to find some way to hide from the possibility of direct sunlight. He could rest properly then, she supposed. Always assuming they found a solution. That would be a conversation to have once they were on the move again.

***

Cam woke for the second time, again aching all over. Before memory could panic him into movement this time, however, the constricted, trapped, claustrophobic, hard to breathe feeling did. He was tightly bound, unable to move so much as a toe. Whatever bound him had some give to it, and enough of a membrane to breathe with only a little difficulty; though the air was a trifle sour and stuffy.

Always by far the most skilled of all his friends at forced relaxation, Cam practised his art now and examined, first of all, the few things he remembered. Moths, complete with teeth that could inject a sedative. Possibly not-quite moths, then, or perhaps more-than moths. But the basis was the same, of this he was sure from the telepathic flutterings he had found. They had been spinning thread around him. That made no sense if they were no longer caterpillars. More evidence towards the more-than moths theory. They were bigger, too, he remembered the furry thing he had grabbed.

Okay. More-than moths, uber-moths, behemoths, whatever he wished to call them—likely enough they had bound him in whatever thread they retained, cocoon silk or whatever it was.

Suddenly Cam wished he had taken a more fervent interest in etymology. Would he be able to rip a hole and wriggle free? Would it rot him free in time?

Would something happen while he gestated here? He almost managed to picture himself with artfully symmetrical butterfly wings and had to stifle a nervous laugh. Someone—something—may be there to watch him.

Cam let his thoughts drop; trying to sense any other presences close by without the risk of raising the alarm by probing. He felt nothing and relaxed a little. Unwatched, at least in the immediate vicinity, he had at least a small chance of escape. Watched over by something that would surely kill him as soon as look at him, would have left him with little-to-none.

He could not tell where he was. The smell told him he remained inside the walls of the faux-castle, there were no other clues. He was unable to tell that he lay on a narrow platform and, should he slip in his attempts to gain free from his cocoon, he would fall a mere 10 feet—barely enough to even register a last thought—to be impaled upon countless long, thin, cruelly sharp spikes.

Inch-by-inch he tested the silk, wiggling his fingers, nudging with his elbows, knees, and head. He found no noticeable weak spot, which left his hands as the best tool; the only real tool. Being left-handed, he presumed that the strongest and began shifting it, feeling the small amount of give, trying to increase it, trying to wriggle it into a position from which it could apply pressure.

His own bitter-sweet odour of sweat and fear combined with the air his exertions forced him to breathe of more deeply and he had to force himself to stay awake as the lungfuls grew bigger and the oxygen flew to his head and made him sleepy. The pain in his hand and forearm was strong. Concentrating on the sensation, as an abstract rather than a physical discomfort, seemed to help. Suddenly he realised it was, in fact, moving. Really, actually moving. Tiny increment by tiny increment, it was moving!

***

Whiling the time away, Bian was telling the story of how he was put into his prison, forced to renege his true form for the humanoid shape he wore now. Back in a time where all humans possessed magic, not all so powerful as Menw, but many, the rest not far behind, demons were kept in check, forced to obey their rules on pain of execution. The young and headstrong got their kicks from pushing the boundaries, bending the rules as far as they could. The humans were strict, however, and most that did such never lived to tell the tale.

Bian was but a foolish child then, and had chosen a young girl to sport with. An only child, a loner like himself, she accepted this, her invisible mischief-maker, and kept him a secret.

Bian gained status amongst his fellow demons with his tales, never letting on what he knew—that the girl allowed him to misbehave, she found it funny. So long as he caused no serious harm.

All little girls, however, must grow up eventually. Bian's was no different. There came the day she had called to him; in the past this had meant a request to cause mischief for another, so Bian went eagerly to her and waited, turning amusing tricks over in his head.

Instead the little girl, now all grown up, told him she was to be married the next day, that Bian must now leave and never return. If he did, she would punish him as she should have done a long time ago, as the law stated she must.

Bian had retreated as if in defeated compliance and watched the girl from a distance. The next day he stood and watched the joining ceremony between his girl and a plain-faced youth. He felt no jealousy, unless it was a petty, possessive sort, he had no romantic love for her. He was demon after all and felt only anger at her rejection, and the knowledge that others would laugh.

He had followed them to their marital bed; closely once realising she was too wrapped up in her new husband to notice his presence.

At their bed he stood by and watched the timid, clumsy fumbling and the grunted thrusting; they did not last long. Then, as the youth reached his climax, Bian reached out and removed his heart through his back. Once the girl's screams began, he dropped the organ and left her.

But she had found him—of course she had. There was nowhere for him to go, and she was powerful. He had missed that, her blossom into a powerful mage, the same way he had missed her growing up. He had not cared enough about her to look.

She came to him alone and terrible with anger. She told him she ought to have caused his execution years ago, but she had not because she was foolish enough to have imagined him to be her friend. She knew now he was nothing, she hated him, but could not bring about his death for memory of the affection she had felt until her wedding day; aye, for it was the murder which had brought her new hatred about, ordering him away had been only another part of her friendship; for she knew he was in danger if he stayed.

She had reached out and pinched reality between her fingers, tearing a hole in it and revealing another world. She had made it for him; she hoped he liked it for he would be there a long time.

175

Before Bian could even begin to understand, she had used the power behind his name to cast him into that world and seamlessly repair the hole.

Bian's son looked at him thoughtfully.

"Why do you look at me so?" the father asked angrily. "I was young and stupid. Now I am neither. I have had countless eons in this prison to hate, to plan. I will destroy that world and everything in it. Just as they deserve."

The boy nodded eagerly. If his father spoke the words they must be true. Already he was trying to forget the emotions given to him by his human mother, being taught to hate the side of him that was like her.

"She trapped me in a physical form as close to human as possible," Bian continued. "I learned some tricks, in time. How to shift my shape a little—although the only thing I can truly become is a human boy. I also learned ways to build and change my world, some which the thought-stealer is finding very unpleasant indeed. Once I am free, son, I shall become my true shape once more. And what rapture shall I feel. And what fear shall they."

***

Somewhere in the human world, a mother awoke from a dark dream she, blessedly, could not recall. She looked at her sleeping husband. She got out of bed and plodded to her child's room to kiss his soft cheek. Then, quietly so as not to disturb her husband, she packed a bag, left a sorrowfully penned note on the fridge, and left the house without looking back.

In the morning her husband would panic and weep, her baby may pick up the feelings and do the same, but her mother would understand the note and, aged and wizened though she was, tell the story.

> *Dear Oz,*
>
> *I hate what I must do. Tell Mother the family legend has risen and I must go. She will explain. I beg you—believe her.*
>
> *If I am never to return, remember the day we bought those ceramic pigs and know I will always love you with every inch of my being. Whatever world I am in.*
>
> *Forever yours,*
> *Mariel*

***

Cam's probing, aching fingers had pulled loose layer after layer of silk until, with a pop, his index finger broke through and felt the coolness of air outside his cocoon. He gave himself a moment to rest before forcing more fingers through. The silk, stretched taut, cut into his skin, but he ignored the extra pain and with a grunt of effort forced his entire hand through.

Now a hole the size of his hand existed in the fabric, Cam began shifting his other into position. With the cool feeling of freedom on the first, the second almost seemed to help him along. In what seemed no time at all, he had one hand on either side of the hole. After a pause for breath, he gathered his strength and shoved all he could muster into those muscles that pulled until they burned and threatened to burst. Still he pulled; sweat beading on his forehead, an ugly grimace on his face, gaining hope with each breaking strand that gave him more movement and more air.

Eventually, with the hole up to his neck and down to his waist, he stopped, resisting the urge to black out but unable to summon any more strength. So he slowed his breathing, cleared his mind and meditated in his tiny, breached, prison.

***

Jodhi was curled up in her sleeping bag inside the van. Lana sat by the dying fire, which still contained enough embers for her to stare into it, entranced by the sparkling, flickering glow.

Something clicked behind her and she whirled on her feet, pulling her knife. Nothing was there, nobody. Yet something was wrong, different. The subtle difference of walking into a familiar room, in which some unknown person has moved an ornament out of place, or straightened a permanently crooked picture.

With a gasp she realised. The thin line of light coming from the crack between the door and the invisible jamb was gone.

Lana gripped the handle and tried to turn it, only to land on the floor a few feet away, sent flying in a fierce crackle of blue light.

"Cam!" she shrieked, trying again to the same effect. She looked at her hand and saw blisters forming, felt the hair on her head crackling. Looking to the left she saw Jodhi, on her feet, a baffled expression on her face.

"It's closed!" Lana sobbed, pointing to the door, unaware that her hair stood on end and her face was a deathly grey. "Cam!" she cried again and stood to try the door a third time.

Jodhi moved quickly, reaching out to stop her. "That's not going to work and you know it."

Lana looked at her and pointed to the door. "Cam," she whispered. "We have to get it open again!"

"I don't think that's gonna be doable," Jodhi whispered back, eyes widening.

The door, once solid and firm—so long as you stood on the correct side to look—was fading. As they watched it became transparent, then little more than a fog, and then it was gone.

Lana ran to where the depressions were still fresh and visible, but there was nothing there now except for the dirt. She let a handful run through her fingers. "It's gone," she whimpered and pummelled the ground with her fists. "No, no you come back! Bring my Cam back to me!"

Jodhi stood aside helplessly, unaware that she was crying too. The door was gone. How now to bring Cam back?

***

Menw & Alnthea were watching a house. Sansé and Arlene were inside, had no doubt raided and pillaged anything of use and now rested, intending to move on shortly. Menw and Alnthea had other ideas.

Without the assistance of Cam they could make no real plan other than to enter the place as quietly as possible and hope Menw could bind them again before they did any harm.

"I see no real reason why it should fail," Menw was murmuring. "We are not attempting to best them, after all; merely cast a spell at them. I need them in my sight, no more than that. So long as you watch for either of them attacking me as I bind the other, this ought to be simple enough."

Alnthea nodded. She knew he was more experienced and prepared than she could ever hope to be, and his earlier arrogance had taught a valuable lesson. So long as their two intended were not master trap-layers or ambushers, they ought to be fine.

It was just that word "ought" that made her teeth want to grind. Alnthea loathed going blind into anything, preferred all doubt first removed. However, there was also the approaching sunrise to consider.

With a nod she told Menw she was aboard and they crept through the damp grass quietly, cursing the gentle drizzle that had begun, subtly soaking and chilling them to the bone.

The house was quiet and still. The front door opened easily at Alnthea's touch. The hallway was empty. Ditto the living room, except for an elderly couple that had, until recently, enjoyed a life of peaceful and contented serenity; interrupted rudely by Sansé's razor-sharp claws before they could so much as rise from their chairs.

Fighting the urge to close their glassy eyes, cover their half-clotted wounds, bury them; do something to make their final awful seconds better, they moved into the dining room, then the kitchen.

Alnthea turned and jerked her thumb upwards.

Menw nodded and Alnthea took the lead once more, back through the house and to the stairs.

They kept their footsteps to the left, where the stairs were mostly unused and less liable to creak, using the wall for balance. At the top, Alnthea tested each board for looseness, skipping some, making no sounds, trusting Menw to simply follow her path—which he did.

Looking through the open door of the first bedroom they saw Sansé. She was curled up on the bed, eyes closed, sleeping; looking peaceful and innocent.

Alnthea stepped back, giving space to Menw, staring at the figure on the bed. She who had caused so much pain.

The wizard raised his hand and cast a binding spell.

Sansé attempted to scream for help but, never freed from her enforced silence, could only loose an impassioned groan. She dropped off the bed to the floor and flailed, fishlike, kicking her legs which were again tied at thigh and ankle.

Watching the scene in fascination, Menw and Alnthea failed to realise that the noise had woken Arlene who now stood dazedly in the doorway at the far end of the landing, rubbing her eyes.

Quickly her confusion evaporated and she reached into a hidden pocket in her woolly jumper and pulled out two vials. Not having time to check what they were, she simply threw the first at Alnthea's feet.

The vampire cried out in pain as she was thrown through the air, breaking her flight headfirst on the bathroom sink.

Menw raised his hand to bind, but his reflexes were too slow. The second vial broke at his feet and a red fog flew into his mouth and nose. He breathed in and tried to scream as a violent pain took over his head. As the red fog dissipated, it was replaced by dark red blood that ran from his ears, his mouth, and his nose and, mingled with tears of pain, from his eyes too.

With his hand still raised, now as if in defence, Menw took one last breath and muttered some words that created a bright flash in his chest before his struggling brain imploded, seeming to suck his face inwards as the bones in his skull turned to powder.

As he fell to the floor, Arlene realised it had been her turn to watch, fascinated, for too long. Alnthea was upon the witch, knocking her to the floor and cracking her head once on the door frame. Hard enough to draw blood and leave the witch helpless to the fangs which sank into her neck and supped her life until she was a sunken grey husk.

Her impending fury slaked for now with the dullishness of a blood-belly, Alnthea sat by Menw. She knew many thought a vampire could not feel, could not love, and could not cry. Not for the first time, she wished they were right.

***

Cam slipped both arms through the tear he had made and began to force the cocoon to bow to him—slipping it over his shoulders and head.

Once his head was free, Cam looked around, startled by the platform he was on—by the fact that his bottom half was mostly hanging off the edge. He reached behind him and realised why—his head must have been only a centimetre or two from the other edge.

Focusing, Cam carefully wriggled his lower half from the limp cocoon. He peered over the side and saw hundreds of tiny pinpricks that might well be nothing more than a trick of the dim light.

He picked up the cocoon and dropped it. Light now, it fluttered down gently and sank peacefully onto what Cam now surmised were incredibly sharp spikes.

A quick glance down each side showed nothing but more spikes and Cam sat back, cross-legged, to survey the room and think. As his eyes adjusted to the gloom, platforms like the one he sat on now revealed themselves to him.

They all sat on one side, seemingly suspended on air, scattered at not-quite-random intervals. He let his eyes relax and soon picked out a path—of sorts—which could only be there for him to follow. As his eyes adjusted more, he thought he could see a wall, and an exit, at the far side, but shut that out until he could see for sure.

The spikes were sharp; the gaps between platforms too long even for his largest stride. Cam stood and stretched the muscles in his legs.

If he had ever been the sort to play computer games, he may have felt like a thousand Atari, Nintendo or Amiga characters; jumping across platforms to escape the spikes, the water, the pit of darkness below.

But Cam was not, and would have scratched his head in confusion were somebody to attempt an explanation. A telepath, he had little use for imagination. A Shadow Walker, he had no use for pretend adventures.

Cam was simply afraid.

He studied the angle and distance; a mis-timed, mis-directed or mis-calculated leap would be his doom across these platforms.

Cam backed to the far edge of his platform, bent slightly at the waist, rocked on his heels, readied himself carefully.

In a sudden burst, he took two long strides, the second hitting the exact edge of his square, and jumped.

He landed smack-bang in the centre of the next, bending his knees to soften the impact, and stood straight.

"One down, plenty more to go," he murmured, checking the urge to celebrate his initial success, and looking ahead. The next platform, though identical, was offset. Cam must jump at an awkward angle. "Difficult," he admitted aloud—it was unpleasant for the eye to see and the brain to contemplate and control. "But not impossible."

He backed up and crouched, angling his body as well as he could before standing, preparing and striding into his jump.

He landed with bent knees again and found his right foot scrabbling for purchase on the edge. Quickly righting this by pulling it into his other and dropping to his knees, Cam sighed in relief.

He looked ahead again and saw the wall was indeed real; he could see it, and a rectangular hole which he could walk—or, presumably, jump—through.

Concentrating again on the next platform, Cam saw it was lined up once more, but farther away. He stood, he contemplated, he readied, and then he leapt, landing neatly in the middle and immediately moving his gaze to the next.

This was farther away again, but lower down.

"You are a tricksy one," Cam informed it and spent a few moments judging his jump. On his first stride he stopped, backed up, shook his legs out, and readied himself again.

On his second, he shot forwards and jumped.

It was long. His left foot missed entirely, but enough of his right found stone for Cam to throw his weight backwards and land on his back with a thud that snapped his teeth together and knocked the air from his lungs with a sharp *whoosh*.

He stayed where he was until his breathing had eased, his heart had slowed, and his right ankle had decided it was merely twisted, rather than truly injured, and stopped hurting. Then he stood and looked. The next platform was closer again, but higher. Cam sighed and then gave himself a mental kick and studied the leap he would make.

He took his time, flexing his legs, his arms, his neck, trying to quash the fear and regain the adrenaline rush. Slowly he prepared; eyes lowered, spine curved, a coiled spring waiting to be set free.

With a grunt he dashed into his stride and leapt...

...just as a searing pain shot through his chest.

He screamed and mis-jumped, hitting the platform at stomach height and holding on for dear life while the burning threatened to burst his chest wide open. When it stopped, Cam's eyes filled with tears at the emptiness that replaced it.

Struggling up onto the platform his only thought was of Menw, and once safe he forced his tired body into the lotus position. Even now he was able to clear his head and visualise the string that enjoined him and his life-force to the mage.

Except that this time visualise was all he could do. The string fell flat, with nothing on the other end to hold it up. Then, before his mind's eye, it shrivelled up and vanished into nothing, filling his chest with a yawning void.

Cam opened his eyes. "Menw..." he wept. "Menw...y-you can't be..." But he knew his visualisation told no lie. Confusion arose in a flash. "Then why aren't I-I should be—" And then he understood. The shrivelling disappearance was Menw's death. But the disconnection beforehand...that was Menw setting him free—making him a mortal man, with his own life-force that would age him, in time, as mortals did.

Even in his last breath, Menw had thought of him.

The aching loneliness in Cam's chest doubled him up in tears. And there he lay, crying, lost, on a small platform surrounded by a deadly river of spikes, in another world, attempting to find a demon who promised to set him free. While in another place his friend, his mentor, his hero had left behind his long, long life and passed into whatever awaited him in the darkness that was death.

Chapter 19

Julio watched the door close and disappear, watched Lana and Jodhi grieve together for their lost one. He raised his face to the sky. "Where are you now then, you omnipotent chingado?! The door's gone anyway!"

He expected no answer, but the voice of the Shadow Council spoke in his head. *"There are things in motion you do not see, young one. Be on your way or remain to watch but remember you have no part in them."*

"That's it? Something else is going on, I'm not allowed to help, but I can sit on my calabazo and watch the pinché show?!"

There were no more answers forthcoming, it seemed, leaving Julio no choice but to sit and watch through his binoculars, knowing his friends needed him, but unable to go on pain of being cast from them entirely.

Refusing to leave, however, needing to see, needing to be close by, he watched the campsite with his binoculars until he fell asleep in his cross-legged position and, slowly, fell to one side until his face rested on the rough blanket he sat on and the binoculars slipped from his hands and he curled up to sleep through the dawn.

When he awoke, the cold and damp had sunk into him, making his teeth chatter and his bones shudder and ache. He looked at his numb hands and saw the skin was tinged blue-grey.

I think I'm sick, he decided, and thought about thinking up a solution. Then he shrugged to himself, slurring his words slightly. "Don't care," and with that thought in his head, he dragged his stiff body to his sleeping bag, curled up, and shuddered his way back to sleep again.

***

"Get Menw," Lana said. She was sat against the outside of the van, staring at the spot where the door used to be.

Jodhi, perched on the inside and staring glumly into space, shook herself and looked up. "Huh?"

"Get Menw," Lana repeated tonelessly.

"But you said——"

"I know what I said. That was before this. It's daylight, he'll be holed up somewhere with Alnthea. Get him. Bring him here."

"Okay, if you're sure." Jodhi stood, pulling herself into a stretch and loosening her clothing again. *I need a more convenient mode of dress,* she thought.

"I'm sure. Go. Hurry." Lana watched as Jodhi's stretch shrunk into a transformation and she leapt forwards, out of her clothes and after the scent.

Once she was out of sight, Lana turned her face back to where she wanted the door to be and stared, willing it to reappear.

Jodhi raced until her muscles screamed, spurred on as the scent grew steadily stronger. She came within view of the house and slowed down, scenting Sansé and Arlene too.

Remembering her lack of attire she remained in her wolf's guise and, hoping it would gain the attention of whoever held sway within enough for them to show their face to her, she sat back on her haunches and howled.

A familiar face appeared briefly at an upstairs window and Jodhi trotted to the door, pawing it open and lolloping up the stairs.

Alnthea stopped her at the top, tear-stained and sorrowful. "Jodhi…" she whispered, and could say no more as the wolf nudged past to see.

For a moment or two the wolf surveyed the scene, every muscle frozen. Then she padded shakily over to Menw and nuzzled his sunken cheek, whimpering softly. After a while, she turned and looked at the other body with vague interest before stalking, hackles raised, into the bedroom where Sansé lay.

Sansé had flipped herself onto her back. Her head now cricked upwards to stare at the animal. The bindings prevented her own change and the wolf smelt her fear as she suddenly realised how vulnerable she was.

Jodhi growled deeply and crouched, ready to pounce.

A hand fixed on the scruff of her neck and pulled her back sharply. "No," Alnthea said and pulled the wolf outside, closing the door firmly and remaining inside. She spoke to Sansé coldly, loud enough for Jodhi to hear. "I could have let her kill you. Would more likely have killed you myself if I didn't think we still need the blood that runs so temptingly through your veins.

"Understand, though, that this is not a permanent situation. You live on borrowed time. The very second we're done with you, I will kill you. It will be fast, it will be soon, and believe me I will enjoy it an awful lot more than you will." She turned on her heel and exited onto the landing, closing the door behind her and lowering her voice. "You heard that?"

The wolf nodded and sat down by Menw, head dangling towards her paws.

Alnthea looked at her thoughtfully, then stepped over the witch with a sneering expression and opened the wardrobe in the smaller bedroom.

Jodhi jumped and looked up sharply as clothes hit the floor in front of her. Alnthea had her back turned politely. Jodhi took the hint.

"Okay, I'm dressed. Thanks," she said shortly.

Alnthea turned round to see her holding Menw's hand and weeping softly.

"You know, in some ways it's simpler to be a wolf. It's all so much more black and white, if you let it be. And it doesn't hurt so much."

Alnthea nodded. "Times like this I wish I could let the evil side take over again, just so it didn't tear me apart. Maybe, right now, we can both do that—just a little. It might help."

"Okay," Jodhi straightened her back, "tell me what happened."

Alnthea related the events sadly. "It was my fault," she finished.

"No it wasn't. No more than it was Menw's fault they got away in the first place. It lies on the person who set them free." Now it was Jodhi's turn to tell her story; Julio, the vanishing door, her headlong dash after Menw at Lana's behest. "What do we do now?" she asked, once done.

"First we do by our fallen," Alnthea said. "Cam would likely know what Menw wanted, but we can't ask him right now. I'd suggest we burn the house, take Sansé and Menw back to Lana and go from there. Maybe we'll think of something on the way, maybe she'll know, maybe…anything. Or nothing."

"Sounds about as close to a plan as we're gonna get," Jodhi agreed, standing uncomfortably in her new clothes. "I'll see what I can find to burn this place."

"I'll figure out a way to get us all back to the camp," Alnthea said.

They left each other to their necessarily solo tasks.

Jodhi went downstairs to find the kitchen. First, she found the bodies in the living room. *More death. Everywhere,* she reflected sadly before allowing her wolf to stay the emotion and move her on.

She found matches in the first drawer she opened. It was where her mum would have kept them, with the candles and other sundries. The "junk" drawer, she always called it. Or, when there was a power cut or some other event that caused an object in the drawer to be useful, the "just in case" drawer.

185

Jodhi sent a loving thought back home, just in case it could be felt, and took the matches.

Next she turned the key in the back door and went outside. She spotted the old-fashioned shed immediately and slid the bolt holding it closed. The door, warped with time and damp, swung open and she looked inside.

Directly in front of her eyes was a barbecue, next to which lay two cans of lighter fluid. Content with her mini hoard of pyromania tools, she turned back inside to see how Alnthea was faring.

The vampire was kneeling on the floor with her back to Jodhi. "Got something?"

Alnthea nodded and shifted to one side. "Sort of. Got this camp bed and some castors. We can take Menw on it."

"And her?" Jodhi nodded to Sansé.

Alnthea shrugged. "Dunno. How'd you get on?"

Jodhi showed her finds and Alnthea nodded approval then stood and flipped the camp bed over. "Not great, it'll be a bitch of a journey, but it's the best we've got."

Jodhi nodded her own approval, turning over the problem of transporting their prisoner.

"Well, we've got till sundown to think of something," Alnthea said, guessing the others' thoughts.

"Think I've got it!" Jodhi galloped down the stairs, was silent for a minute, then yelled up to Alnthea. "Thought I saw something!"

Alnthea came to the top of the stairs and looked. Jodhi was posing, with one hand resting on the handle of a wheelchair and a pleased smile on her face.

"Excellent!" Alnthea applauded quietly. "Now make the sun go down so we can leave!"

Together they hefted the camp bed down the stairs and into the hallway, then carefully carried Menw down and strapped him in place with some thin rope from the shed.

Sansé made it easy for them to put her in the wheelchair, hopping most of the way and settling herself in comfortably with a defiant face that both captors found almost unbearably comical.

"Well, don't know about you but it's well past my bedtime." The vampire yawned.

Jodhi yawned in unison. "You go to sleep, I'll watch her. I'll wake you if I start dozing off." Jodhi made shooing gestures. "Go, rest."

Too tired to argue, Alnthea obeyed and went to rest in the as yet unopened third bedroom of the house. It was obviously little-used at any other time. Though it was spotlessly clean, the wallpaper was faded and old, the bed unmade, the window curtainless. The room itself gave off an air of abandonment.

Alnthea looked at the bed with a sigh. It was bound to be lumpy, but it seemed so long since she had slept on anything even remotely soft. However, with the light filtering through the clouds and in the window, all it would take was one well-placed ray of sunshine to break through and hit her sleeping form.

With a sigh she took the lonely-looking pillow and lay down on the floor, feeling the floorboards creak and give beneath her. She closed her eyes, thankful for the fact that vampires rarely dreamed, and allowed sleep to rush up and overtake her.

Jodhi sat herself on the stairs, resting her chin on her hands and wondering how to pass the time. She had turned Sansé's chair away to avoid the malicious stare, then covered Menw and the two elderly occupants of the living room with blankets.

During her forays through the living room her eyes had repeatedly fixed on an overflowing bookcase. Her fingers itched to pick one up and read for a while to pass the time and take her mind away from everything. But something in her rebelled against taking and using what she still considered the property so recently owned and used by the real residents of the house.

Shortly, though, boredom began to set in and cause Jodhi's eyes to grow heavy. She stood and paced to and fro in the hallway, unwilling to push Sansé into the living room with her victims to gain more space, yet needing to remain within sight of her. Her legs moaned and begged for rest and her eyes began to close despite the exercise and Jodhi eventually went to study the books. One might keep her awake for at least an hour or two, and that was important. She took one that looked interesting and lively and took it back into the hall, propping herself up against the wall and holding the book up to keep her head high and remain alert.

***

Lana hardly even noticed as the day passed and Jodhi did not return. She dozed a little, always jerking awake to the sound of Cam's voice before realising it was not real, that the door was still gone and he had not returned. Thoughts of Jodhi and Menw were few, far between and short-lived.

187

Her ears barely registered the drone of a car engine drawing steadily closer, not even when it pulled up a stone's throw away, bathing her in headlights before the engine was killed and the occupant exited, slamming the car door shut to rouse the attentions of the lone person leaning against the van. She was short, dumpy, mousy-haired and rheumy eyed.

As she walked closer, Lana raised her face, managing a half-hearted curious expression. "Who you?" she asked, her voice thick with tears.

The woman smiled a trifle nervously. "Mariel." She held out her hand for shaking, then dropped it back to her side as the other showed no sign of movement. "And-and you?"

Lana ignored her question. "What do you want?"

Mariel opened her mouth, and then closed it, unsure of how to explain.

There was a growing commotion from behind a hillock and Lana leapt to her feet, the stranger forgotten as a strange collection of figures approached.

Lana recognised Alnthea, Jodhi, and Sansé in a wheelchair looking annoyed. "Menw?" she asked, when they drew close and stopped, unwilling or unable to draw her eyes to the prone figure on the clattering metal gurney.

Jodhi looked at her, then at the body, then at Alnthea.

Alnthea was studying the newcomer. "Who're you?"

"Mariel…" the woman repeated, extending her hand again, only to be ignored a second time as Alnthea turned o Lana.

Lana's eyes had finally registered Menw's body. Her face showed incomprehension. "What's that?" she asked, timidly. "Looks like…it looks like…" She took a hasty step backwards, flinching as she connected with the van.

***

Julio groaned in his sleep as a cry of grief echoed through the hills. He made a vague thrusting gesture with one hand, then muttered incoherently to himself and faded away again, his breathing short and ragged.

***

Mariel, still ignored, stood respectfully to one side and watched as a tearful trio dug a grave, working until Alnthea smelled the dawn once more and called a halt, climbing back out onto solid ground. "I can't work much longer," she told them, "it has to be deep enough."

Lana and Jodhi climbed out, grimy and sweating, and stood by while Alnthea encased Menw in tarpaulin and threaded rope through holes on either side. Together, Lana and Jodhi carried him to the grave and lowered him in, the vampire reciting a druidic player and blessing from a book found in Menw's bag.

Alnthea was forced to retreat inside the van, leaving Lana and Jodhi to fill in the grave. Glad of the distraction, she called the stranger to her. "Mariel, what're you doing here?"

Mariel hesitated, then registered what she had just seen and, looking into the somehow glowing eyes of the woman who avoided the sun, spoke. "There's a demon, and he's trying to get free of his prison, and only I can stop him if he does that."

Alnthea stared at her in shock. "You-what? How? Wait, when we're all sat down tell us. Okay?"

Mariel nodded. "Sure, okay."

"Alnthea, by the way." The vampire proffered her hand and Mariel shook it gratefully. "That's Lana, there on the left. The younger one's Jodhi."

Mariel nodded. "And the others?"

"In the wheelchair, that's Sansé—keep well away from her. The last…that was Menw. Best we not talk too much of him right now." Alnthea turned her face away, hiding the tears that slipped down her cheeks, leaving small tracks in the smears of mud from the digging.

"Of course," Mariel said, understanding, and was quiet.

Jodhi and Lana finished filling the hole, patting the soil down carefully, and joined Alnthea and Mariel at the van. Alnthea had gotten together some food, rationing now Menw and his magic were absent, and gave it to them. It was wolfed down gladly and the two workers allowed themselves to cool off and relax.

When they seemed ready, Alnthea indicated Mariel. "This lady seems to have a story to tell us."

Mariel nodded and thought for a while, finding a way to begin. "There's been this legend, passed down generations, through name changes and everything. Everyone in the family knows it and eventually passes it onto the next. It's been around so long I can't even comprehend it, but it's there and fixed firm.

"I don't know as I ever thought it was much but a tale. A myth, perhaps. I never really examined it that much. It was just…there, is all.

"The story in it's most basic form says that one of my ancestors imprisoned a demon, and swore us all to be guardians of his name until such time as he may escape and we be needed to defeat him.

"I've been having dreams, visions, sometimes when I'm not even asleep. Something has been pulling me away from home, more urgently every day, but I ignored it. I mean, I don't know who you are but you're very different to me. I'm a wife, a mother. I work in a shop and drink coffee with my friends. I thought I was going insane!

"Then last night I had another dream and there was something about it, like red flashing emergency lights—I was in my car and halfway out of town before I realised what I was doing. So I stayed in my car, and when something said 'turn this way' or 'take this road,' I did just that." She looked around at the three carefully expressionless faces. "As I was driving, I kept picturing this door. It led into His prison and it was open, and he was close—so close— to being out. That voice told me to close it, so I visualised it closing and then disappearing." She saw the three faces now register surprise, understanding and, one, anger, and rushed on to finish her story. "Then I kept driving, going wherever I was pulled, and when I got here and saw your van and you, Lana, something said to stop and so I did," she ended and watched Lana, expecting the outburst that sat behind her eyes.

It did not come. Alnthea spoke instead. "A friend of ours was trapped in that world."

Mariel looked at Lana again and understood. "Oh, oh no, oh I'm so sorry. it's not gone—the door?—it's still there; I just closed it and made it disappear so nobody could open it again, so he couldn't get out. it's still there, I think, I don't know anything about this sort of thing but I think I can just bring it back…"

"We're running almost as blind as you are on this one," Alnthea replied. "We opened the door using me and her blood." She nodded at Sansé.

Mariel looked confused, then nervous. "You and her blood? I don't, I—"

Alnthea raised an eyebrow. "You don't?" she said through eye teeth that had suddenly extended.

"You're a vampire," Mariel said, sounding relieved to have it spoken. "But you're not a bad one. I knew that."

Alnthea nodded.

"What about Jodhi?" Lana spoke up. "Is she just as she seems? And me— am I just your normal, average person?"

Mariel frowned a little. "Jodhi's got something else inside her—an animal? No, that can't be…a werewolf? You're a werewolf, Jodhi?"

Jodhi nodded.

"You, Lana, I think you're all human, but with something extra. Your head, it's full of…so many things…you remember, is that what you do?"

"Close enough for toffee," Lana agreed. "Mariel, might your family have a history of magic? Or psychic ability? Mediums, readers and the like?"

Mariel nodded.

"Your ancestor, when she named you all to be guardians, she ensured that within you all would be a spark of her power. Active enough to know things, to call you when you were needed, but dormant enough to allow you to live as normal, everyday people until that time. I would even hazard a guess that you have some hidden depths, wherein hides whatever is required to hold sway over this demon by using his name."

Mariel smiled. "I think you may be right. My family has always had, as you say, mediums and readers and the like. I never entered that field, though my mum is a much respected psychic amongst the small circle she keeps, but I was always encouraged in my interest of what you might call the occult."

"What is it about the name, though?" Jodhi asked.

"Names hold power," Lana explained. "Your name is attached to you at birth, it becomes how you are known and identified to the world. A nickname can do similar thing, though to a lesser extent. A name is your identity; who you are, how you are known to others. It is your spiritual self, if you like. For a demon no less, and often even more, than a human."

Mariel took over. "A witch or someone who possesses such power can take control of you by using your name. A voodoo doll, for example, becomes you not simply by a lock of your hair being attached; it is the name attached to the owner of lock of hair that binds the two together and allows magic to be worked. A photograph, a portrait, a hairbrush or something belonging to you; all these can allow someone with the right power to control you from afar."

Lana nodded and carried on. "But it works better if you have in sight the person you want to control. Bind a spell to somebody using an intermediary like a hairbrush and you have a limited control. Bind a spell to their name while looking them in the eyes and it becomes immediately and 100% effective."

"In the case of this demon," Mariel took up the thread, "his name can be used first to prevent him from doing any harm in this world, and then to either cast him back into his prison or make him mortal enough to destroy entirely. I just…I don't know how. Or if I can. It needs magic." She looked chastened. "I've never…"

"Hidden depths," Alnthea reminded her.

"If Menw were still…" Jodhi trailed off.

"But he's not," the vampire countered glumly, "and so he can't. But we have a person who likely possesses the power somewhere within, a person who can find us the information we need—be it in her head or elsewhere—and then we have a vampire and a big bad wolf to do the dirty work once we get him."

"What about Cam?" Lana asked.

"Anyone trapped in a demon prison should be released once the demon dies. It is the demon that has your friend trapped, isn't it? Demons work different to humans, once he's dead any spell he cast should lift."

Lana thought, and then nodded. "You're right, of course. Except that the demon can't get free without killing Cam."

Mariel shook her head. "Unless somebody with the right power and connection lets him loose by choice."

Lana's eyes widened. "You can do that?"

Jodhi cleared her throat. "What about…his son?"

Mariel's mouth dropped open. "He has-how did he get a son?"

Jodhi's eyes closed painfully and her head dropped onto her clasped hands.

"Oh, you dear, dear thing…" Mariel reached out a hand and stroked Jodhi's hair.

Jodhi shook herself and looked up, angrily fighting what was in her head. "That's for later," she growled, allowing the wolf to come forward and block her emotions, struggling to keep her voice from wavering. "He has a son. My son. That makes it half-human, though if it has a name it's not one I gave him."

"If he's half-human," Lana thought aloud, "and only so young, and he hasn't really done anything yet. Maybe we can save him."

"Why?" Jodhi spat.

"Because he is half able to think like us, and given a chance might have a hope of being good," Lana said.

"It wasn't his fault he was born the way he was," Alnthea said gently. "And he saved you, he brought you back to us. That shows something good is in him—something good that came from you. If we have to destroy him then we have to destroy him, but if there's a chance? Surely we should save him and give him the opportunity to choose what he wants to be. Isn't that a part of what we do? Give people—even half-people, people with vampires or wolves or demons inside of them—the chance to be good despite those things?"

Jodhi lowered her head again. "Every part of me that hurts wants to make them both suffer. You're right, though. it's not the son's—my son's—fault how he came to be. He didn't ask for it. And yes, he saved me. If, in return for that, we can save him…if we can give him a chance to be something good, I know that's what we should do. Just don't expect me to do it. Don't expect me to ever look at him not see his father, and want to hate him for it." She uttered a bitter, barking laugh. "My mum once said all rapists were demons in disguise." With that, she buried her head in Lana's shoulder and was silent, Lana hugging her tightly to stop the tremors that rattled through her slender frame.

"Right then," Alnthea pressed on carefully, painfully aware that time was passing. "Some form of plannage might be in order. Lana, get those brain cells of yours working, we need to know everything we can. Mariel, me and you get to raid Menw's magical bag to see what we can see. Jodhi, get some rest. If you can. If you can't, at least keep Isabel company."

Mariel looked around, confused. "Isabel?"

Alnthea indicated the unconscious figure at the back of the van.

"Oh. Is she…?"

"Not dead. Very long story. But, like I said—keep well away from Sansé," Alnthea said.

Mariel looked at Isabel, then at Sansé, and then nodded vigorously. "As far away as I possibly can! Are you sure we have to look through this stuff?" she grimaced as Alnthea undid the straps on Menw's bag.

"Well…for one, I know that Menw would moan at us until we did. For two, we might find something useful; information, supplies we might need for now or later, something."

Jodhi was halfway past the two of them, heading for Isabel and her own sleeping bag, when she stopped suddenly. "Julio!"

"Who?!" Mariel asked, this time looking a little exasperated.

Lana and Alnthea looked at Jodhi for a moment, then in unison. "Get him."

Jodhi nodded. "I'll bring him back. Only…if he fights, what do I do?"

"Wheelchair?" Alnthea suggested.

Jodhi thought. "I can't take that and be wolfy at the same time—slight lack of opposable thumbs, but if wolfy can guide me…?" she asked her wolf politely and nodded with a smile. "Alright. Wheelchair and rope."

Shortly, equipped with rope and a change of clothing just in case, leaving Sansé on a blanket at the other side of the camp and pushing the wheelchair ahead of her, Jodhi set off at a speedy clip, following her wolf's directions along her earlier route.

As they examined Menw's supplies, Lana and Alnthea tried to explain why and how they had come to be there, making no mention of Shadow Walkers and keeping their story as succinct as possible.

Mariel listened intently, taking in every morsel with an open mind that was attuned to listening for the truth of things. At the end she was silent for a while before speaking. "I accept there are things you need to keep from me. I believe everything you have been kind enough to tell me. I'm suddenly very glad that you're here, I know that without you I'll fail, and that with you there's a chance." She nodded to herself as if satisfied and bowed her head to examine the dark leather binding of a book.

Land and Alnthea exchanged a glance of approval and kept to their tasks.

***

Cam awoke from his doze, still lying on the platform. The ache had left his chest, now leaving an empty disconnected feeling in its place. He sat up and shook his head groggily as the grief came back to the forefront and threatened to overwhelm him again.

Cursing himself for it, Cam pushed the tears aside. *Later,* he told them, *not while I'm still here. Later, when this is over and we've won the day. If I fail because I'm too busy crying and puling it's the worst tribute I could ever give him, and he would likely rise from his death just long enough to clout me around the head and call me a clot.* Cam felt a small smile play on his lips at this image and took it gladly. *Remember him alive,* he told himself. *Do what he would have you do. Grieve for him when all is well and dedicate your victory march to him.*

Cam hefted himself to a standing position, shakily at first, then firm and strong. With Menw fixed in his head to give him strength, Cam leapt the next three platforms without pause and found himself facing the door that was his escape—from this particular room, at least. It was level, there was more room than he could possibly need, but it was farther away than he could possibly jump.

He crouched at the very end of his platform for a time. Then he stood, stretched his muscles out and took his position. He had room for three strides, if he hit the end at exactly the right spot.

Cam bowed his head. "Menw, help me," he begged. "Help me live, help me get through this and back to Lana, help me celebrate your memory. Help me jump this gap." Something surged through his muscles, hot and strong, and it moved him forwards. One stride, two—gaining momentum, three—his foot coming down at the perfect spot and he flew forwards, legs bicycling, arms reaching for the edge that drew closer.

Cam's feet fell short and he landed with a breathtaking thud, his arms scrabbling for purchase, finding it and heaving him forwards until he lay flat on his stomach, shins still hanging over the edge, gasping for breath. "Thank you," he said, once he could speak, and dragged himself into a sitting position. He was in a wide corridor, lit softly by whatever lay beyond.

Cam shuffled to the wall and leaned against it, exhausted, refusing to even consider what came next.

As he rested, he registered the sounds of music and people talking. Though he strained his ears, the conversation remained elusive and he gave up trying, willing to wait until his legs could carry him to the sounds.

He rested, losing track of time, drifting in and out of drowsy sleep in his corridor until, eventually, his legs itched for movement and he stood. He faced the light, the music, and the voices and walked forwards. The light grew brighter as he neared until it finally gave way and opened the corridor out into a large ballroom, filled with people.

Cam smiled wryly as he recognised where he was, trying to think which particular occasion this could be.

Then it came to him. Of course. What else? It would be his sister's coming of age ball.

Cam tried to back up out into the corridor again but walked, instead, into solid wall. No exit there, then. And here was his sister now, looking as fresh-faced and lovely as ever she did—in life or death.

And there was he. Younger than he had looked for a long time, for Menw had not taken him under his wing for a few more years yet, and even on the un-ageing face he had possessed ever since, the lines of experience could form. There he was, and on his arm…that hair, that tinkling laugh, that stunning and evil beauty.

"Sansé…" Cam breathed.

The laughing beauty whispered something into his younger self's ear with a smile. Camlaidh-the-younger flinched and forced a smile that came nowhere near his eyes.

Nobody was paying any attention to the tired, wounded, dirty Cam at the edge of the room. He experimented, reaching out to touch a nearby guest, and nodded grimly as his hand passed straight through. A similar experiment with an inanimate object—namely, a glass of sherry placed on a table—afforded the same result.

Attempting to exit the ballroom proved equally fruitless as, instead of walking through the doorway, Cam crashed into something solid and cried out in pain.

He turned back to the room and thought hard. This was after the speeches, after the meal and ceremony. Outside was dark, the guests slightly tiddly. And…yes. As he listened, the band struck up a new song. A nameless waltz he knew note-for-note, having heard it in his dreams for over 200 years.

"It's now." he thought and, no sooner did the thought cross his mind, it was. The doors slammed shut. Half of the guests, including Cam's sister, parents, aunts, uncles, cousins; including his friends, acquaintances and those of his sister; all screamed, knowing immediately that something was wrong.

The other half merely smiled, awaiting their signal.

Sansé had dropped the arm of the younger Camlaidh and now hopped nimbly onto a table, kicking over a bowl of punch as she did so.

"Ladies and gentlemen!" she cried. "Welcome!"

Her half of the guests cheered. The others seemed to shrink into themselves.

"I would like to thank you all for coming, and hope you have all enjoyed yourselves so far this evening! It is now my pleasure to inform you all that dinner is served!" Her elegant dress tore open and dropped away from her changing body. A second later a wolf leapt from the table and into the crowd. Her invited guests, a small army of wolves, followed suit.

The image faded as Cam saw his bewildered other self, standing protectively in front of his sister, be tossed aside by a slathering wolf who hesitated none in grasping the helpless girl and aiming its teeth at her neck.

Cam blinked and found himself standing in a large, empty room. From another corridor, light touched his face and beckoned. He followed it, dazed and unthinking. This was a warmer light; one that he finally realised was leading him towards the combined smells of fresh air, flowers, grass and trees.

Cam walked faster, leaving the dark, musty castle behind, craving the outside world—even the disturbed, endless sunshine of this was better than none at all!

He came out onto a simple, peaceful garden. A gazebo sat in one corner, a small pebble fountain in another. The grass was freshly green, dotted with paving stones. Around the edge, thick hedges grew tall, frequented by trees bearing apples, pears, oranges and other fruit; some he knew, some he did not.

Inside the gazebo was a figure, sitting in the somehow exaggerated shade.

Cam walked closer until he saw properly, and stopped once he recognised the creature that had brought Jodhi to him so tenderly.

The creature saw his recognition and spoke in a voice that was shaky and quiet, though gaining confidence with use. "She is my mother. I did not want my father to kill her."

Cam nodded. "Thank you. We are grateful to you for that."

The creature stood. "I am half like you and that half fights what my father tells me. But I will never be accepted as one of you."

"Perhaps not to walk amongst people, but then neither are all of us. I am a thought-stealer, your mother a werewolf. I have known vampires, wizards and many others; both of my own species and others who cannot walk properly amongst the human race."

"Then what is there? If you cannot be as they are, what else is there to be?"

"Yourself?" Cam suggested. "You have had no option to discover who or what you truly are. Would you like to?"

The creature hesitated. "I would. Perhaps."

"I can help."

"You would kill my father."

"Yes."

"Then I cannot trust you. Though neither will I hurt you or yours. Your small band is safe from me, though not from my father who cannot wait to kill you all."

"Your father sent you to kill me. Somehow that will lead to his escape."

"Yes." The creature pointed to a path hidden in the hedgerow. "Follow that path and you will emerge into your world unharmed. I cannot say where, I have no strength to direct, it will bring you out to a place with the power to attract it, wherever that may be, but from there you can surely find your way home."

"Your father will not be happy," Cam said, walking to the edge of the path. "Or perhaps this is a trick, and upon this path is my death."

"My father I can handle. Go, there is no trick."

My life in the hands of a monster, Cam thought with mild amusement. "Very well, but remember my offer. I and my friends will help, if you would let us."

The creature nodded and then faded back into the shadows.

Cam stepped onto the path, leaves filtering the sunlight until what came through was a faint, dark green. He trod carefully but confidently along the soft soil and, when once he blinked and opened his eyes, he saw the path, the hedges, even the sunlight had gone.

Without pausing to examine his surroundings, Cam reached out his mind for his loved one and called her name.

Chapter 20

Jodhi came within sight of Julio's camp and stopped, searching for him. She saw the lump in the sleeping bag and approached, purposely making enough noise to alert and wake him.

When she reached his sleeping bag and he slept on, unroused, she frowned and shook his shoulder. He grumbled and rolled onto his back.

Jodhi saw the blue-grey colour of his skin, the sheen of cold sweat on his brow and stepped back in shock. "They, uh, didn't cover this in the manual," she told him.

Hesitating only long enough to decide it was probably better to force him awake than leave him like that and, what the hell, he deserved it anyway, she drew back her hand and delivered a ringing slap to Julio's ice-cold cheek.

His eyes flew open and he babbled incoherently, unable to fix on her face or recognise her if he could.

When he began to drift off again, Jodhi grabbed his shoulder and forced him into a sitting position. "Oh no, you don't get off that easily you son of a bitch," she said and slapped him again.

This time he seemed to realise where the blow originated from and his hollow eyes fixed pitifully on her for a second without recognition, before clouding again as another spout of drivel spilled from his mouth.

Jodhi let him babble, so long as he did he was awake, and pulled the wheelchair close. Asking her wolf for assistance, she hooked her arms under him, holding his sleeping bag in place, and let out a groan of effort as she lifted and dropped him heavily into the wheelchair.

He began to fall forwards and she held him up, pulling on his feet until he sat back enough for his head to loll, but his torso to remain mostly upright. Using the rope, Jodhi tied him firmly in place, cursing him under her breath and, with an effort, started the chair rolling and set off as speedily as she could manage, once again following her wolf's directions.

***

199

Lana sat bolt upright. "Cam!" she cried.

Alnthea jumped. "What?!"

Lana held up a hand for her to be quiet, her eyes closed and a smile on her face.

Alnthea shrugged and, taking a quick glance at Mariel's befuddled expression, but seeing she intended to obey, sat quietly and waited.

Eventually Lana opened her eyes and seemed to remember they were waiting. "It's Cam! He got out! The—Jodhi's son—he let Cam go free!" She told them the story she had been given, taking longer in words, unable to share the pictures Cam's telepathy had presented her with.

"So where is he?" Alnthea asked when the story was told.

Lana's answer was interrupted by Jodhi's reappearance, almost flying over the hill and landing at the campsite.

Lana was by her side just in time to break the fall as her legs collapses, muscles cramped and screaming for oxygen.

"Julio…" Jodhi pointed.

"Mariel!" Lana called, before realising the woman was already there. "Take care of Jodhi."

Mariel nodded and obeyed.

Lana wheeled the chair over to the van where Alnthea handed over Cam's knife and caught Julio as he was cut loose of the ropes and flopped forward.

Lana climbed into the van and pulled him out of the damp sleeping bag. Alnthea checked his pulse. "Not great, but steady enough."

"Help me," Lana said as she hauled over all the blankets and sleeping bags piled at the other end of the van. She used the knife to cut off Julio's wet clothes and then, with Alnthea's help, bundled him up in warm, fresh clothing from Cam's backpack before wrestling him into a sleeping bag and wrapping him in the blankets.

Alnthea checked his pulse again and nodded. "Better, a little. Any tricks in the first aid box?"

Lana shook her head. "Nothing we can do." She flashed a cheeky grin. "Unless you fancy drinking his blood, warming it up, and then feeding it back to him."

Alnthea grimaced. "Not particularly." She checked his pulse again. "So fortunately I think he'll be okay, it's stronger."

As she spoke, Julio moaned and opened his eyes.

Lana stroked his hair. "Julio? You hear me?"

He mumbled and gave a small nod.

"You know who I am?"

He narrowed his eyes, forcing them to focus, then nodded, fear clouding his face and feeding some colour back into his cheeks.

"Now, don't be afraid. Jodhi found you. We know what you did. But right now we have to get you well. We'll talk about it all when you're able. Deal?"

Julio nodded again, the fear fading. He opened his mouth and tried to speak.

"Never mind that now. Alnthea will stay with you, okay? I'm going to get you something warm to drink."

Lana had a fire lit in no time, a pan of water heating slowly. Once it had boiled and cooled, she poured some into a cup and gave it to Alnthea, who helped Julio sit up a little and held it to his lips to sip slowly.

Next, she repeated Cam's story to Jodhi, who was pale but recovering quickly.

Alnthea repeated her question. "Where is he now?"

"He wasn't sure, he said he hadn't looked yet—he wanted to talk to me first. But Jodhi's son, he said it would be drawn to somewhere powerful."

"Depot E?" Jodhi asked. "And can we please stop calling him my son if we can help it? I know he is and everything, I just…I'm not ready to…"

Lana gave her a hug. "Of course, I'm sorry. Depot E, you think?"

Alnthea shrugged. "Makes sense. If the door was opened with a mind to returning Cam to us, and the best he could do was let it be drawn to somewhere powerful. I don't think there's a place on the planet with more overall power than Depot E. Not just all the people it contains, also the equipment, all the things it does, creates, tests, everything; plus it's built on ley lines, surrounded by various supernatural barriers, and probably contains enough leftover power in it's walls to draw anything looking for a fix."

"Probably a good guess, then," Jodhi affirmed. "But what does Cam say?"

"Nothing yet," Lana replied. "He'll let us know when he has something."

***

Cam, satisfied his beloved was well, updated as much as she was able on their situation, realised his face was getting wet. He opened his eyes to a gloomy, raining day, remembering the sun in the world he had just left, and smiled. Glad to be home.

In front of him was a low-rise office building and as he probed it for life, a smile spread across his face. "Department E," he murmured, changing tactic and sending a cheery hello directly to the telepaths inside.

In no time at all, he was greeted and escorted down to a large, oval meeting room where he was served food and drink and told that Morgan would be down to see him shortly.

While waiting, he sent a speedy update to Lana, who replied with a smile—telling him they had already guessed his likely whereabouts and would wait on more news.

Morgan entered in due course, smiling at Cam's tanned face. "Been somewhere nice?" she asked, once small talk was done.

"Not exactly…" he grimaced. "I'm hoping that open mind of yours will be useful here. He told what parts of the story that he could, his own and that which he knew of the others, holding back his grief at Menw's death long enough to finish before breaking down into sobs.

Morgan comforted him as best she could, aware that she was woefully inadequate, especially encased in her own sadness at the same event. "Menw was a good man," she said, at long last. "I thought him a friend."

Cam smiled. "As did all who met him. He was a friend to everybody, even when he was being a grumpy, stubborn old fool you wanted to strangle."

Morgan smiled back. "I'll do everything I can to help you, you know that. Menw wouldn't have us let his death be for nothing."

"My thoughts exactly," Cam agreed. "According to what Lana has told me, they have the person who can open the door, call out this demon and bind him enough for him to be destroyed. As for the son…they want to save him, if they are able, and give him the chance to be good. But I don't know as anybody but you should know of him—I told him I would help, I'll not let him be taken away and experimented on. We'll find our own way, unless you can promise me he'll be treated well."

Morgan nodded her understanding. "I agree with you, Cam, I really do. I think we can take him in and teach him, though we will want to learn from him also I think that certain recent events will allow certain people to agree that the tests should remain unintrusive. Though you know, don't you, that, if he is deemed untameable, he will be destroyed without asking consent."

"I realise that, but I'm willing to take the chance. If you can give me your word that you will personally make sure he is treated well, then I will gladly entrust him to your care."

Morgan thought deeply for a few moments, considering, and then nodded. "You have my word. The half-human creature shall be treated well, and allowed to grow as he sees fit and, provided he does not grow into a being which causes harm or poses a threat to others, I promise I will make sure he is unharmed and submits to nothing he does not wish to."

Cam took in each word and turned it over in his head before holding out his hand and shaking hers. "You know you have my trust, Morgan. Now, we need to help the others, where can I find the information I need?"

Morgan pressed a switch under the table and a computer rose in front of her, behind Cam a large screen opened up and, as Morgan tapped at the keyboard, showed a virtual library. "We've been upgrading," Morgan said with a smile. "All the things we can do, yet we were still hunting down books in the library. Not anymore. You comfortable on one of these, Cam?"

Cam shook his head. "I still live mostly in the era I was born into," he said, "but I suppose I could learn a little."

"It's easy, scoot over here." Morgan took him through a crash course, pleased at the speed with which he picked it up, and then popped up a computer for him to use, doubling their efforts and pulling together anything useful on the large screen for later use.

***

Julio, pale and weak, was propped up against the door of the van.

"Not until you're well, we said," Lana scolded.

"I'm well enough," he said. "I know the things you're thinking, and until I at least try to explain that'll prevent me from getting better."

"If you're ready, talk," Alnthea told him.

He smiled wanly and began with his stormy exit from Lana's house, what seemed like a hundred years ago now.

He avoided mention of the Council as much as possible, aware both that Mariel was not supposed to know of the Shadow Walkers, and obeying their own request that he keep them as much a secret as he was able; but Lana, at least, seemed to get the information between the lines he drew.

When he was done, he coughed weakly and allowed Alnthea to soothe him with some more warm water and then settle him back inside the van for more sleep.

"I believe him," Mariel said, nervously. "I know he kept some things back, but I think that was partly because of me. I believe him, though."

"Me too," Jodhi said.

Alnthea raised her hands palm-up. "I'm with the flow, here—I think he told us the truth; everything he could, anyway."

"Me too." Lana sighed. "Poor Julio. He did the only thing he could. He must know Menw would still be here if he hadn't. I don't know what you all think, but I'm sure that knowledge will be more than enough punishment for him." Three murmurs of agreement were returned to her and she smiled at them all. "So it won't be for us to make him feel bad; but it might be for us to forgive him. Can we all do that? Even you, Mariel." More agreements followed, then silence.

"So, what do we do next?" Jodhi asked her usual question.

"I suppose we just wait for Cam to give us anything he finds out down at Depot E. Morgan should be helping him."

"There has to be something we can do," Jodhi said. "We can't just sit here and hope Cam and Morgan come up with the magic formula that lets Mariel and us make everything all better again."

Mariel cleared her throat. "Maybe we should try something to make sure I can do anything at all in the first place?"

"Like what?" Lana asked.

"Bring the door back," Alnthea chipped in. "You got rid of it, but you said you think it's still there and you can bring it back. Why not give it a go? Now Cam's back with us, the demon can't get out until we call him. And anyhow, if you can get it back and open it then we can get rid of our surplus werewolf once and for all."

All eyes turned to look at Sansé. She had obviously heard and was struggling in her bonds.

Mariel turned to study Alnthea. "You would simply kill her, if she were not needed to reopen the door?"

"I would. And why the hell not? She would do the same for us—almost did—and with a gleeful laugh. I would merely be ridding the world of a murderous pest. Would you ignore greenflies or slugs that ate your plants? A spider that tried to bite your child? A dog that attacked you? Or would you attempt to rid yourself and your world of it?"

"I don't believe in the death penalty..." Mariel said, looking timid. "People can be punished, some can be rehabilitated, but nobody has the right to remove the life of another human being. Even if that human being has taken it upon herself to remove the life—or lives—of others. Doing that makes you just as bad as the killer."

"You know, mostly I agree with you, Mariel," Jodhi said. "But Sansé isn't strictly a human being in the sense you speak of. She's a wolf who takes pleasure in torturing and killing others. Left alive, she'll only keep doing it.

Try to imprison her, she'll only try to escape and kill people both in the process and afterwards—and once loose, she'd be worse than ever. How can we ever ensure that doesn't happen?"

"What of this Depot E you spoke of? Can they do nothing?"

Jodhi looked suddenly thoughtful and turned to Lana.

Lana fidgeted and looked at Alnthea.

Alnthea bared her teeth. "I promised I would kill her as soon as she was no longer any use to me," she growled.

"I didn't mean to question anything. I just, I never could keep my mouth shut is all. I know you have your ways, and whatever it is you really are, they must work else people like Sansé would probably be all over..." she trailed off, leaving whatever else she wanted to say hanging in mid air.

Jodhi plucked it out with ease. "However, if we can try and save the half-human, half-demon creature, why not Sansé too? Right, Mariel?"

Mariel nodded.

Alnthea looked at Lana for her thoughts.

"I understand your view, Alnthea. I'd like to see that wolf ripped in half too. But...Mariel does have a very valid point. By giving one a chance and another death, aren't we showing ourselves to be worse than Sansé, who merely hates everybody equally?"

Alnthea hit the floor of the van with her fist, the growl turning into a snarl. "Very well. Save her miserable life. Give her to Depot E. But when she escapes and kills again, don't expect me to accept any blame."

"Very well," Lana said impatiently. "So we keep our eyes on Sansé and, provided she causes no trouble, we get her to Department E with the demon's son. Alnthea, if she makes one wrong move then go ahead and be rid of her. Until then, however..."

"I'll be good," the vampire promised with a poisonous scowl directed at the back of Sansé's head.

Mariel was looking between Lana and Alnthea with a frightened expression on her face, as if waiting for world war three to begin. As the strained silence grew calmer, she relaxed a little and waited for somebody to speak. When she realised they were all waiting for her, she swallowed a few times and almost did, then thought better of it, closed her eyes and visualised the blank spot where once there had stood a door, aware that she was within view of the spot itself, but following the instinct that said the door must first reappear in her own mind.

She pictured the reverse of what she had done earlier, the empty space becoming foggy, the fog slowly forming into the correct shape then solidifying. She stopped before she pictured it opening again and looked up.

Alnthea was staring, open-mouthed at a spot just behind Mariel and, slowly, Jodhi and Lana turned to see what had shocked her so. Mariel followed suit, knowing she had been successful, grateful and surprised at the ease with which her hidden depths seemed to be willing to reveal themselves to her.

"So I guess that's question one answered," Jodhi said with a grin.

Mariel felt a smile flicker onto her own face. "So it would seem," she agreed. "I know I can open it, too, when we're ready."

"So all we're missing is how to release the demon and his son, bind them both—one by name, the other by any means we can, then destroy one and capture the other while making sure the wolf back there doesn't cause any more mischief," Alnthea said.

"Thanks for that Little Miss Positive Thinking," Lana shot back, and then grimaced. "Sorry, that was probably uncalled for, but Alnthea, please, for the sake of what we have to do, can you put this aside? Just for now?"

Alnthea rubbed her face with both hands then ran them through her hair. "Yes, of course. I'm acting like a spoiled kid who didn't get what she wanted for her birthday. I'm sorry, I'll be good." She gave them a smile, small but genuine.

"No apology required. This whole thing is getting all of us, especially when all we can do is sit here and wait."

Mariel was staring blankly at the ground, deep within her own head, seeming to have forgotten what else was going on, she spoke. "According to the story, my ancestor opened a hole in the fabric of this world, bound the demon using his name, sent him through it and sealed it up again."

Lana looked at her. "You think we can use that?"

"Well," Mariel said, "what if it's more than just a metaphor? What if it isn't just a way to tell the story, but an actual description of what she did? What if she actually took hold of whatever holds this world to itself and opened it up onto the prison she had made for him?"

"Menw rarely talked about exactly how magic functions," Lana said, thoughtfully, "but when he did it was often in terms that sounded metaphorical but…perhaps weren't. Cam's telepathy, he talks about it in the same way."

"Maybe it's, like, half a metaphor," Jodhi suggested. "Like…oh, I don't know how to explain it—"

"Like visualisation," Alnthea said. "How you meditate, Jodhi; you picture a beach, visualise all stress leaving through your toes or whatever. it's a way to override the brain and help coax it into an extrasensory state so that the extraordinary part of it is allowed to do what it does without being impeded by the logical side, which would otherwise snap it back to 'reality.'"

"Wow, Alnthea, that's about as good an explanation as I ever heard." Lana smiled. "Mariel, could you try it?"

Mariel nodded. "It might help if...well, I did the door when you weren't waiting for me to do it...if I just go a little way out?"

"Of course, being self-conscious isn't going to help. We'll be right here, take your time."

Mariel stood, wincing a little as her back creaked in complaint at the kneeling position she had been sat in. "Not quite as young as I used to be." She smiled wryly and looked around. "I'll be over the hill, there," she said at last. "I know that building is more...I don't know, appropriate? It just doesn't feel right."

"And for a bloody good reason," Alnthea agreed. "Like Lana says, we'll be here."

Mariel strolled over hill and, once out of sight, sat cross-legged on the grass. It was slightly damp, but not cold, and soft enough to be comfortable. She closed her eyes and pictured the door, pleased with the ease it came to her, and then waved it away. It was not quite what she needed.

Thinking of the story, how her ancestor reached out and opened a hole, Mariel reached out with her mind, trying to find a place to push against.

Reality invaded, telling her she was being silly, and she pushed it aside time and time again. She was vaguely aware of the changing light of the passing day each time she was forced back out of her self-induced trance, but barely registered it as she put herself straight back in it again.

Finally, remembering Alnthea's comparison to meditation, she tried to stop forcing it, instead closing her eyes and listening to the day. The breeze, an animal scurrying, the faint sounds of her new-found companions. She allowed her mind to relax and take in everything, little-by-little, until everything took on its own little spark of significance; right down to the air moving in and out of her lungs. Slowly, not thinking, she reached out a hand and touched something. Something that gave a little before resisting gently. Opening her eyes, Mariel saw a faint golden shimmer around her hand, as if it was in contact with something else.

Mariel pushed a little harder, seeing the gold spread under the pressure she applied. Afraid it would give, not sure what it would give way to, she dropped her hand. The gold disappeared and she doubted herself a little until, with minimal effort, she reached out and felt for it again, in a different spot, and found it with ease. The membrane, if that's what it was, though difficult to find was seemingly harder to lose.

She stood up, smiling and feeling rested, and made her way back to the camp, checking once to be sure she could still find it.

"Hey, how'd you do?" Alnthea asked, helping prop Julio up on some pillows.

Mariel smiled and touched the membrane. "I don't know if you see anything, but I've found it. If I tore it open, we'd be through to somewhere. I think there has to be something like this keeping the demon in. Once I open the door and I have a focal point I should just be able to rip it open and set him free. I won't know until I try, though. I may be entirely wrong."

"Hidden depths," Alnthea told her. "It's in untold generations of your blood. Does it feel right?"

Mariel nodded without hesitation.

"Then it's right. Lana, anything at all from Cam yet?"

Lana nodded. "They're pulling it all together. He and Morgan. Just a bit longer to wait."

"Great. Sun almost down, too. I say we'll have it covered by morning and be on our way to London with a wolf and a Halfling creature in tow. How "bout you?"

Her buoyant confidence found mirrors in the faces Jodhi, Lana and Mariel. Even Julio managed a weak agreement.

And so they waited.

Chapter 21

Cam sent his thoughts out to contact Lana. "We have everything Depot E knows," he told her. "Do you have a pen?"

He waited for Lana to find a pen and reply in the affirmative before asking if they had discovered anything themselves.

Lana told him and he smiled. "Excellent work, that was exactly my theory." He went on to talk Lana carefully through a ritual to bind the demon by his name; how to prepare it beforehand ready for immediate casting. He then gave another to bind the Halfling and keep him sedate. Lastly, he told her how to mortalise the demon so Alnthea and Jodhi could destroy it.

"What about transporting them to Depot E?" Lana asked, after checking each detail twice.

"We're already on the way," he said. "We've got a secure van for Sansé and a demon trap for the other. What with Sansé bound up and the Halfling sedated, there should be little room for error. All you have to do once it's over is sit tight until we arrive, it should only be a short while at this speed. Our drivers seem to have taken the same reckless driving class as you, Lana."

"My driving is just fine." Lana grinned. "And I'll see you very soon. I love you."

"I love you too," he replied, smiling happily. "Go to it. I know you can do this."

"But if I can't, Cam…I want you to know. I never dreamed it was possible to love someone the way I love you."

"I never dreamed it was possible for me to love anyone at all. Lana, you took the cold place in my heart and made it warm, brimming with love. I have never been as happy as I am when near you. I will see you very soon," he repeated, firm and confident, refusing to accept any other possibility.

"Sure will," she replied, trying to convey as much surety back at him.

Cam let her go with a twinge of sorrow and guilt that he was not there to help.

Morgan sensed his feelings and patted his shoulder. "You've done everything you possibly can. Lana, Jodhi, and Alnthea—they're more than capable of doing this with ease. And if they believe in this Mariel, then so do I—and so should you."

He nodded wearily. "I know that, I do. I just feel so helpless. What if something goes wrong? What if something happens and I'm not there? Again!"

"There's nothing I can say to that and you know it," Morgan told him. "All we can do is hope and trust in the strength and wisdom we know they possess.

***

Lana read over her instructions twice before raising her head to talk to the others.

"They came through like we knew they would," she confirmed. "Alnthea, go through Menw's supplies again and find me these." She ripped a sheet of paper from the pad and handed it to her via Jodhi.

Alnthea read it quickly and began rummaging, setting aside what she found, measuring some powders and double-checking everything. Once done, she checked the list a third time and nodded. "That's all of it. Menw sure was a well-stocked wiz."

"He was a well-practiced, well-travelled wiz," Lana mused. "That taught him well, I suppose."

"Now what?" Jodhi asked, and then shook her head ruefully. "I know, that's all I ever seem to say, but I never seem to know the answer."

"Now we set up our two bindings and one mortality spell, ready ourselves, and free the beast." Alnthea said, looking at the sun, which was almost down; would be in time for her to venture out of the van. She picked up three stubby candles and juggled them. "So, Lana, it's like a jigsaw puzzle—and you're the only one who can see the picture on the box. What goes where?"

Jodhi grinned. "My mum does Wasgijs."

"Your mum does what now?" the vampire replied, dropping a candle and swearing lightly.

"Wasgijs. it's a backwards jigsaw. You get a picture of people looking at you, and you have to build what they see."

Alnthea nodded approvingly. "Very cool. Wasgij it is. Lana?"

Lana studied the first binding spell carefully. "Okay. Four candles, placed at four points so they can be joined to make a circle. Mostly symbolic, for focus. Apparently we don't really even need to light them, but we will anyway." Jodhi took the candles Alnthea held out and set them down as required, lighting them as the wind kindly dropped to nothing.

"Mariel, stand in the middle."

Mariel did so.

"Jodhi, create the circle by pouring the jars of salt—that's pouring, not sprinkling, the circle has to be completely unbroken."

Jodhi obeyed, pouring carefully through the attached spout, sure to leave not even the smallest gap. "What if it gets windy again and blows it around?" she asked.

Lana thought for a second and gave the reply she thought Cam would have gone for. "Let's just hope it doesn't. Next, without stepping inside the circle—or you out of it, Mariel—Jodhi, give her one of those small bottles with the purple smoke inside. They're meant to be unbreakable, but best be careful not to drop them anyway. This is not a good time for beta-testing."

Alnthea grinned at this, amused to see her own attitude rubbing off on the normally completely non-goofy researcher.

The vial was handled carefully and Mariel held it protectively to her chest.

Lana looked at her instructions again and wrote something neatly on another piece from her pad. She tore it off and held it out for Jodhi to pass on. "That and the matches," she said.

"Can't we just use a lighter, like for the candles?" Jodhi asked, looking doubtfully at the matchbook.

"We could," Lana nodded, "but these are special matches. Don't ask me how, but they were made especially for tasks like this and are supposed to enhance the magic somehow."

Jodhi shrugged and handed Mariel the paper and matches.

"How many hands are required for this?" Mariel asked nervously.

"Just the two, I promise." Lana read her notes again. "As the Guardian and Possessor of the Demon's Name, you and you alone must do this for he will bow only to you."

"Lana, you fill me full of confidence," Mariel said quietly.

"You can do this," Lana told her. "You have the power, you've already proved that. You will do this."

"I will do this," Mariel said, standing straight and firm. "What am I doing?"

"You are going to place the vial on the ground and remove the cap. Then, as the smoke rises, you will read what is on that piece of paper three times. You will then roll of the paper, put it in the neck of the vial, then leave it— the spell is prepared."

Mariel put one knee to the floor and gently placed the vial down; pushing it a little into the ground to be sure it remained upright. She removed the cap and placed it beside the tiny jar.

Inside, the purple smoke swirled and a tendril edged its way out, gaining confidence and pulling the rest along with it, flowing out of the glass and hovering expectantly in the air as if waiting.

Mariel stood and looked at the words closely. Lana had written them both as spelt and phonetically. Mariel studied the clearer syllables and made her voice strong as she spoke them aloud.

The language was ancient, alien and, nearing the end of the first recital, Mariel's voice changed to a two-toned cry; herself, plus her ancestor, channelling through the ages, speaking in unison.

The second recital she spoke with her head up and the words flying from her mouth in that eerie voice.

The third seemed to rock the hills themselves, the words so strong they were almost visible, almost a tangible entity to be absorbed into the purple fog that grew in definition with each one it accepted.

Having recited three times, Mariel rolled the paper, knelt again and tucked it into the neck of the jar.

After a moment she came partway back from where she had been taken, her eyes shining with some form of raw power, and looked at Lana for instruction.

Lana looked back in some wonder. "Next...n-next—" she shook her head sharply to clear it and read her note, "as soon as the demon is free and completely out of his prison and into our world, light a match and burn the paper. That should stop him in his tracks. Then, order the fog there to bind him—point him out and use whatever name you have then order them to bind him into doing no harm."

"Can do. Will do," Mariel agreed, trembling slightly with the sudden energy that was rushing through her.

"Jodhi, I need you for the next one," Lana said cautiously. "For the Halfling. Because you're, I mean your connection to him, it means that—"

"I'm his mum, so I can boss him around," Jodhi said simply.

Lana nodded, seeing the pain behind her eyes. "If you're up to it. If not—"

"I am," Jodhi said. "Same deal?"

"Different words, but otherwise yes."

Jodhi went to work quietly, taking the vial, matches and words to the centre of the candles and building her circle before tossing the jar back to Alnthea.

She studied the words, mouthing them to herself, careful not to actually speak them until she was ready.

Finally she took a deep breath and knelt to uncap her vial. As the smoke breathed free, she spoke her words almost caressingly. The second and third repetitions were the same and the fog seemed to fold lovingly around her.

Jodhi rolled up the paper and set it into the neck of the vial then she looked at Lana and nodded.

"The last one, Alnthea, is for you."

"What?" the vampire replied, startled. "Hey, Lana, I don't know any magic. I trust it in the hands of other people who know magic and aren't trying to kill me. I don't practice it!"

"We need to make the demon mortal. The safest, easiest and most effective way to do that is to oppose your own immortality."

"Then who kills him?"

"Once the spells are cast, the circles break themselves to allow the magic to go free. Something like that, Cam wasn't sure, not being a mage himself. But once you're done, you can leave and do what you have to do."

"Are you absolutely certain of that?" Alnthea asked.

"As certain as I can be. Not absolutely, but very."

"And if exiting the circle breaks the spell or something? Or if we're just unable to do so?"

"Then I'll just have to do my best," Lana said. "I have Cam's knife, and I'm not as soft as you think. If the spell breaks, then I-I don't know…"

"It won't," Mariel said in her doubly-pitched voice, neither brooking any argument. "The circle will break once the spell is cast, and the spell will hold."

"Good enough for me," Lana said. "but if you don't want to, Alnthea, I can do it. Cam gave me another spell that can use me."

"Nope, you said allowing it to use my contrast would make it easier and more effective. Well, so be it. What do I do?"

Lana flipped over two pages and read intently. "First, make the circle as the others did. that's all a part of holding it and protecting you until you're ready to cast the spell, I think. But you'll need the little cauldron-thing and the powders you measured out, instead of a vial."

Alnthea created a circle around herself and her tools and waited for instruction.

"Okay. Now put all the powders into the cauldron. In no particular order, but be very careful not to mix them up—leave them exactly as they lie."

Alnthea obeyed, dropping in her various measurements of colourful and smelly powders, careful to leave them just as they fell, though the fact that she had been ordered to do so activated the contrary section of her brain and made her fingers itch to mingle them into some sort of colourful pattern. She quashed the urge and nodded for her next instruction.

Lana stood and handed her a piece of paper. "Read that once. Then, it might hurt, but you have to dip your hands into the cauldron."

"It might hurt?" Alnthea asked doubtfully.

"I was told to warn you. It'll hurt, but you mustn't stop or hesitate or jerk your hands back. When the demon is bound, you have to grab two handfuls of powder and throw it at him. After that, it will hurt a lot more for a moment, but it will have made him flesh and blood mortal, so you can kill him."

"Well, okay then," Alnthea said. Her ancient vampire race showed through as she took in the words speedily and spoke them back. It was a long passage and, as she cried the words, the world seemed to grow dark and stormy as black clouds concealed the moon and stars.

At the last word, the paper burst into flames and was gone without a trace. Unhesitating, even in surprise, Alnthea plunged her hands directly into the cauldron and screamed as her skin sizzled in the suddenly searing hot powder that swirled around itself, like desert sand blown by an unusual breeze.

The pain gradually eased into a sharp cutting, peeling sensation and Alnthea spoke through gritted teeth. "Smarts a little bit. Can we move on at as speedy a pace as possible?"

Lana acknowledged the request by obeying. "Mariel, your turn. Open the door, break the seal and drag them out. Then be ready. Ditto for you, Jodhi. Alnthea, watch Mariel for your cue. Mariel, as soon as your Demon is bound, give Alnthea the nod. It's all down to your own judgement; I trust it, do what you feel, but the demon must be killed and the Halfling must be bound. Ready?"

All three nodded and steeled themselves. Lana retreated to the van and stood guard with her knife.

Mariel looked around to check all were prepared, her newly-discovered persona giving her an assurance she could not recall ever feeling before.

Satisfied, she closed her eyes and pictured the door swinging open, knowing as she opened them that it had.

Once again she checked the others. All looked tense, alert, and as ready as they ever would be. Alnthea's face was averted from the sun which barely missed her carefully-placed circle, pain registering even in her squint. Jodhi's eyes registered cold readiness. Mariel turned back to her own task.

Unable to physically touch the door from the confines of her circle, she closed her eyes and visualised the membrane holding the demon in place. Then she simply melted it away into nothing, opened her eyes and waited.

They all heard the roar of triumph from deep within that other world as the demon felt those inexplicable-yet-repressive bars fall from his cage.

Mariel felt him searching, locking onto the door. Felt the two of them surge towards it.

Blocking out the Halfling, she waited for hers to throw himself into this world, a match held ready to strike, and his name on her lips ready to command his binding.

Jodhi, in her circle, was trying to block the approach of the demon, her attacker, from her mind; trying to keep the memories from surfacing, along with their psychosomatic pain. She felt the son close in, heard his confusion and a flash of fear, then his excitement as he caught up to his father's furious headlong gallop.

Mariel tensed more as she felt her target near, knowing he would be first out, sensing no thoughts of caution.

He was upon them in the blink of an eye; one moment the door spilled its sunlight out onto the ground, in the next it shattered and was gone as they both emerged.

The demon screeched as his scaled human-esque form began to shift into his true one.

Mariel struck her match and lit her paper.

Jodhi did the same as her son revealed himself to her and stood still, as if waiting.

"Bian!" Mariel stood and cried out. "his name is Bian—now bind him!"

The purple fog immediately stopped its aimless swirling and flew across to Bian, surrounding him as his figure completed its change.

He was tall as a house and a little more. His body had slimmed and, as the fog gathered around him, still oblivious he shook out veined, grey wings, stretched two sets of long, muscular, quadruple-jointed arms and screamed victory through a mouth that now contained two rows of sharp, pointed teeth and a split-tongue that spat poison. His eyes glowed bright emerald green as they fixed upon Mariel and he took a step towards her on thick, powerful legs that ended in scimitar-like claws. He was halted, bound by the fog even as he rejoiced, and his cry of rage cut through the ears of all until they felt something must burst.

While this happened, Jodhi had lit her paper and motioned to the Halfling creature that looked at her with a sorrowful love. "Bind him. He is my son who has no name, I ask you to bind him from doing harm."

Her fog obeyed, almost sauntering over to the Halfling and wrapped itself around the creature who submitted gracefully, cowering from his father's wrath.

Mariel nodded at Alnthea who drew her hands, full of powder, from the cauldron and threw it in the direction of the raging, moth-like demon. For a second she despaired, she was too far away, it would never reach. But the powder hovered, formed itself into two darts which launched themselves, one at Bian and one at the vampire. Both let out screams of agony as the darts pierced their hearts.

The remaining powder rose into the air itself and formed a line between the two, linking them. Then, Alnthea's dart ripped from her and disintegrated as she dropped, breathless, to the ground, her chest gripped by iron.

When she looked up, Jodhi was already upon the demon, worrying at his legs, trying to knock him down with scratches and bites.

Bound, mortal, unable to fight back, it took only a well-timed charge at the back of his thighs from Alnthea to bring him crashing to the earth with a ground-shaking boom.

Alnthea started for his throat, growling, but checked her fury and stood aside. This was not her kill.

Jodhi saw her move back and understood. She leapt onto the demon's segmented torso and walked up to the top. There, she sat on her haunches and howled a victory to the moon before closing her jaws on the tender flesh of his neck and tearing it asunder with a fearsome strength. A bloody snarl of relish fading from her wolfish features, Jodhi stepped down and padded to one side.

"He's dead," Mariel said, stepping up. She looked at the others, her voice and eyes her own once more. "I can feel it. Or rather I can't feel him any longer."

Lana, ever prepared, dropped some clothes by Jodhi and all politely turned and walked a few paces away to allow her privacy to return to human form and dress.

"How are we all?" she asked anxiously upon joining them, still straightening her waistband.

"If my heart actually still beat, I'd say it was about to stop," Alnthea said, cradling her hands in obvious discomfort. "But as that's not the case, I'll be fine shortly."

Lana nodded. "I'm alright."

Mariel nodded too. "I'm okay. I feel strange, though."

"Well, you drove up here on a whim, found a random assortment of rather odd people and discovered you had hidden depths, then channelled an ancient ancestor and helped to destroy an ancient demon. I'm not surprised you feel a little unusual." Alnthea chuckled.

"That, of course." Mariel was smiling. "Also like...like something is missing."

"Centuries of dormant power and responsibility, perhaps?" suggested Lana.

"Probably it," Mariel agreed.

Jodhi turned away from them and walked over to where her son stood, looking very afraid. "Why did you let Cam go?" she asked coldly. "And why did you let me do this to you?"

"He was freed? I thought, when we were allowed out, that it had gone wrong, somehow." He paused and then answered the questions put to him in a cracked voice. "I did not want to hurt one who loved you, so when given the chance I let him go. I let you do this to me because I had no choice and saw no reason to resist against you, my mother." He saw her flinch at that name and his head dropped. Her pain and hatred were clear enough. "Are you going to kill me?"

"No. You will be taken to a place that will give you a chance to become good, useful. So long as you do, you'll be alright."

The Halfling nodded, tears in his eyes. Simple emotions were as yet all he possessed. Black and white. Shallow. His mother hated him and that made him sad. Yet he was to live and be helped and that made him happy. If he was good, he reasoned, maybe one day he could make her like him a little.

Jodhi saw this in his differently-coloured eyes; one green like his father, one brown like her own, and turned away, not wanting to let her heart soften.

She joined the others in the van as they awaited Depot E. Lana had slipped into herself to talk to Cam. Mariel dozed lightly and soon Jodhi joined her, leaving Alnthea awake and keeping her eyes on Bian, the Halfling, Sansé and the sleeping Julio.

When she heard an engine approaching she woke the two dozers and smiled as Lana leapt out to watch for the vehicles.

When they arrived, Cam barely waited for the car in front to slow down before leaping from the passenger side, running to Lana and enveloping her in his arms.

The other Shadow Walkers and Mariel smiled and left them to each other.

Morgan, driving the lead car, parked, exited and did likewise. She set the occupants of a large, steel-caged flatbed truck to work loading Bian and walked over to Jodhi, Alnthea and Mariel.

"We've got Julio here with a touch of hypothermia," Althea said immediately. "In the back is Isabel, she—"

Morgan cut her off kindly. "Cam has explained." She waved over a group of medical workers from an ambulance disguised neatly as an overlarge van and the two sick were quickly transferred for treatment.

"Now the other..." Morgan said, looking at Jodhi. "Would you like to?"

Jodhi nodded and led Morgan to the Halfling who nodded an amiable, if fearful, greeting.

"He can't hurt anyone," Jodhi assured Morgan, though it was meant more for herself than the other woman.

"I know. We have the spell to unbind him when we're ready." She nodded to four burly occupants of a secure prison van and they came over, sporting guns. "This one goes in the van. Be gentle—no harm comes to him."

They nodded and two made to take him arms and lead him away.

"Wait. Please," he begged. They did. "Mother..." He frowned in pain as she flinched again, but knew no other way to address her. "Would you...you called me your son with no name. Would you, could you, give one to me?"

Jodhi's lip refused to curl in the disgust she wanted to express but felt only partly. She turned away, stopped and turned back to him, tears brimming in her eyes and his. "I name you Antranig," she told him.

His tears broke free as he smiled, looking shockingly human as he did so. "Antranig." He tasted the word. "Thank you," he said as his voice cracked beneath new emotion and walked over to the van by himself, the guards following behind.

Jodhi watched him climb inside, then felt Morgan's arm around her shoulder and realised she was crying too.

"Antranig?" Morgan asked, curiously.

Jodhi nodded. "It means First Son."

Printed in the United States
107814LV00004B/372/A